WITHDRAWN

ALSO BY

BOUALEM SANSAL

The German Mujahid

2 0 8 4
THE END OF THE WORLD

Boualem Sansal

2084
THE END OF THE WORLD

*Translated from the French
by Alison Anderson*

Europa
editions

Europa Editions
214 West 29th Street
New York, N.Y. 10001
www.europaeditions.com
info@europaeditions.com

Library of Congress Cataloging in Publication Data is available
ISBN 978-1-60945-366-4

Sansal, Boualem
2084. The End of the World

Cover art and illustration by Emanuele Ragnisco
www.mekkanografici.com

Prepress by Grafica Punto Print – Rome

Printed in the USA

CONTENTS

BOOK ONE - 13

BOOK TWO - 71

BOOK THREE - 109

BOOK FOUR - 195

EPILOGUE - 241

ABOUT THE AUTHOR - 253

*Religion might make us love God
but there is nothing stronger than religion
to make us despise man and hate humankind.*

WARNING

The reader is advised to refrain from believing that this is a true story, or that it is based on any known reality. No, in truth, everything has been invented, the characters, the events, and all the rest, and the proof of this is that the story is set in a distant world, in a distant future that looks nothing like our own.

This is a work of pure invention: the world of Bigaye that I describe in these pages does not exist and has no reason to exist in the future, just as the world of Big Brother imagined by George Orwell, and so marvelously depicted in his novel 1984, did not exist in his time, does not exist in our own, and truly has no reason to exist in the future. Sleep soundly, good people, everything is sheer falsehood, and the rest is under control.

BOOK ONE

In which Ati returns to Qodsabad, his city, the capital of Abistan, after two long years of absence, one spent in the sanatorium at Sîn in the mountains of the Ouâ, and the other trudging along the roads from one caravan to the next. Along the way, he will meet Nas, an investigator from the powerful Ministry of Archives, Sacred Books, and Holy Memories, who is returning from a mission to a new archeological site that dates from before the Char, the Great Holy War; the discovery of this site has been cause for strange agitation within the Appartus and, so it is said, at the very heart of the Just Brotherhood.

Ati was losing sleep. The anxiety came over him earlier and earlier, as soon as the lights were out and even before then, when twilight unfurled its pallid veil, and the patients, tired from their long day of wandering from room to corridor and corridor to terrace, began to return to their beds, dragging their feet, calling to one another with doleful wishes of happiness for the passage of the night. Some of them would no longer be there in the morning. Yölah is great and just, he gives and takes as he sees fit.

Then night came, falling so quickly in the mountains that it was unsettling. Just as abruptly, the cold turned biting, breath became mist. Outside, the wind prowled, relentless, ready for anything.

The familiar sounds of the sanatorium calmed him some-what, even if they spoke of human suffering and its deafening alarms, or the shameful expression of bodily functions, but they did not manage to conceal the ghostly rumblings of the mountain: a faraway echo more imagined than heard, emerging from the depths of the earth, laden with miasma and menace. And this mountain of Ouâ, at the far reaches of the empire, was indeed a gloomy and oppressive place, and not only because of its vast and wretched aspect; there were stories that circulated in its valleys, and which reached the sanatorium together with the throng of pilgrims who crossed the region of Sîn twice a year and always stopped at the hospital to beg for warmth and sustenance for the road. They came from afar, the four corners of the land, on foot, tattered and feverish, in what were often perilous conditions; their sibylline stories were full of marvels, sordid, criminal, and all the more troubling in that they were uttered in hushed tones, until at the slightest sound the story-teller broke off to peer over his shoulder. Like everyone, pilgrims and patients never let their attention slip, for fear of being caught out by the guards, or perhaps the terrible Vs, and denounced as *makoufs*, propagandists of the Great Heathendom, an unspeakably ignominious sect. Ati appreci-ated this contact with the long-traveled voyagers; he sought them out, for they had collected so many stories and discover-ies in the course of their peregrinations. The country was so vast and so thoroughly unknown that it seemed a desirable thing to lose oneself in its mysteries.

The pilgrims were the only people who were allowed to move about the country, not freely but according to precise calendars, on specified roads that they could not leave, roads that were staked out with way stations in the middle of nowhere, in the middle of arid plateaus, boundless steppes, deep canyons, abandoned hamlets, where the pilgrims were counted and divided into groups like armies on the move, bivouacking around a thousand campfires while they waited for their marching orders. At times the pauses lasted so long that the penitents put down roots in vast, spreading slums and behaved like forgotten refugees, at a loss to remember what only a day before had nourished their dreams. In this eternal limbo there is a lesson: the important thing is no longer the final destination but the way station, however precarious it might be; it offers rest and safety, and in so doing, it displays the practical intelligence of the Apparatus, and the Delegate's affection for his people. Apathetic soldiers and commissars of faith, tormented and highly strung as meerkats, took turns along the roads at each nerve center to watch the pilgrims go by, with an aim to surveillance. No one knew whether anyone had ever escaped, or whether there had been any manhunts; people went their way as they were told, dragging their feet only when the fatigue overwhelmed them, and their ranks began to thin. Everything was perfectly regulated and carefully filtered; nothing could happen without the express volition of the Apparatus.

The reasons for these restrictions are not known. They date from long ago. The truth is that the question had never occurred to anyone, harmony had reigned for so long that no one knew of any reason for disquiet. Even disease and death, which took their turn more often than was fair, had no effect on people's morale. Yölah is great, and Abi is his faithful Delegate.

Pilgrimage was the only reason anyone was allowed to move about the country, except for administrative and commercial requirements, for which agents used a travel permit that had to be stamped at every stage of their mission. Controls of this nature were repeated ad infinitum, and mobilized hosts of counter clerks and ticket-punchers, but they no longer had any reason to exist: they were a relic of some forgotten era. The country was built on recurring, spontaneous, and mysterious wars about which one thing was certain: the enemy was everywhere, could suddenly appear from east or west, or from north or south; there was wariness, no one knew what they looked like or what they wanted. They were called the Enemy, with a capital letter in the intonation, that was enough. People seemed to recall that one day it had been announced that it was wrong to refer to them in any other way, and that had seemed legitimate, and so obvious, there was no reason to give a name to a thing no one has ever seen. The Enemy acquired a fabulous and frightening dimension. And one day, without warning, the word Enemy disappeared from the vocabulary. To have enemies is an admission of weakness; victory is either total or it is not. There was talk of the Great Heathendom, of the *makoufs*, a new word signifying invisible, omnipresent renegades. The internal enemy had replaced the external enemy, or vice versa. Then came the time of vampires and incubi. During the grand ceremonies a name filled with every fear was uttered, the Chitan. Or the Chitan and his assembly. Some saw this as another way to say the Renegade and his circle, an expression people could grasp. That was not all: he who utters the name of the Devil must spit on the ground and recite the consecrated formula three times: "May Yölah banish him and curse him!" Later, after other obstacles were overcome, at last the Devil, Satan, the Chitan, the Renegade was given his true name: Balis. His followers, the renegades, became Balisians. Things suddenly seemed clearer after that, but nevertheless, for a long time there was much questioning as to why so many false names had been used for such an eternity.

The war had been long, and worse than terrible. Here and there, everywhere in fact (but no doubt there were a number of disasters that came to compound the warfare—earthquakes and other maelstroms), traces remain, piously preserved, arranged like so many installations ceremoniously offered to the public by artists with a taste for excess: blocks of gutted buildings, walls riddled with bullet holes, entire neighborhoods buried in rubble, eviscerated corpses, gigantic craters transformed into steaming dumping grounds or putrid swamps, hallucinatory masses of twisted, torn, melted metal, where people come to read signs, and in some places, vast forbidden zones of several hundred square *kilosiccas* or *chabirs*, enclosed by rough stockades at points of passage, or torn away in other places, bare land swept by icy or torrid winds, a place where something has happened, something beyond comprehension, fragments of the sun fallen to earth, or black magic sparking blazing infernos, what else could it be, because everything—earth, rocks, things wrought by the hand of man—has been vitrified through and through, and this iridescent magma emits a shrill crackling sound that makes hair stand on end, ears buzz, and hearts beat wildly. Curious onlookers are drawn to the phenomenon; they hurry to these giant mirrors and find it entertaining to see their hair rise to attention and their skin flushing and swelling before their eyes and their noses bleeding profusely. That the inhabitants of these regions, man and beast alike, suffer from strange maladies, and their offspring come into the world burdened with every imaginable deformity, and that there has been no explanation for any of it—this has not provoked fear, the people continue to thank Yölah for his blessings and to praise Abi for his affectionate intercession.

Signs posted in strategic spots inform the visitor that after the Great Holy War, known as the Char, the destruction spread as far as the eye could see, and the newly martyred dead numbered in the hundreds of millions. For years, for entire decades, for as long as the war lasted and well beyond, some hardy types began to collect the bodies, to move them and pile them and incinerate them, to cover them with quicklime and bury them in never-ending trenches, to stack them in the bowels of abandoned mines or deep caves forever sealed with dynamite. For as long as was necessary a decree from Abi authorized these age-old practices so unlike the funeral rites of the people of believers. For a long time, corpse collecting and incinerating were fashionable professions. Any man with brawn and a good back could go in for it, full-time or as the fancy took him, but in the end only the truly solid men remained at the front. They went from one region to the next with their apprentices and their tools—handcart, ropes, hoist, lantern, and for the better-equipped, a draft animal; they obtained a concession within their capabilities and got to work. The elders still recall seeing those austere, placid giants in the distance, making their way along footpaths or over mountain passes, their thick leather aprons flapping against their massive thighs, pulling their heavily laden carts, followed by their apprentices and sometimes their families. The smell of their profession preceded them, followed them, permeated everything, everywhere, an emetic stench of putrefied flesh, burned grease, effervescent quicklime, polluted earth, obsessive gases. With time they vanished, the country was sanitized, all that remained were a few slow, taciturn old men who sold their services for a song outside a hospital, a hospice, a cemetery. A sad ending for these heroic dustmen of death.

As for the Enemy, he had simply disappeared. No trace of his passage through the country was ever found, or of his miserable presence on earth. The victory over him had been "total, definitive, and irrevocable," according to the official teaching. Yölah had prevailed; to his people, more fervent believers than ever, he had offered the supremacy promised to them since the dawn of time. One date stood out, although no one knew how or why, it had penetrated minds and appeared on all the commemorative signs erected near the ruins: 2084. Was it something to do with the war? Perhaps. Nowhere was it specified whether it corresponded to a beginning, an end, or a particular episode during the conflict. People imagined one thing, then another, more subtle, to do with the holiness of their life. Numerology became a national pastime, there were additions, subtractions, multiplications, they did everything it was possible to do with the numbers 2, 0, 8, 4. At one time the notion was adopted that 2084 was simply the year of Abi's birth, or of his illumination by divine light, which occurred when he was on the threshold of his fiftieth year. The fact remains that, already, no one doubted that God had given him a new and unique role to play in the history of humanity. It was at this time that the country—

which had been called simply "the land of believers"—
adopted the name Abistan, quite a lovely name, used by
authorities, by the Honorables and Sectarians of the Just
Brotherhood and by agents of the Apparatus. The common
people continued to use the old designation "land of believers," and in everyday conversation they simply said, mindless
of the danger they incurred, "the land," "the house,"
"home." That is what the people's gaze is like, carefree and
truly not very imaginative; they do not see beyond their own
doorstep. As if it were a sort of courtesy on their part: elsewhere has its masters, and to look elsewhere is to violate pri-
vacy, to break a pact. There was a stressful official side to calling themselves Abistanis, something that suggested trouble,
calls to order, even the occasional summons; so they referred
to themselves as "people," convinced that this would suffice
for them to know one another.

There was another time when the date was linked to the
founding of the Apparatus, or earlier still, to the creation of the
Just Brotherhood—the congregation of forty dignitaries chosen among the most faithful believers by Abi himself, after he
had been appointed by God to assist him with the colossal task
of governing the people of believers and bringing them all to
the afterlife, where they would each be questioned by the
Angel of Justice about their works. They were informed that
the shadow hid nothing in this light, that it revealed all. It was
during the period of successive cataclysms that God was given
a new name, Yölah. Times had changed, according to the pri-
mordial Promise; another world had been born, on an earth
that was cleansed, devoted to truth, beneath the gazes of God
and of Abi; everything must be renamed, everything must be
rewritten, so that the new life would not be sullied by bygone
History, which was now null and void, effaced as if it had never
existed. The Just Brotherhood granted Abi the humble but
eminently explicit title of Delegate, and it conceived a sober,

moving salutation for him: "Abi the Delegate, may salvation be upon him," while kissing the back of one's left hand.

So many stories went around, until everything was snuffed out and restored to order. History was rewritten and sealed by the hand of Abi. Anything that might have clung on from the olden times, deep in purged memories, shreds, smoke, was fuel for vague delirium among the elderly, afflicted with dementia. For the generations of the New Era, dates, the calendar, History were no more important than the stamp of the wind on the sky; the present is eternal, today is always here, time in its entirety can fit in Yölah's hand, he knows things, he decides upon their meaning and instructs whomever he chooses.

Whatever the case may be, 2084 was a founding date for the country, even if no one knew what it referred to.

That is how things stood, simple and complicated, but not absurd. Candidates for the pilgrimage enrolled on a list for a designated holy place that the Apparatus chose for them and waited to be called to join a caravan due to leave. The wait could last a year or a lifetime, without remission, in which case the eldest child of the deceased inherited the certificate of enrollment, but never the second son and never the sisters: holiness cannot be divided nor does it change sex. A grandiose celebration would follow. Asceticism was passed on through the son, and so the honor of the family was reinforced. There were millions and millions of them throughout the land, from every one of the sixty provinces, of every age and condition, all counting the days until the great departure, the Bidi, the Blessed Day. In some regions it had become customary to gather once a year in huge crowds for a mass self-flogging with studded whips, amid a joyful uproar, to show that suffering was nothing compared to the happiness of awaiting the Bidi; in other regions, people came together at extraordinary jam-borees, sitting cross-legged in a circle, knees touching, and they listened to the oldest candidates, who'd reached the limits of exhaustion but not of hope, tell of their long and blessed ordeal, known as the Expectation. Every sentence was met with an encouraging response from a powerful megaphone: "Yölah is just," "Yölah is patient," "Yölah is great," "Abi supports you," "Abi is with you," etc., echoed by ten thousand throats tight with emotion. Then there was prayer, elbow to elbow, everyone chanting their heads off, singing the odes written by Abi, until they began over again unto exhaustion; then came the high point of the ceremony: fatted calves and entire herds of sheep were slaughtered. The most skillful butchers in the region were required, for this was a sacrifice, and as such a difficult process, slaughter is not killing, but an exaltation. Next all the meat had to be roasted. The flames were visible from afar, the air was redolent with fat, and the good smell of grilled meat went on to tantalize everything within a radius of ten *chabirs* that had nose, snout, muzzle, or beak. It was something of an orgy, interminable and vulgar. Electrified clusters of beggars hurried over, drawn by the aroma; they could not resist the abundance of meat dripping with tasty juice, they were overcome with an extreme intoxication that led them to behave in ways that were anything but religious—but in the end, their voraciousness was welcome, for what else was there to do with so much sanctified meat? To throw it out would have been sacrilege.

The passion for pilgrimage was maintained by never-ending campaigns, a mixture of publicity, sermons, fairs, contests, and various manipulative events orchestrated by the very powerful Ministry of Sacrifices and Pilgrimages. A very old and very holy family, much-loved by Abi, controlled the monopoly of the Hype, the *moussim*, which they exercised in a manner befitting piety: "Neither too little nor too much" was their commercial slogan, and even children knew it. Many other professions gravitated around the sacrifices and pilgrimages, and an equal number of noble families endeavored to provide their best. In Abistan, the only economy was religious.

These campaigns were spread throughout the year, with a high point in summer, during the Siam, the holy week of Absolute Abstinence, which coincided with the return of the pilgrims from their distant, enchanting sojourns in one of the thousand and one sites available for pilgrimage all over the country: shrines, sanctuaries, sacred lands, mausoleums, and places of glory and martyrdom, where the people of the believers had won sublime victories over the Enemy. A stubborn coincidence had arranged things in the following manner: all these sites were at the far reaches of the globe, nowhere near roads or inhabited areas, and this meant that every pilgrimage was a long, impossible expedition, taking years; pilgrims crossed the country from one end to the other on foot, along rough, solitary roads, as tradition would have it, which made the return of the old or sick improbable. But in fact this was the true dream of all the candidates—to die along the path to holiness. As if they thought that it might not be such a good thing to attain perfection in one's lifetime after all; perfection placed so many duties and responsibilities on the chosen one that he would be bound to fail, losing in one fell swoop all that had been gained from so many years of sacrifice. And then how—unless he were to behave as a potentate—could a little saint find pleasure in perfection in a world that was so imperfect?

No one, not one single worthy believer, ever thought for an instant that these perilous pilgrimages might be an effective way to rid the cities of their teeming masses and offer them a beautiful death along the road to fulfillment. Similarly, no one ever thought that the Holy War might have been waged for the same purpose: to transform useless, wretched believers into glorious, lucrative martyrs.

It went without saying that the holy of holies of all the saints was the little house of rare stones that was Abi's place of birth. The hovel was the most pitiful in creation, but the miracles that had taken place there were more than merely extraordinary. No Abistani was without a reproduction of the holy dwelling in his home; it might be made of papier-mâché, or wood, or jade, or gold: all reflected the same love for Abi. No one pointed it out, the people had not noticed, but every eleven years the little house changed its location, this by virtue of a secret arrangement on the part of the Just Brotherhood, who organized the rotation of the prestigious monument out of a concern for equity among the sixty provinces of Abistan. Nor did anyone know that one of the most discreet programs of the Apparatus prepared the reception site long in advance, and trained the local inhabitants in their role as future historic witnesses, whose job it would be to teach the pilgrims what it meant to live in the vicinity of a cottage that was unique in all the universe. The penitents paid them back in kind, they were generous with their acclaim, their tears, and their little gifts. The communion was total. Without witnesses to testify, History does not exist, and someone must begin the story so that others may tell the end.

The dense network of restrictions and prohibitions, the propaganda, preaching, and obligatory worship, the hurried succession of ceremonies, the display of personal initiative that counted so much in both the assessment and conferral of privileges: all of this added up to create a particular state of mind among the Abistanis, and they were constantly bustling about in support of a cause about which they knew not the first thing.

To welcome the pilgrims when they returned from their long absence, with their aura of recent holiness; to celebrate them, and ply them with delicacies; to obtain something from them—an object, a lock of hair, just any old relic: this was an occasion and an opportunity which the populace and the candidates for the Bidi would not have missed for the world. Such treasures were beyond price on the market for relics. But what was more, there were wonders to be learned from these beloved pilgrims; theirs were the eyes that had seen the world and reached its holiest places.

In the weave of routine and sacrament, the Expectation was a trial the candidates endured with ever-increasing happiness. Patience is another name for faith, it is the path and the goal: this was the first teaching, along with obedience and submission, which made for a good believer. And during this period, at every moment, day and night, while God and man looked on, one had to remain a worthy among the worthies. No Expectant would ever survive for one minute the shame of being withdrawn from the most glorious list of candidates for pilgrimage to the sanctuaries. But this was an absurd rumor that the Apparatus liked to keep alive, for no one had ever failed, no one had died of shame, everyone knew that the people of the believers did not harbor any hypocrites in their midst, just as they knew that the vigilance of the Apparatus was infallible; the Indusoccupants were said to have been eliminated before the idea ever came to them to delude anyone. Intox, provoc, agitprop: nothing but a scourge, the people needed clarity and encouragement, not false rumors or veiled threats. Sometimes the Apparatus went too far with their manipulation, they grew careless, even made up bogus enemies whom they then went to great lengths to track down—only, when all was said and done, to find themselves eliminating their own friends.

Ati nurtured a passion for those long-distance adventurers; at first he would listen ever so casually, so as not to frighten them off or alert the watchman's antennae, but then he would get carried away by his enthusiasm and begin to question them avidly, like a child, firing off a battery of "whys" and "hows."

And yet he was always left unsatisfied, and had sudden fits of anxiety and rage. Somewhere there was a wall that prevented one from seeing beyond the gossip of these poor wanderers; they were on probation, conditioned to propagate illusions throughout the country. Ati was sorry to think this way, but he was convinced that their frenzied stories had been planted on their tongues by the people deep within the Apparatus who controlled their brains from a distance. What better means than hope and wonder to chain people to their beliefs, for he who believes is afraid, and he who is afraid believes blindly. But this was something Ati would think of only later, in the throes of torment: for him it would mean breaking the chains that bind faith to madness and truth to fear, to save oneself from annihilation.

In the darkness and tumult of vast, overcrowded rooms he was seized by strange, urgent spasms of pain, shuddering like a horse in a stable that senses danger lurking in the night. The hospital did indeed seem to house death. Panic was not long in coming, and it hounded him until dawn and did not recede until daylight banished the swarming shadows of night and the morning service began in a commotion of casseroles and quarrels. The mountain had always terrified him, he was a city man, born in the warm fug of crowding and close quarters, and here, in his wretched bed, sweating and gasping for breath, he felt he was at the mountain's mercy, crushed by its mass and severity, oppressed by its sulfurous emanations.

And yet it was the mountain that had cured him. He had arrived at the sanatorium in a calamitous state, tuberculosis was bleeding him dry, he was coughing up great clots of blood, and the hacking and fever were driving him mad. In one year he had regained a semblance of health. The fresh, chill air was like an ardent fire, ruthlessly consuming the little worms devouring his lungs—that was how the patients liked to depict their ailment, although they knew full well that it came from Balis the Renegade, and that it was divine will that ultimately decided the order of things. The nurses—crude, rough-hewn mountain men—did not think otherwise, and at set times they handed out roughly fashioned pills and emetic concoctions; nor did they forget to renew the talismans when new ones came in, preceded by enticing rumors. As for the doctor, who would sweep through once a month without saying a word to anyone, other than to snap his fingers: no one even dared glance at him. He was not a man of the people, he belonged to the Apparatus. There was a great murmuring of excuses as he went by, and a rush to hide wherever possible. The director of the asylum cleared the way for him, slashing the air with his switch. Ati knew nothing about the Apparatus, other than that they had power over everything, in the name of Abi and the Just Brotherhood; Abi's giant portrait was on every wall from one end of the country to the other. Oh . . . that portrait, it must be said, was the identity of the country. It consisted, in fact, of no more than a play of shadows, a sort of negative of a face: at its center was a magic eye, pointed like a diamond, endowed with a consciousness that could pierce armor plating. It was a well-known fact that Abi was a man, a most humble man, but he was not a man like other men, he was Yölah's Delegate, the father of the believers, the supreme leader of the world, and in the end, by the grace of God and the love of humankind, he was immortal; and if no one had ever seen him it was simply because his light was blinding. No, truly, he was too precious: to expose him to the gaze of the common people was unthinkable. Around his palace, at the heart of the forbidden city, in the center of Qodsabad, hundreds of well-armed men were massed, aligned to form concentric, hermetic barriers that not even a fly could get through without the permission of the Apparatus. These massive guards were selected at birth, painstakingly trained by the Apparatus, and they obeyed no one else; nothing could distract them, divert them, unsettle them; no compassion could restrain their cruelty. No one knew whether they were actually human; their brains had been removed at birth, which would explain their terrifying stubbornness and haunted gaze. The common people, who never miss an opportunity to find an appropriate name for something they do not understand, called them Abi's Fools. It was said they came from a faraway province in the south, from a remote tribe bound to Abi by a mythical pact. The tribe, too, had been named by the people, a name which described it well: the leg-abi, for Abi's legion.

The safety measures were so excessive that some people thought these unshakeable robots guarded an empty nest, or nothing at all, just an idea, a premise. It was a way of finding entertainment in the mystery; at such levels of ignorance, everyone adds their own bit of folly, but they all knew that Abi was omnipresent, simultaneously here and there, in one provincial capital and in another, in an identical palace that was just as hermetically guarded, and from that palace Abi radiated light and life over the people. This is the power of ubiquity, the center is everywhere, and so, every day, enthusiastic crowds flocked in procession around his sixty palaces to offer him their ardent devotion and costly gifts, and all they asked from him in return was paradise upon their death.

The idea of representing him in this way, with one eye, was cause for debate, and theories were advanced: it was said he was one-eyed—from birth, according to some, or due to the suffering he endured in his childhood, according to others; it was also said he actually had an eye in the middle of his forehead, and that this was the mark of a prophetic destiny, but equally firmly it was posited that the image was symbolic, signaling a spirit, a soul, a mystery. With such mass distribution, hundreds of millions of copies a year, the portrait might have provoked madness by indigestion had art not endowed it with an ultrapowerful magnetism emitting strange vibrations, and these vibrations filled space the way the spellbinding song of whales saturates the oceans during mating season. At first glance a passerby was subjugated, then before long he was happy, and felt intensely protected, loved, promoted—crushed, too, by the majesty and all it conveyed of formidable violence. Crowds would form before the richly illuminated giant portraits that clothed the facades of major administrative buildings. No artist on earth could ever have produced such a marvel, this portrait was the work of Abi himself, inspired by Yölah—and as all were taught from an early age, this was the truth.

One day someone wrote something in the corner of one of Abi's portraits. An incomprehensible word, scribbled in an unknown language, an ancient written form from before the first Great Holy War. People were not only intrigued, they expected a great event to occur. Then the rumor went around that the word had been translated by the Apparatus cipher office; the mysterious wording was equivalent, in *abilang*, to "Bigaye is watching you!" It didn't mean anything, but as the name had a pleasing sound, the people immediately took it up, and Abi was affectionately baptized Bigaye. All anyone heard now was Bigaye this and Bigaye that, Bigaye the beloved, Bigaye the just, Bigaye the all-seeing, until the day a decree from the Just Brotherhood prohibited the use of the barbarian word under pain of immediate death. Not long thereafter, communiqué number 66710 from the *NeF*, the *News from the Front*, triumphantly proclaimed that the loathsome scribbler had been found and immediately executed along with his entire family and all his friends, and their names had been stricken from the registers all the way back to the first generation. Silence fell through the land, but many people, deep down, were wondering: why had the forbidden word been spelled *Big Eye* in the aforementioned decree? Where did that mistake come from? Was it the scribe at the *NeF*? The editor, the Honorable Suc? Someone else? It could not be Duc, the Great Commander, head of the Just Brotherhood, let alone Abi himself: he had invented *abilang*, and even if he had wanted to he could not have made a mistake, of any kind.

The fact remained that Ati had regained some color and put on a few pounds. His phlegm was still thick, he had trouble breathing, he moaned a lot, coughed a great deal, but he was no longer spitting blood. For the rest, there was not much the mountain could do: life was hard, everything was in short supply, days were filled with a steady accretion of deprivation, in a manner of speaking. No sooner did you begin life than you were already ruined, and this was natural. So high up in the mountains and so far from the city, the decline was rapid. The sanatorium was a guaranteed end of the road for many—old people, children, the seriously disabled. That's how it is with the poor, they are resigned to the end, they begin to seek treatment only when life is leaving them behind for good. There was something funereal and grandiose about the way they cloaked themselves in their *burni*, an ample woolen coat water-proofed with filth and patched in a hundred places, as if they were draping themselves in a king's shroud, ready to follow death forthwith. They would not take it off, day or night, as if they were afraid they'd be caught out by fate and would have to go naked and ashamed to meet death—which, incidentally, they awaited without fear, and welcomed with a familiarity that was not at all feigned, even obsequious, or so it seemed. Death did not hesitate, it struck there and there and there, and continued on its way. Those who prayed to death merely whetted its appetite, until it gobbled down double portions. Their departure went unnoticed, there was no one to mourn them. There was never a lack of sick people, more arrived than departed, no one knew where to put them all. An empty bed did not stay empty for long, the suffering patients who slept on pallets in the wide windy corridors fought over it bitterly. Even prior arrangements did not always suffice to ensure the succession went smoothly.

And it wasn't just penury, there were also the hardships of the terrain, which made people forget the rest. Food, medication, the supplies necessary for the running of the sanatorium were sent from the city by truck—huge shapeless juggernauts, tattooed all over, that were as old as the mountain and feared nothing, or at least not until the first foothills, where the oxygen began to be a bit too thin for their huge pistons—then on the backs of brave and hardy men and mules, climbers who were highly skilled, but execrably slow: they got there when they could, depending on the vagaries of the weather, the state of the trails and ledges, their mood, and the level of tribal bickering, which had the knack of bringing everything on the chosen route to a halt, with immediate effect.

In these mountains at the end of the world, every step was a challenge to life, and the sanatorium was as far as one could go along this fatal dead end. Some people, in long gone, obscure days, may have wondered why it was necessary to climb so high and far away into the cold and wilderness to isolate these tubercular patients, who were no more contagious than others: lepers roamed where they liked, throughout the country, as did the pestilent, and those who were still referred to as the terminally febrile—who, it is true, had certain seasons and zones of proliferation. No one had ever died as a result of coming into contact with them or meeting their gaze. The principle of contagion has not always been fully understood; people do not die because others are sick, but because they themselves are sick. At any rate, that was how things stood, every era has its fears, and now it fell to tuberculosis to carry the banner of supreme disease spreading terror among the populace.

Then things changed, and other horrible ills appeared, laying waste to luxuriant regions and filling the cemeteries, then those ills ebbed away, but as the sanatorium was still there, impressive in its mineral eternity, consumptives and other bronchitics continued to be sent there instead of being allowed to die at home or nearby, among other sufferers. They would have had a natural death, surrounded by the affection of family and friends, but instead they were crammed into the attics of the world, where they died shamefully, harassed by cold, hunger and cruelty.

There were times when the caravan simply vanished—men, beasts, and supplies. Sometimes the soldiers who were appointed to protect them vanished, too, sometimes they didn't; after a few days of searching they were found at the bottom of a ravine, mutilated, their throats cut, half devoured by beasts of prey. No sign of their rifles. No one said as much out loud, but some people reckoned that the caravan had taken the forbidden road and crossed the border. That was what the elders thought; their gaze was so eloquent. *Who talked?* The atmosphere was suddenly oppressive, the old folk scattered, coughing as if they were apologizing for having said too much, whereas the young ones pricked up their ears. Their thoughts could be heard from afar, so noisily were they pounding in their heads.

The forbidden road! . . . the border! . . . What border, what forbidden road? Isn't our world the entire world? Aren't we at home wherever we go, by the grace of Yölah and Abi? What need have we of boundaries? What are we to make of this?

The news would plunge the sanatorium into stupor and despondency, men flogged themselves in keeping with the tradition of their region, or banged their heads against the wall, or clawed at their chests, or screamed at the top of their lungs: such an act was a heresy that would bring ruin to believers. What world could exist beyond that so-called border? Was there even light there, or a patch of earth where one of God's creatures could stand? What sort of mind could conceive of the intention to flee the kingdom of faith for nothingness? Only the Renegade could inspire such thoughts, or the *makoufs*, the propagandists of the Great Heathendom: they were capable of anything.

And suddenly the event became an affair of state, and disappeared from public view. As if by the wave of a magic wand the lost shipment was replaced with a hefty supplement of sweetmeats, costly medication, and miracle-working talismans, and nothing remained of the rumor, not an echo; better still, over the land there settled a stubborn, hypnotic impression that nothing untoward had ever happened. Transfers, arrests, and disappearances might occur, but no one ever witnessed them, all their attention was elsewhere; not all embers were cold in the kingdom and there was no lack of ceremonies. The dignity of martyrdom was conferred upon the murdered guards, and the news would be broadcast by the *NeF*, the *nadirs* (electronic wall newspapers found all over the globe) and through the network of *mockbas* where nine times a day it was preached that the guards had fallen on the field of glory, during a heroic battle qualified as "the battle to end all battles," just like all those real or imagined battles that had come before and would come again, century after century. There was no hierarchy among martyrs, nor ever any end to the Holy War; it would only be proclaimed once Yölah crushed Balis, in accordance with the Promise.

What wars, what battles, what victories, against whom, how, when, why? were questions that did not exist, were not asked, and so there were no answers to expect. "The Holy War, it is known, is at the heart of the doctrine, but it is one theory among others! If speculations can be floated this simply, and in one's lifetime, then there is no more faith, no more dreaming, no more sincere love, and the world is doomed": that is what the people thought when the ground opened beneath their feet. It was true, what else could one cling to, other than what was incredible? Only the incredible is credible.

And doubt brings anxiety, and misfortune is not long in coming. Ati had reached this point, he could no longer sleep, and he was filled with the foreboding of unspeakable terrors.

Shortly after he arrived at the sanatorium, in the middle of the previous winter, a caravan disappeared along with its guards, who were later found at the bottom of a ravine, trapped in the ice. While waiting for more clement weather to take them back to the city, they placed the bodies in the morgue. The hospital was buzzing, nurses running in every direction with their pails and their brooms, patients wandering aimlessly, swarming in the courtyard by the outbuildings, squinting over at the dark narrow ramp that spiraled down to the mortuary fifteen *siccas* below, which was in fact the end of a partially-collapsed tunnel that wound its way under the fortress; it had been built in the rock wall back in the days when the first Holy War was raging in these remote parts. No one knew where the other end was; it disappeared somewhere in the bowels of the mountain. It was an escape route, or a wretched dwelling, a dungeon or a catacomb, or perhaps a hiding place for women and children in the event of an invasion, or a place of forbidden worship like the ones that were found these days in the most unbelievable locations. This tunnel was an unsavory place, filled with the furies of past worlds, incomprehensible and so terrifying that there were days when the bottom of the well let out mournful gurgles. The temperature was conducive to rapid freezing.

Horror of horrors: it was said that, in addition to the injuries they had sustained during their vertiginous fall, the soldiers had been savagely butchered. No more ears, or tongue, or nose; their genitals in their mouths, their testicles crushed, their eyes gouged out. A convulsive old man uttered the word "torture," but he didn't know what it meant, he had forgotten the meaning or didn't want to say, which only made the terror worse. He crept away, recoiling, murmuring things: ". . . conjure . . . democ . . . against . . . may Yölah preserve us." In Ati, the event triggered an insidious process that led him to rebellion. Against what, against whom, he could not imagine; in a motionless world there is no way to understand, one only knows if one does rebel—against oneself, against empire, against God—and no one can do that—but then how to move in an ossified world? All the greatest knowledge in the world gives way before the speck of dust that obstructs thought. Those who confronted death on the mountain, who set off along the forbidden road and crossed the border: they knew.

But to cross a border, what does that mean—to go where?

And why massacre those poor devils in uniform when they could have taken them with them, or simply left them to their fate on the mountain? What's the answer? There were soldiers who had been spared by the renegades and had gone home, only to receive the punishment reserved for cowards, traitors, and heathens; they had ended up at the stadium, on the day of great prayer, and were executed to the sounds of great cheering after they had been paraded through town. To conclude a matter of state necessitates the disappearance of witnesses, in one manner or another.

Ati found his hospital outside of time unsettling: every day he learned of dreadful things that would have gone unnoticed in the commotion of a city, but here they filled the space and invaded minds that were constantly heckled, crushed, humiliated. The isolation of the sanatorium was one explanation. In a void, life becomes strange, nothing restrains it, it doesn't know where to look for support, where to go. Going around in circles without moving is a horrible feeling; living too long by oneself and for oneself is mortal. As for illness, it destroys many certainties: death will not tolerate any truths that try to be greater than it is, so it reduces them all to nothing. The notion that a border might exist was shattering. The world might be divided, divisible, and humankind might be multiple? Since when? Since always, what else could it be, if a thing exists it has existed for all eternity, there is no spontaneous generation. Unless God wills it—he is almighty—but does God work toward the division of mankind, does he do piecework, from time to time?

What is the border, dammit, what is on the other side?

It is known that the heavens are inhabited by angels, that hell is teeming with demons, and that the earth is covered with believers—but why should there be a border at its extremities? Who was it keeping from whom, and from what? A sphere has no beginning or end. What would that invisible world be like? If its inhabitants are endowed with consciousness, are they aware of our presence on earth and do they know of this unthinkable thing, that we do not know they exist, other than in the form of a horrible and unbelievable rumor, the improbable remains of an obliterated era? So the victory over the Enemy during the Great Holy War was not so "total, definitive, irrevocable!" Failure was right behind us, covering us with its dust while we went on celebrating our victory.

So where does that leave us? In this calamitous state, obviously: we were defeated, dispossessed of everything, and driven back behind the wrong side of the border. Our world does indeed seem to be the losers', bric-a-brac after the debacle, embellishing reality is nothing more than painting a dead man's face and offering him up to ridicule. And Yölah the almighty and Abi his delegate: what are they doing with us on this raft that has been cast adrift? Who will save us, from which side will rescue come?

The air was dense with questions: Ati did not dare look at them, but he heard them, and suffered.

Sometimes, in spite of the strictness of the surveillance and "purification" system, some felt doubt graze their minds; in others it wormed its way inside. Once it gets going, imagination can invent as many leads and riddles as it likes, to be borne far away, except that those who are bold are careless and are soon caught. The internal tension that dwells inside them charges the air around them and that is enough; the Vs have ultrasensitive antennae. It is a common error to believe that the future belongs to us because we possess knowledge. In a perfect world, there is no future, only the past and its legends, articulated in a tale of fantastic beginnings, without evolution or science; there is the Truth, single and eternal, and the Almighty always nearby, watching over it. Knowledge, doubt, and ignorance stem from a corruption that is inherent in an active world, the world of the dead and the wicked. There can be no contact possible between these worlds. It is the law: a bird that leaves its cage, even just for a single flap of its wings, is doomed to disappear; it cannot return to the cage, it would sing off-key and sow discord. Nevertheless, what one person has seen or glimpsed or even only dreamed, another, later, elsewhere, will see and glimpse and think, and perhaps this new person will manage to bring it into the light in such a way that everyone will see it and rebel against the dead man lurking inside them.

Something disturbing, leading to a question; anger to despondency; dreams to disappointment: Ati had lost his way, that was the only thing he could be sure of. All over the country, in every one of the sixty provinces, nothing ever happened, nothing visible, life was limpid, order was sublime, communion had been achieved within the Just Brotherhood, beneath the gaze of Abi and the benevolent surveillance of the

Apparatus. After such a crowning achievement, life comes to a halt: what is left to imagine, to revive, to surpass? Time stands still: what is there to count, what use is space in immobility? Abi had worked his miracle; a grateful humanity could cease to exist.

"Our faith is the soul of the world, and Abi is its beating heart."

"Submission is faith and faith is truth."

"The Apparatus and the people are ONE, *as Yölah and Abi are One."*

"To Yölah we belong, to Abi we obey."

etc.;

were the ninety-nine key phrases one learned from earliest childhood, and one recited for the rest of one's life.

When the sanatorium was built, many many years ago—a cartouche, etched in the stone above the barrel vault of the fortress's monumental portal, indicated a date, if it was indeed a date, between two fading cabalistic signs: *1984,* the year which might have been that of its inauguration, but the short text that served as a caption, no doubt to confirm and describe the building's vocation, was in an unfamiliar language; things had been going rather well, according to what a few old madmen, long gone, used to say, but no one ever understood what they were talking about, in any case no one recalled them being able to explain anything—the world has always turned in the same admirable and canonical way, yesterday and today, as it will tomorrow and the day after. Sometimes, for days and weeks at a time, life was nothing but penury, and nothing could hold back the misfortune unleashed on the cities and their inhabitants—only this was normal and just, it was everyone's duty to constantly reaffirm their faith and learn to scoff at death. The prayer meetings that marked the rhythm of the hours and days did all the rest; they installed the flock into a blissful stupor, and the chants that were broadcast from tireless loudspeakers located in strategic spots around the sanatorium in the intervals between the nine daily prayers resonated from partitions to walls, corridors to dormitories, unendingly inter-weaving their lenitive strains to maintain people's attention on the verge of abulia. The background noise was such an inti-mate part of the substratum that no one even noticed when it wasn't there, when there were power cuts or the aging sound system broke down; something in the walls or in the inmates' subconscious took over and began to chant as authentically as the truest of realities. In the absent gazes of the praying figures shone the same gentle, vibrant light of acceptance, and it never left them. Acceptance: in *abilang Gkabul* was actually the name of the holy religion of Abistan, and it was also the title of the holy book where Abi had recorded his divine teachings.

At the age of thirty-two, or thirty-five, he wasn't really sure, Ati was already an old man. He had preserved some of the charm of his youth and his race: he was tall and slim, and his fair skin was burnished by the biting upland winds, which caused the green of his gold-flecked eyes to stand out, and his natural nonchalance imbued his movements with a feline sen-suality. When he stood up straight, and closed his mouth over his rotting teeth to give a smile, he could still pass for a hand-some man. He had surely been handsome once, he remem-bered it drove him to despair because physical beauty is a defect, much appreciated by the Renegade; it attracts mock-ery and aggression. Sheltered beneath their thick veils and *burniqabs*, compressed by bandages, and always well guarded in their quarters, women did not suffer too greatly, but for the man who had even an touch of grace the ordeal was never-ending. A wild beard could make one ugly, and coarse manners or a scarecrow's rags were repellent, but unfortu-nately for Ati the people of his race were hairless, and their demeanor was gracious, Ati's particularly so; in addition he had a youthful shyness that filled hefty sanguine types with lust. Ati's memories of childhood were of one long nightmare. He had stopped thinking about it, shame had built a wall. But at the sanatorium those memories resurfaced: the patients, with nothing better to do, gave free rein to their baser instincts. It pained him to see the poor boys trying to get away, constantly having to fight someone off, but the harassment was so extreme that they eventually gave in, they could not withstand both their assailants' brutality and their cunning. At night Ati could hear their heartbreaking moans.

He despaired of ever understanding how vice proliferates in proportion to the perfection of the world. He did not dare conclude with a misinterpretation; virtue did not increase with disorder, and it was impossible to believe that depravity was a relic from the Dark Ages, before Abi brought the Light, a relic kept alive to test the believer and keep him under threat. Change, however miraculous it might be, needs time to materialize; good and evil cohabit until the former's final victory. How to know where one begins and the other ends? After all, good might be merely a substitute for evil; evil is that clever, it knows how to put on fine clothes and sing in tune, just as it is in the nature of good to be conciliatory, even to the point of spinelessness or sometimes treason. It is said in the *Gkabul* in title 2, chapter 30, verse 618: *"It is not given to man to know what is Evil and what is Good, he need only know that Yölah and Abi are working for his happiness."*

Ati did not recognize himself; he was afraid of this other self who had invaded him and behaved so carelessly, getting bolder by the day. He could hear him prompting him with questions and whispering incomprehensible answers . . . and he listened, pricked up his ears, urged him to be more specific, to provide conclusions. The confrontation was exhausting. He was terrified at the thought that he might come under suspicion, that they might find out he was a . . . he did not dare say the word . . . a nonbeliever. He didn't understand that bloody word, a word no one dared say for fear of making it happen, for common sense, after all, is founded on familiar things one says over and over without thinking . . . Non . . . be . . . lie . . . ver, it was obviously a deceitful abstraction, never, ever was anyone in Abistan obliged to believe, and there had never been any attempts to win his sincere adherence; the behavior of the perfect believer had been imposed on him, that was all. Nothing in his speech, attitude or clothing must set him apart from the robotic profile of the perfect believer, as conceived by Abi, or one of his right-hand men inspired by the Just Brotherhood and in charge of indoctrination. Ati had been trained from early childhood, and before puberty loomed on the horizon with its raw revelations of the absolute truths of the human condition, he had already become a perfect believer, who could never imagine there might be any other way to exist in life. *"God is great, he needs his believers to be perfectly submissive, he hates pretention and calculation"* (*Gkabul*, title 2, chapter 30, verse 619).

The word was more disturbing than that: to disbelieve is to reject a belief to which one has been signed up as a matter of course, but—and here's the rub—man cannot free himself from one belief without turning to another for support; like treating addiction with drugs, another creed will be adopted, invented if necessary. But how could this happen, since in Abi's ideal world there is nothing enabling one to do this, there are no competing opinions, not a hint of a premise on which to hang the tail of a mutinous idea, imagine a future, construct a story to oppose the accepted dogma? Every path down which one could play truant has been accounted for and wiped out; every mind has been strictly calibrated according to the official canon, and is adjusted regularly. Under the empire of Unique Thought, nonbelief is therefore unthinkable. But then why does the System prohibit nonbelief when it knows that such a thing is impossible and has done everything in its power to ensure it will remain so? Ati had a sudden intuition, so clear was their plan: the System does not want people to believe! That was their secret goal, because when one believes in one idea, one can believe in another—its opposite, for example—and use it as a warhorse to combat the first illusion. But since it is ridiculous, impossible, and dangerous to forbid people from believing in the idea that has been imposed upon them, the proposition has been worded in such a way as to forbid people from disbelieving: in other words, the Great Ordainer has said: "Do not seek to believe, you are in danger of straying into another belief, forbid yourself only from doubting, say and repeat that my truth is unique and just and thus will you have it constantly in mind, and do not forget that your life and your property belong to me."

In its infinite knowledge of artifice, the System realized early on that it was hypocrisy that made the perfect believer, not faith; given its oppressive nature, faith trails doubt behind it, or even rebellion and madness. The System also understood that true religion can be nothing other than well-regulated sanctimoniousness, set up as a monopoly and maintained by omnipresent terror. "As detail is the essence of practice" everything has been codified, from birth to death, from sunrise to sunset; the life of the perfect believer is an uninterrupted succession of words and gestures to be repeated, and it leaves no latitude to dream, hesitate, think, or possibly disbelieve—or even believe. Ati found it hard to formulate a conclusion: believing is not believing but deceiving; not believing is believing the opposite idea, thereby deceiving oneself and eventually making one's idea into a dogma for others. That held true for Unique Thought . . . was it also true in the free world? Ati recoiled at the difficulty, he did not know the free world, he could simply not imagine the connection between dogma and freedom, or which of the two might prove stronger.

Something in his mind had snapped, and he couldn't see what. And yet he was fully aware that he did not want to go on being the man he had been in this world, a world that suddenly seemed horribly wicked and base to him; he desired this transformation that had begun in pain and shame, even if it killed him. The man he had been, the faithful believer, was dying, that much he knew, and another life was being born inside him. This new life was exalting, even though he knew it was doomed to violent punishment—he would be crushed and cursed, his family ruined and banished, because—and this was as clear as day—he had no means of escaping from this world, he belonged to it, body and soul, as he had always done and always would until the end of time, when nothing would remain of him, not a speck of dust, not a memory. He could not even deny it in silence, he had nothing to reproach it with—basically, nothing to oppose it with—it was what he was, true to his nature. And who could contest the *Gkabul*, who could cause it any trouble, and how? Nothing touched it; on the contrary, everything strengthened it. That was the way it was conceived, supreme and sublimely indifferent to the world and to humankind, just as the madness and the colossal ambition of its promoters wished. That was the explanation: he was like God, everything proceeded from him and everything was resolved in him—good and evil, life and death. In fact, nothing exists, not even God; he alone exists.

The Apparatus was sure to hunt him down and annihilate him—soon, no doubt, and perhaps the machinery had already been on the alert for a long time, or forever, waiting for the right moment to strike, like a cat pretending to sleep when the mouse thinks it has gotten away. He was one cell in an organ, an ant in the anthill: dysfunction in one spot is instantly felt throughout the body collective. The distress tormenting him would surely goad the System to its depths; unusual signals would have been exchanged somewhere, driven by instinct, a vibration of chords or a mental flow among the Vs, automatically triggering some process in the nerve center to localize the source of the disturbance, to verify and analyze it with infinite complexity, which in turn would set in motion other equally complex mechanisms to correct and adjust and if need be destroy, and then reinitialization and oblivion would come to ward off any harmful reminiscences and the ensuing surge of nostalgia that could follow; and all of it, down to the most minute quantum of information, would be encoded and archived in a slow infallible memory, to be chewed on over and over, endlessly, until this rumination disgorged sovereign rules and practical teachings to reinforce the whole system and prevent the future from being anything other than a strict replica of the past.

In the Book of Abi it is written, in the first title, chapter 2, verse 12:

"The Revelation is one, unique and universal, it calls for neither addition nor revision, nor does it call for faith, love, or criticism. Only Acceptance and Submission. Yölah is all-powerful, he will punish the arrogant severely."

And further, in title 42, chapter 36, verse 351, Yölah is more specific: *"He who is arrogant will suffer the thunder of my wrath, he will be mutilated, dismembered, burned, and his ashes will be scattered to the winds, and his kin, ascendants, and offspring, will know a bitter end, and death itself will not protect them from my prosecution."*

The mind is basically nothing more than a mechanism, a blind, cold machine by virtue of its extraordinary complexity, which mandates that it must apprehend everything, control everything, and increase interference and terror without pause. Between life and the machine there is all the mystery of freedom, which man cannot attain without dying, and which the machine transcends without acceding to consciousness. Ati was not free and never would be, but armed solely with his doubt and fears he felt truer than Abi, greater than the Just Brotherhood and its tentacular Apparatus, and more alive than the inert, swelling mass of believers; he had acquired the consciousness of his condition, and therein lay his freedom, in the perception that we are not free but possess the power to fight to the death to be so. It seemed clear to him that true victory lies in the losing battle that, despite everything, is fought to the end. By virtue of this knowledge, he understood that when death came for him, it would be his own and not that of the Apparatus; it would occur through his own volition, his inner rebellion, it would never be punishment for any deviation from or failure to obey the laws of the System. The Apparatus might destroy him, erase him, it could shake him and reprogram him and make him adore submission to the point of madness, but it could never take from him that which it did not know, had never seen, never possessed, had never given or received, although it was something it hated above all else and sought endlessly to crush: freedom. Ati knew this, the way man knows that death is the end of life—that thing that is elusive in essence is its disavowal and its end, but it is also its justification—the System having no aim other than to prevent freedom from appearing, to enchain men and kill them; though driven by self-interest this was also the only pleasure it could find in its miserable existence. The slave who knows he is a slave will always be freer and greater than his master, even if that master is king of the world.

So Ati would die like that, with a dream of freedom in his heart, it was what he wanted, it was vital, because he knew he could never have anything more, and that living in a system like that was not living at all, it served no purpose, it was a life lived for nothing, for no one, only to die and disintegrate like an inanimate object.

His heart was beating so fast it hurt. A strange sensation: the more fear overwhelmed him and twisted his guts, the stronger he felt. He felt so courageous. Something was crystallizing deep in his heart, a little seed of true courage, a diamond. He was discovering—without knowing how to express it other than through a paradox—that life deserves for us to die for it, because without life we are dead creatures who have never been anything but dead. Before dying, Ati wanted to live his life, the life he sensed emerging from darkness, even if for only a split second.

Not that long ago he had been among those who called for the death of anyone who failed to obey the rules of the Just Brotherhood. When it came to gross misconduct, he rallied with the hard-liners who insisted on spectacular executions, for he believed that the people were entitled to these moments of intense communion, where blood flowed and splattered profusely, and purifying terror erupted like a volcano. His faith emerged enhanced, renewed. It was not cruelty that inspired him, nor any base emotion; he simply believed that to Yölah man must offer his best by showing hatred for the enemy and love for one's kin, by rewarding good and punishing evil, in wisdom as well as madness.

God is ardent; to live for him is an exaltation.

But now with each passing moment Ati was increasingly convinced that all of this was mere words, words that could have been etched onto his memory at birth, automatic, delayed-action responses inserted in his genes and constantly perfected with each generation. And suddenly there came to him the revelation of the deep reality of his conditioning: it had made him, and everyone around him, into a stubborn machine who was proud of the fact, a believer who was happy to be blind, a zombie congealed in submission and obsequiousness, living for nothing, out of simple obligation, useless duty, a petty creature capable of killing all of mankind with a snap of his fingers. This revelation was an enlightenment, and showed him the insidious self that dominated him from within and against whom he wanted to rebel . . . but then again he did not. The contradiction was flagrant, and indispensable, it was at the very heart of his conditioning! The believer must be constantly maintained at the point where submission and rebellion are enamored of each other: submission is infinitely more delightful when one sees the possibility of setting oneself free, but it is also for this reason that mutiny is out of the question. There is too much at stake—life and the heavens—and nothing to gain; freedom in the wilderness or in the grave is another prison. Were it not for this complicity, submission would be a vague state unable to awaken the consciousness of the believer to his absolute insignificance, let alone to the munificence, omnipotence, and infinite compassion of his sovereign. Submission engenders rebellion and rebellion resolves itself in submission: that is what is needed, this indissoluble pair, in order for one's self-awareness to exist. That is the path: one can only know good if one knows evil, and vice versa, by virtue of the principle that holds that life does not exist or move other than within and in opposition to hostile forces. A strange, underhand spirit is lodged in everyone; it thinks of life, goodness, peace, truth, brotherhood, and gentle, reassuring perpetuity, and endows them with every virtue, but does not seek them out—and oh how passionately—other than through death, destruction, lying, cunning, domination, perversion, and brutal, unjust aggression. And so the contradiction vanishes into confusion, the struggle between good and evil comes to an end, as they are two modes of a single reality, just as action and reaction are one, and equal, to ensure unity and equilibrium. Suppressing one implies suppressing the other. In Abi's world good and evil are not in opposition; they merge, since there is no life to recognize them, name them, and construct a duality, they are one and the same reality, that of non-life, or death-in-life. All of belief is there, the question of good and evil from a moral viewpoint is a pointless, subsidiary question, set aside once and for all, good and evil are no more than the pillars of stability, with no meaning of their own. The true holy religion, Acceptance, *Gkabul*, consists of this and only this: proclaiming that there is no god but Yölah, and that Abi is his Delegate. The rest belongs to the law and its tribunal: they will make man into a submissive, diligent believer, and crowds of tireless cohorts who will do what they are told, with the means placed at their disposal, and all will proclaim, "Yölah is great and Abi is his Delegate!"

The more men are diminished, the more they see themselves as strong and great. Only at the hour of their death do they realize, dazed, that life owes them nothing because they gave it nothing.

But what does their opinion matter: they've had their blood sucked dry by a system they have both defended and been victim to. Predators and prey, inseparable in absurdity and madness. No one will tell them that in the equation of life, good and evil have been reversed, and that in the end good has been replaced by a lesser evil; life has left them no other way, given the fact that human society can only be governed by evil, an ever greater evil, so that nothing, ever, from without or within, will come to threaten it. And so the evil that opposes evil becomes good, and good is the perfect expedient to support evil and justify it.

"Good and Evil are mine, it has not been given to you to distinguish them, I send them both to you to show the way to truth

and happiness. Woe to those who do not heed my call. I am Yölah the almighty," so it is written in the Book of Abi, title 5, chapter 36, verse 97.

He would have liked to speak to someone about his trouble. To put his thoughts into words and say them, hear mocking replies, criticism, perhaps encouragement—it all seemed vital to him at this stage, where perdition was already well advanced. More than once he was tempted to strike up a conversation with a patient, a nurse, or a pilgrim, but he caught himself just in time; they'd call him crazy, accuse him of blasphemy. One word and the world collapses. The Vs would come running: evil thoughts were like nectar to them. He knew how people were trained to denounce others; he himself had gone about it with fervor at his work, in his neighborhood, against his most reliable neighbors and friends. He had been highly rated and more than once he'd received praise during the R-Days, the Days of Reward, and been mentioned in *The Hero*, the renowned and very honorable newsletter of the VLBs, the Volunteer Law-enforcing Believers.

As the days and months went by, Ati began to feel out of his depth with the most familiar notions; they took on a new resonance. Outside the yoke of society and police machinery that keep belief on the straight and narrow path, everything falls apart: good, evil, true, false no longer have borders, or at least not those they had been known to have—other borders emerge in filigree. Everything is blurred, everything is dangerous and far away. The more one looks for oneself, the more one is lost.

The isolation of the sanatorium made everything difficult: wretchedness grew by the day, indoctrination was getting lax. There was always something preventing classes from being held, or the beneficial sessions of scansion, or the restful prayers, and even the sacrosanct Thursday Imploration: patients were missing at roll call, an avalanche or a landslide had blocked the road, high waters had washed away a foot-bridge, lightning had struck a cable, the schoolmaster had fallen into the ravine on his way back from the city, the direc-tor had gone to see what had happened or was required in high places, the tutor had lost his voice, the janitor could not find his key-ring, there was hunger, thirst, an epidemic, penury, car-nage, a thousand futile, sovereign things. Far from everything, nothing worked, calamity had a free rein. Left to their own devices, idle as stones, surrounded by want, they were all unnecessary, in the way; the patients gathered together, pathetic and ashamed, to watch each other die, to tell of their suffering, to wander from one wall to the next, and at night, in their icy beds, adrift in the dark like a raft on the ocean, they stirred up happy memories to keep warm, always the same ones, for they had taken on an obsessive significance. It was as if they wanted to announce something: they receded, returned, clashed. Sometimes, for a short while, which the patients tried to prolong by watching the film again, adding adventure and color, they might be aware of how far they had come, and that in a way they did exist, someone in the ether wanted to talk to them, to listen, to offer help, a compassionate soul, a long-lost friend, a confidant. So there were things in this life that did belong to them, not in the way of some venal piece of property, but as a truth, a comfort. It was bliss to be able to surrender to trust.

Bit by bit, an unfamiliar world appeared, where strange words were in use, words no one had ever heard—glimpsed, perhaps, like shadows passing in the commotion of murmurs. One word fascinated Ati; it opened the door onto a world of beauty and inexhaustible love, where man was a god who could work miracles with his thoughts. It was insane, it caused him to tremble; not only did the thing seem possible, it told him that it alone was real.

One night, he heard himself murmuring beneath his blanket. The sounds emerged of their own will, as if forcing their way through his pinched lips. Gripped by fear, he resisted, then he let go and listened to his words. An electric shock went through him. He gasped for breath, he heard himself repeating that fascinating word, the one he'd never used and did not know, and he stammered each syllable: "Free . . . dom . . . free . . . dom . . . free . . . dom . . . free . . . dom . . . free . . . dom . . . free . . . dom . . . " Did he shout it at one point? Did the other patients hear him? How could he know? It was a cry inside . . .

The cavernous groan of the mountain, which had terrified him ever since his arrival at the sanatorium, suddenly vanished. The wind was light, now that it was rid of fear; it smelled of good mountain air, sharp and euphoric. A bright melody, rising from the deep gorges to the summits. Ati listened, rapt.

That night he did not sleep a wink. He was happy. He could have slept and dreamt, happiness had exhausted him, but he preferred to stay awake and let his imagination roam. This happiness would be short-lived, he must make the most of it. He also urged himself to remain calm, to come back down to earth, to do some planning and prepare himself mentally, for soon he would be leaving the hospital and going home, back to where he belonged . . . his country, Abistan, about which he realized he knew so little. He must quickly learn all he could, to give himself a chance at salvation.

Two more months as heavy as the tomb would go by before the duty nurse came to tell him the doctor had signed his discharge papers. The nurse showed him his medical file. It consisted of two crumpled sheets of paper: the admissions form and the discharge form, to which a nervous hand had added: "Keep under close scrutiny."

Ati suddenly had a bad feeling. Had the Vs heard him in his dreams?

It was with a heavy heart that Ati left the sanatorium, one fine April morning. It was still bone-chillingly cold, but there were hidden pockets of impending summer warmth, the faintest hints, enough to make you want to live again, to run as far as your lungs could carry you.

It was still the deep of night, but the caravan was ready. Nothing was missing, perhaps just an order. All the travelers had gathered outside the fortress and were waiting patiently; the donkeys were in their favorite position, in pairs, head to tail, dining on the scrawny mountain grass; indolent porters stood chewing on magic herbs under the lean-to, guards sipped scorching tea, fiddling with their rifle breeches with a most military alacrity; and off to one side, cloaked with dignity in their polar pelisses around a blazing brazier, were the commissar of faith and his escort (including the invisible and worrying presence of a V whose mind was telepathically sweeping his surroundings), consulting one another while telling their portable prayer beads. Between two mundane deliberations they prayed noisily to Yölah, and to themselves they prayed to Jabil, the spirit of the mountain. Going down the mountain is not an easy task: it is more dangerous than the ascent, and with the added danger of gravity it is easy to succumb to the lure of vertigo. The old hands, devilishly cryptic, repeatedly told the novices that to run in the direction of a fall is a very human tendency.

The caravan passengers stood further off, under a collapsed

awning, contrite and trembling, as if they were about to head off to an unjust death. Only the whites of their eyes were visible. Their shortness of breath betrayed their extreme nervousness. They were patients who'd recovered and were on their way home, or agents from the administration who had come for some bureaucratic reason that could not wait until summer. Ati was among them, wrapped in several *burnis,* waterproof with grime; he leaned on a gnarled pilgrim's staff, and held a bundle with his gear: a shirt, a metal cup, a bowl, his pills, his prayer book, and his talismans. They waited, stamping the ground and thumping their sides. On the horizon the vast sky was ablaze with a blinding, dazzling light, their eyelids were heavy, they had grown used to their slow, twilit existence at the sanatorium. Everything about them—gestures, breathing, vision—had become sluggish, heavy, to enable them to survive this impossible asceticism, clinging as they did above the void at an altitude of more than four thousand *siccas.*

He would miss his icy hell; he was beholden to it for curing him and showing him a reality he never knew existed, although it was the reality of his world and he knew no other. There is a certain type of music we hear only in solitude, away from police surveillance and the confines of society.

He dreaded his return, and at the same time he was eager to be home. It is among one's kin, and against them, that one must fight; it is there, in the steady succession of days and the thicket of the unspoken that life loses its deeper significance and seeks refuge in pretense and shallowness. The sanatorium had restored his vigor and opened his eyes onto the unthinkable reality that in their world there was another country, and that a border—deadly, impossible to find and therefore impossible to cross—lay between them. What sort of world could allow ignorance to reach such a point that a person didn't know who was living in his own house, at the end of the corridor?

It was entertaining to ponder the maddening question: does a man continue to exist if he has been projected from the real world into a virtual world? If so, can he die? What of? Time does not exist in the virtual world, therefore neither does boredom, old age, illness, or death. How could he commit suicide? Would he in turn become virtual, like his new world? Would he preserve the memory of this other world, of life, death, people coming and going, the days passing? Can a world that offers these sensations be virtual?

But enough of all that: theories, mind games, he'd gone over them a thousand times in his mind, without ever gaining anything other than fear and headaches. And anger and insomnia. And shame, and stabbing regret. What was urgent, now, was to go to find those borders and to cross them. To see, from the other side, what it was they had forbidden by means of such a long and perfect conspiracy; to find out, with terror or with joy, who we were, and what sort of world was ours.

These were also some of his thoughts that helped him pass the time; waiting was a source of anxiety and questioning.

Suddenly, out of everywhere and nowhere, from a distant valley, a vast, powerful sound, smooth and harmonious, assaulted the mountain, climbing all the way to the sanatorium: a magnificent, spellbinding chant, its echoes interweaving, undulating, then fading away in a strange, sad, poetic way. Ati liked to listen and follow the languid strains until they vanished into sidereal silence; the beautiful song of the alpine horn!

The vanguard had left the sanatorium at first light, and now they had reached the foothills, where the first stop was a bric-a-brac between bazaar and desert, shaman's cave and multipurpose administrative office, offering multiple services, located far below, over twenty *chabirs* as the crow flies. Only the alpine horn had enough breath to carry that far. And now it was calling out that the route was clear and passable. The signal they had been waiting for.

The caravan could depart.

Every hour the horns on the next foothills would sound to indicate the time and the way, and the caravan's foghorn would reply that time keeps its own rhythm, in accordance with Yölah's will; a rhythm that would not, however, try the passengers' resistance, for they were convalescents with little strength or skill in the ways of the mountain, and poor civil servants who were stiff from head to toe.

The departure was a moment of great emotion at the sanatorium. Crowded onto terraces, around small openings in the thick stone walls, and on the rampart walks, the patients watched the caravan set off into the dawn mist. They waved and prayed as much for the courageous voyagers as for themselves, still prisoners of their debilitating illness. Pale as they were, wrapped in their threadbare, patched, dirty white *burnis*, surrounded by a chiaroscuro halo, they looked like a host of phantoms come to bid farewell to the end of something incomprehensible.

At a bend in the trail, overlooking a sheer ravine, Ati turned around to gaze at the fortress one last time. Seen from below, crowned with a vaporous sky vibrant with light, its hieratic power was impressive, even terrifying. There was a long history behind the fortress; no one knew what it was, but they could feel it. It seemed to have always been there, to have known multiple worlds and peoples, and to have watched them disappear one after the other. Almost nothing remained of all those eras, just a spectral atmosphere heavy with mystery and murmuring, a certain subjacent vanity of things, a few signs carved in stone, crosses, stars, crescents, roughly chiseled or finely drawn, here and there phylacteries bearing scribbles all in gothic accents, or elsewhere, disfigured drawings. They must have meant something, they wouldn't have been sculpted for nothing, the care taken implied they must be of significance, and there wouldn't have been such an effort to erase them had that significance not been powerful. During the Great Holy War, the fortress had been on the front line that ran along the Ouâ range, and it was put to use, for its strategic value made it an irresistible objective; it became a fortified town in the hands of the Enemy and then under the people of believers . . . or the other way around; in short, it changed hands more than once. The fact remains that in the end it was bravely conquered once and for all by Abi's soldiers, as Yölah had ordained. A certain legend had it that there were enough dead bodies in that region to fill every gorge in the Ouâ and cross the rivers as if they were dry. It was possible, after all; the figures they gave were astronomical, the weapons they'd used were more powerful than the sun, and the battles had lasted for decades—it is no longer known how long. It was a miracle that the fortress had remained intact amid the general annihilation. If even half the stories one heard were true, that would mean that wherever we set our feet in this country we step on corpses. It was disheartening, one couldn't help but think that the next time the earth was turned over it would be for us.

After the war that destroyed everything and radically transformed the history of the world, poverty cast hundreds of millions of unfortunate souls onto the roads throughout the sixty provinces of the empire—gaunt tribes, lost families, or what remained of them; widows, orphans, the disabled, the insane, lepers, victims of plague, of gassings, of radiation. Who could help them? Everywhere was hell. Highway robbers pullulated, forming armies that plundered whatever remained of that wretched world. For a long time the fortress served as refuge for any wanderer who had the strength and courage to confront the steep face of the Ouâ. It became an unsavory place, people came from afar looking for asylum and justice, but found only vice and death. Truly, never was there a worse place.

But with time, things went back to normal. The brigands were arrested and executed in keeping with the traditions of each region; the machinery of death operated day and night, there were a thousand ways to make it more efficient, but even a thirty-six hour day would not have sufficed to get the daily job done.

Widows and orphans were housed here and there, and given basic trades to perform. Those who were sick or disabled went on begging wherever the wind carried them, and for a lack of care they died in the millions. It was to make these corpses disappear—for they were stinking up the cities and the countryside and causing countless epidemics—that the mysterious and very efficient guild of corpse collectors was created. Laws were passed to regulate their activity, and the Just Brotherhood promulgated a religious edict attributing sacramental value to something that was above all a matter of public hygiene and corporatist interest. Emptied, cleaned, and restored, the fortress was made into a sanatorium, and those who had tuberculosis were sent there. No one remembers exactly how or why, but it was commonly held that they were the cause of all human woe. People mobilized against them, banned them from the cities, then from the countryside, which had to be plowed again. Superstition vanished with the thaw, but the practice remained, and consumptives were still consigned to the fortress.

Between the patients and the pilgrims Ati learned a great deal. They came from all four corners of the vast empire. Learning the name of their city, and something of their customs and history, hearing their accents and observing them on an everyday basis: it was all surprising, an incredible education. The fortress offered a global vision of the people of believers in their infinite diversity, each group with its own color and manners, not found in the others. Similarly, they had their own language which they spoke among themselves, in hushed tones, far from foreign ears, with such eagerness that everyone else was burning to know what was being said. But they immediately broke off their discussions: they were cautious. Once Ati had regained some strength, he ran from room to room to fill his eyes and ears and nose, too—for these people had their typical smells, you could follow any one of them just by his or her odor. You could also place them by their accent, their way of walking, their gaze, who knows what else, and before exchanging even two words, there they would be, in each other's arms, sobbing with emotion. It was moving to see how they sought each other out, as if they were at a crowded market, then went to gather in a shady corner to carry on in their dialect to their hearts' content. What were they on about all the livelong day? It was words, nothing more, but it cheered them up. It was magnificent, but ever so wrongheaded, according to the law all inhabitants must speak *abilang*, the sacred tongue Yölah taught Abi in order to unite the believers as one nation; all other languages were the product of contingency, and they were pointless, they divided mankind, shut them off into the particular, corrupted their souls through invention and falsehood. Whosoever utters the name of Yölah cannot be sullied by the bastard languages that exhale the fetid breath of Balis.

He had never thought about it, but if someone had put the question to Ati, he would have replied that all Abistanis looked alike, that they resembled him, were in the same mold as the people from his neighborhood in Qodsabad, the only human beings he had ever seen. And now it turned out they were infinitely more varied and so different that at the end of the day they were worlds unto themselves, unique and unfathomable, which in a way went counter to the notion of *a people*, unique and valiant, made of identical brothers and sisters. So *the people* was a theory, yet another one, contrary to the principle of humankind, which was entirely crystallized in the individual, in each individual. It was fascinating and disturbing. What then was *a people*?

The fortress disappeared in the mist, behind the curtain of his tears. This was the last time Ati would see it. He would preserve a mystical memory of the place. It was there, in its walls, that he had learned he was living in a dead world, and it was there, at the heart of the drama, in the depths of solitude, that he had had the extraordinary vision of another, permanently inaccessible, world.

The homeward journey took nearly a year. From cart to truck, from truck to train (in those regions where the railroad had withstood rust and war), and from train back to cart wherever civilization had disappeared yet again. And sometimes on foot, or on mules, across steep mountains and deep forests. The caravan was at the mercy of chance and of its guides, and it made headway by clinging on wherever it could.

In the end the voyagers had covered no less than six thousand *chabirs*, interrupted by endless stops spent fretting in this place or that; there were reunification camps, there were dispatch centers, where huge crowds mingled together, drifted apart, came together again, a constant confusing assembly of milling, teeming throngs, until docile and patient they settled into apathy, to confront time. The caravan leaders waited for orders that did not come, the trucks waited for spare parts that could not be found, the trains waited for the tracks to be repaired and the locomotive to be brought back to life. And once everything was finally ready, there came the issue of drivers and guides, who must be found, quickly, and in the meantime there was nothing for it but patience. Later, when after multiple searches the missing individuals were joyfully located at last, it was only to learn that they were now otherwise occupied. There were all manner of excuses, familiar and novel: they'd gone to bury someone, or visit friends who were ill; they had problems to deal with, ceremonies to attend, sacrifices to catch up on, but most often—and this was the Abistanis' particular indulgence, for they were devilishly opportunistic—they were busy doing volunteer work to rack up points for the next R-Day, the Day of Reward, giving a helping hand wherever it was needed—here to raise the tower of a *mockba*, there to dig graves or a well, paint a *midra*, check a list of pilgrims, provide backup to rescuers, take part in searches for missing persons, and so on. Their good deeds would be validated by a certificate at their local R-Day office, there could be no cheating, it was delivered under oath. All that remained now was to find the high-ranking official who would issue the permit to leave the camp. Obviously, so much wasted time could never be made up, the road wouldn't allow it; that was another ordeal, as dreadful as they came during the rainy season.

So it all took a year. With a sturdy truck, roads that were in good condition from start to finish, decent weather, serious guides, and total freedom to maneuver, six thousand *chabirs* would have taken no time at all, scarcely a month.

Along with all the others—except the pilgrims and caravan leaders who were a bit better informed—Ati had no idea what the country was like. He thought it must be huge, but what does huge mean if you cannot see it with your own eyes, cannot touch it with your own hands? And what are limits, if you never reach them? The word "limit" itself raises the question: what is there beyond the limit? Only the Honorables, the great masters of the Just Brotherhood, and the leaders of the Apparatus knew these things and everything else; they defined and controlled all of it. For them the world was a small place, they could hold it in the palm of their hand, they had planes and helicopters to dash about the sky, and speedboats to cross the seas and the oceans. You saw their vehicles go by, you heard them roar, but you never saw *them*; they didn't mingle with *the people*, they addressed them through the *nadirs*, the wall screens you could find all over the country, and they always resorted to emphatic presenters whom the common people referred to as "parrots," or to the oft-heard voices of the *mockbis* confessing the faithful nine times a day from their *mockbas*, and surely (but no one knew how) they must have used the channel of the Vs, those mysterious beings, formerly known as djinns, who mastered telepathy, invisibility, and ubiquity. It was also said that the masters—but no one had seen this with his own eyes—possessed submarines and flying fortresses, propelled by a mysterious energy, vessels which endlessly probed the depths of the oceans and of the skies.

Later, Ati would learn that the distance on the diagonal from one end of Abistan to the other was a fabulous fifty thousand *chabirs*. It made him dizzy. How many lives did it take to cover such a distance?

When the decision was made to send him to the sanatorium, Ati was half-conscious. He saw nothing as they crossed the country, just fragments of landscape between two dizzy spells or two comas. He remembered that the journey had seemed endless, and that his bad spells were ever more frequent and painful, draining him of his blood, and that more than once he had called out to death to come and rescue him. It was a sin, but he reckoned that Yölah would know how to forgive those who were in agony.

There was nothing luxurious about these journeys; a nomad's everyday life consisted of digging vehicles out of the sand, clearing the road, closing gaps, towing, sawing, propping, filling in, dismantling, loading, and unloading. The voyagers helped out, enthusiastically, encouraging each other with calls and cries. The hours between chores were devoted to worship. The rest of the time, while the landscape rolled monotonously by, they counted the hours.

There was one thing bothering Ati, but in the long run he was forced to accept the hallucinatory reality before him: the country was empty. Not a single soul anywhere, no movement, no sound, only the wind sweeping along the roads, and the torrential rain, sometimes washing everything away. The convoy was literally sinking into the void, a sort of grayish-black fog streaked here and there with luminous flashes. One day, between two yawns, it occurred to Ati that the dawn of creation must have been something like this, the world did not exist, either as container or as content; emptiness dwelling in emptiness. This gave him a disquieting, troubling feeling, as if that primeval time had returned, and now everything was equally possible, the best and the worst—all one had to say was "I want" for a world to emerge from nothingness and be ordained according to one's wishes. Ati would have liked to share his thoughts, but he held his tongue, not because he believed his desire might be heard, but because he felt that he himself was in this original state of indetermination, and to utter his wish might act on him first of all and transform him into a . . . toad, perhaps, since the first creatures who ever appeared on earth were toads—slimy, pustular, born of the failed wish of some inexperienced god . . . One must never tempt life, or rush it; it is capable of anything.

Two or three times over, in the distance, they glimpsed military convoys advancing stiffly, a movement that was hieratic and mechanical but even more than that, stubborn and resolute, like the invincible force that orders great herds on the savannah to surge into action and begin their migration toward life or death—who knows, the only thing that matters is the forward motion and the anticipated encounter. It all gave the impression of a mysterious expedition come from another world. The caravan of trucks, heavily laden with cannons and missile launchers, was dragging in its dusty wake an interminable legion of soldiers, loaded down with equipment. Ati had never seen more soldiers than a truck patrolling in town could carry—a dozen or so, supported by an indeterminate number of casual militia, turbulent and indefatigable, armed with machetes, rods, or truncheons—and this was when there were major ceremonies in the stadiums, such as mass executions or religious services calling for holy war, and during these events the exaltation became trancelike, and then there were more militia than there are ants at the height of summer. Were these soldiers on their way to war, or on their way back? Which war? A new Great Holy War? Against whom, if the only country on this earth was Abistan?

Ati was further convinced of the reality of war when one day in the distance they saw a military convoy towing an endless column of prisoners, thousands of them, chained together in threes. From that distance it was impossible to make out any details that might have enabled him to give them an identity—but which identity? Were they old, young, bandits, heathens? There were women among them, of that he was sure, he could tell from certain signs, shadows draped in blue, the color of the female prisoner's *burniqab*, and they followed far behind, keeping the distance—forty steps—prescribed by the Holy Scriptures so that neither soldiers nor convicts would be able to see them, or get a strong whiff of their musky female smell, which fear and sweat compounded to make unbearably sharp.

They also met pilgrims, in columns that were just as impressive, trudging along, scanning verses from the Book of Abi, as well as hikers' slogans: "Pilgrim am I, pilgrim I go, with a hey and a ho, and onwards I go!" "We walk on the earth, we fly in the sky and life goes on, do or die!" "One more *chabir*, a thousand more *chabirs*, all in good cheer, may beggars live in fear!" and so on, and always the same formula that punctuated every sentence, every gesture of the believer's life: "Yölah is great and Abi is his Delegate!" Their bombastic chants resounded in the distance, adding a moving refrain to the silence embracing the world.

From time to time they nearly stumbled upon a village, an invisible hamlet. Clearly life had never really lingered there; there was absence in the air, and a great deal of parsimony. With so much discretion, there is no difference between a village and a cemetery. Cows grazed in surrounding pastures but there were no cowherds; did they even have any owners? In their childlike gaze was that gray, pale fear that comes of emptiness, solitude, boredom, and too great a poverty. At the sight of the caravan, they rolled their eyes in every direction. That evening their milk would have turned.

But there are no journeys without an end; it was long in coming. It was not much further to Qodsabad, three days as the crow flies. As they neared their goal, the caravans marked time: it was a deep-rooted habit, they sent scouts to reconnoiter, and an envoy to negotiate a friendly welcome, and so the waiting was put to good use, to recover from the fatigue of the journey, because a mass arrival in a friendly city would be cause for exhausting displays of effusion—one party after the other, nonstop and round the clock. It was important to make a good impression, and to remain vigilant. And one does wonder, after all, when there is a homecoming: will we recognize our loved ones, will they recognize us, after such a long time?

Something in the air told them that they were approaching a major city; before their eyes the countryside was losing its wild and sovereign aspect to take on the colors of abandonment and depletion, along with the smell of things rotting in the sun; it was as if a blind, evil force were at work, corrupting everything around it—life, the soil, the people—and spitting them back out, horribly damaged. There was no explanation for it; it was a decay that seemed to exist of its own volition, feeding on whatever remained and throwing it back up only to feast on it all over again, and although the first circle of suburbs was still far away, at several dozen *chabirs*, the poverty here was Pantagruelian. Ati seemed to recall that the air in his neighborhood in Qodsabad was no better, but you could breathe it all the same, because you always feel better at home than at your neighbor's.

The caravan Ati had been assigned to at the last dispatch center included civil servants on their way home from a mission; various kinds of stewards; students trussed up in their school *burnis*, which were long black gowns that stopped a hand's width from their ankles; they were on their way to the capital to perfect their knowledge of certain very recondite branches of religion. There was also, somewhat off to one side as befits nobility, a posse of theologians and *mockbis* coming back from a spiritual retreat on Abirat, the sacred mountain where Abi liked to go as a child, all alone, and where he had had his first visions.

Among the voyagers was a civil servant called Nas, no older than Ati but in fine form, suntanned, on his way home from a dig at an archeological site that was still secret but that was destined to become a celebrated place of pilgrimage. All that was left to be done was to polish up the history behind the place: Nas was in charge of gathering the technical elements that would enable theoreticians from the Ministry of Archives, Sacred Books, and Holy Memories to finalize that history, to stage it and connect it to the history of Abistan as a whole. It was a truly miraculous business: an ancient village had been found perfectly intact. How had it survived the Great Holy War and the ravages that had followed? Why had it not been discovered before now? Unthinkably, this meant that the

Apparatus had failed—worse, that it was fallible; it meant that in the holy land of the *Gkabul* there were people and places who eluded Yölah's light and jurisdiction. The other mystery was the absence of skeletons in the streets or in the houses. What had the inhabitants died of, who had removed the bodies, where had they been placed?—these were the questions to which Nas had to find an answer. One evening, as they sat talking around the campfire, he let slip that it was rumored among the clerks at the Ministry that a certain Dia, a great Honorable of the Just Brotherhood and head of the powerful Department of Investigations into Miracles, had his heart set on that village: he wanted it in order to serve his personal legend, to lay claim, as his own property, to a pilgrimage of prime importance. Nas went about his task with passion and growing disquiet, because he could see there was a great deal at stake, and that he was smack in the middle of an infinitely complex rivalry between clans in the Just Brotherhood. One day, throwing caution to the wind, he told Ati that the dig had unearthed relics likely to shake the very symbolic foundations of Abistan.

Ati was drawn by his gaze; it was the gaze of a man who, like him, had made the disturbing discovery that religion can be built on the opposite of truth and so become the fierce wardress of the original falsehood.

BOOK TWO

In which Ati returns to his neighborhood in Qodsabad, his friends, and his work, and discovers that the daily routine quickly makes him forget the sanatorium, his woes, and the dark thoughts that had troubled his ailing mind. But what is done is done, things do not disappear simply because we are far away from them; behind sovereign appearance lies the invisible, with its mysteries and obscure menace. And then there is chance, like an architect at work, coordinating everything with art and method.

A ti had recovered from his illness and his prodigious voyage. If he suffered any aftereffects, they were hardly visible—a waxy complexion, gaunt cheeks, a little wrinkle here, a little necrosis there, some creaking in his joints, an untimely wheezing in his throat: nothing life-threatening, and he did not stand out amid the ambient pallor. Neighbors and friends greeted him warmly and accompanied him as a worthy cohort wherever he went. Reinsertion meant errands, waiting, documents to file and to fetch, arrangements to make; it was easy to get muddled. But eventually all the loose ends were tied up, Ati was home at last, life was back to normal. And in fact he had ended up better off: before, he had been a temporary employee in some vague municipal office, but now he was at the city hall, with a sensitive position in the patent office, where they issued important documents to tradespeople; his job, under the authority of his boss, was to make certified copies and archive them. At that level of responsibility, he had the right and the obligation to wear the green-and-white-striped armband of a basic councilor, and for prayer at his *mockba* he had a spot reserved in the eighth row. He used to live in a damp basement room that smelled of rats and bedbugs, and which had been the cause of his tuberculosis; now he was granted a lovely little studio on the sunny terrace of a building that was run-down but still solid. Back in the days when water ran through pipes, to the delight of households, the place had been a washhouse, open to the winds and the pigeons, where women came to do the laundry, and while it was drying in the sun they would revel in ribald tales and raucous laughter while observing the world of men milling idly outside the building in the dusty streets below, but eventually a civic committee found out about their Sabbath and the place was raided, requisitioned by a decree from the Bailiff, released from its spell and granted to an honest schoolteacher who spent a great amount of time fixing the place up and draftproofing it until at last it was a cozy nest. He had just died, leaving nothing behind him, neither family nor memory, only a teacher's illegible scribble and the impression of a retiring individual. Solidarity among believers was a duty, and carried particular weight in the monthly appraisal, but affection and admiration also counted: Ati was a hero in the neighborhood. To vanquish the dread tuberculosis and return alive from so far away was an exploit worthy of a believer whom Yölah looked kindly upon, and so it went without saying that he would be favored. The little he had shared about the sanatorium, the climate, and the journey had sufficed to astound colleagues and neighbors. For people who have never transcended their fear, elsewhere is an abyss. Later, much later, he would learn that his magnificent promotion was not due to the good will of others, or to his exploits, any more than it was to the benevolence of Yölah, but only to the recommendation on the part of an agent from the Apparatus, made in the name of the all-powerful Ministry of Moral Health.

Then people forgot about him, discreetly, and everything evaporated into mumbling and silence. The duties of religion, para-religious activities, the attendant ceremonies—it all left little time for daydreaming and idle chatter, and people simply refused to indulge in either. It was not so much that they feared they might be rebuffed, or tapped and scanned by the Vs, or taken to task by the Volunteer Law-enforcing Believers or the

Volunteer Militia, or even handed over to the police and the justice system, but in truth their deep sense of conformity was just that way, they quickly got bored with anything that distracted them from their religious and para-religious duties and that might in the end make them lose points and expose them to the public condemnation of Yölah. This suited Ati fine, he hoped for nothing better than to resume his life as a good believer who was attentive to universal harmony, and he did not feel he had the strength or the courage to become a committed nonbeliever.

He displayed a grave vigor in his new life, both in his work at the city hall and at the neighborhood *mockba*, and he outdid himself in his volunteer service, hopping from one construction site to the next without even taking the time to wipe his brow. There is no better way to forget oneself and everything else than wearing oneself out at work, because something was eating away at his thoughts, and obsessed him. Even when he was dead tired, he could not sleep, so he would prolong his evenings of study at the *mockba* as late as possible, which greatly flattered the *mockbi*, his response-givers, and the cantors. Ati explained that he had fallen behind in his studies and devotions during his stay at the sanatorium; the hospital chaplain and his deputies did what they could, but were manifestly lacking in science and penetration: at the first difficulty they would lapse into fairy tales and magic if not downright gobbledygook and heresy. There had also been the disease and the suffering it brought, and death mowing people down as in wartime, and hunger and cold, and homesickness, all of which numbed the spirit and prevented him from understanding everything as he should.

Where everything else was concerned, Ati did what he could to be elusive and shy away. Things that used to delight him, and which he had taken pride in, now disgusted him: spying on neighbors, telling off distracted passersby, cuffing children, lashing women, joining a dense crowd to run through the neighborhood in a display of popular fervor, swinging his cudgel left and right during his crowd control work at stadium ceremonies, lending a hand to volunteer hangmen in the course of their duties. He could not forget that at the sanatorium he had crossed a red line: he had been guilty of high nonbelief, a crime of thought; he had dreamt of rebellion, of freedom, and of a new life beyond the borders; he had a presentiment that some day this madness would rise to the surface and cause untold misfortune. In reality, even simple hesitation is dangerous; one must walk straight ahead and keep on the right side of the shadow without ever arousing suspicion, because then nothing can stop the machine of inquisition; he who falters will never know how he came to be in the stadium, surrounded by all the acolytes that have been found for him, right down to the very last one.

What Ati once performed so naturally now cost him heavily, and the affliction was worsening. He no longer knew how to say, "Yölah is just," or "Hail to Yölah and to Abi his Delegate" and seem sincere—and yet his faith was intact, he knew how to weigh the pros and cons, to tell good from evil according to the proper belief, but alas, something was missing to make things right—emotion, perhaps, or stupor, emphasis or hypocrisy, yes, and surely that extraordinary sanctimoniousness without which belief would not know how to exist.

What his spirit was rejecting was not so much religion itself as the crushing of mankind by religion. He could not remember by what train of thought he had convinced himself that man could only exist and know himself in and through a state of rebellion, and that that rebellion could only be authentic if it turned, before all else, against religion and its troops. Perhaps he had even thought that truth, be it divine or human, sacred or profane, was not man's true obsession, but that his dream, too vast to be apprehended in all its madness, was to invent humanity and live in it like a sovereign in his palace.

Over time Ati found some peace, which allowed him to settle into the routine he dreamt of. At last he was a believer like all the others; he was no longer in danger. He rediscovered the pleasure of living from day to day without worrying about tomorrow, and the joy of believing without asking any questions. Rebellion is impossible in a closed world where there is no way out. True faith is in surrender and submission, Yölah is omnipotent, and Abi is the flock's infallible shepherd.

With relief and solemnity Ati greeted the news one morning that the Como, the Committee for Moral Health, would be coming to the city hall the next day for the monthly personnel inspection, and that he was summoned to appear, like everyone else. He felt he had truly reintegrated the community of believers. Until now people had kept him at a certain distance, since he was exempt from saying confession and demonstrating piety; it was generally assumed that in his convalescent state he was not in full possession of his faculties, and could still succumb to delirium and involuntarily offend divinity and its representatives. Upon his return from the sanatorium it had been decided that until he had completely recovered he could be given an audition at his neighborhood *mockba*, and that they would make a report to the local Como unit. In the Book of Abi, several verses insisted on the necessity for the believer to be master of his words in order to be properly judged.

The periodical Inspection was, in a manner of speaking, a sacrament: it occupied a signal position in a believer's life; it was a powerful liturgical act, as important as the nine daily prayers, or Siam, or the Great Thursday Imploration, or the eight holy days of Absolute Abstinence, or the Caesura for boys and the Resection for girls, or the R-Days, the Days of Reward that honored the worthiest believers, and just as important as the long-lasting Expectation, or the Bidi, the incredible Blessed Day which marked the departure of the happy chosen ones on their pilgrimage to the Holy Places. The point was not so much to receive a "rating" from the Como, but rather the fact that everyone took part, including the Como, in what was a consolidation of general harmony in the light of Yölah and the perfect knowledge of the *Gkabul*, and Yölah knows what is just and what is necessary. Everyone impatiently awaited the Inspection. The result, which was a rating out of a scale of sixty, along with various pertinent remarks, was recorded in a green notebook with purple stripes called the Booklet of Worth, the Bowo, which everyone kept on their person all through their life. It was a moral identity card which everyone displayed proudly: it established hierarchies and opened doors.

In the administrative services, the Inspection took place on the fifteenth day of every month. So many things depended on it, the worker's remuneration for a start (the rating could increase it by fifty percent, or cut it by half), career advancement, access to social benefits, housing allocation, scholarships for children, birth bonuses, ration cards, inscription on the list of pilgrimages, nomination for R-Days, and all manner of privileges relating to one's status as a person. Sixty out of sixty was the miracle everyone dreamt of: it would confer upon the laureate the status of a living legend but—naïve aspirants always failed to remember this—such a degree of recognition would turn the recipient into a freak, to be shown off to exhaustion from one place to the next. But not only that, jealous sorts would treat him like dirt and single him out as a renegade. The Inspection evaluated a believer's faith and morality and, behind the scenes, it provided useful information to the various services of the Apparatus. Its "self-criticism" moment, if properly planned, sometimes led to emotional collapse and elicited spontaneous confessions that could give rise to the most interesting witch hunts. In short, the rating was a master key, opening and closing every door in life. If a deceased person had had excellent ratings his entire life, his family was entitled to request his canonization. No one had ever obtained it, but the procedure did exist, and everyone was encouraged to resort to it by active publicity campaigns launched by the Funeral Company. This planetary monopoly belonged to an influential member of the Just Brotherhood, the Honorable Dol, who was also the director of the Department of National Historical Monuments and Real Property of the State. The powerful argument was that to have an official saint in one's family meant that every member of the family was guaranteed entry into paradise, and that they would have the possibility to see Abi in person one day, or at least his shadow behind a curtain. The first-class funeral given to candidates for canonization cost a thousand times more than the funeral of even the most outstanding of citizens, and who knows how many zeroes one would have to add in comparison to a worker's burial—this was how profitable beatification could be for insurers and other gravediggers.

But if the rating was negative six months in a row, and the defendant's state of health was not the obvious cause of his failing, the matter was referred to the jurisdiction of another institution, the Core, the Council of Reformation. And after a summons in due form the inadequate individual simply vanished. No one knew anything about the Council, but it was often in their thoughts: it was like death, the living have not experienced it and can say nothing about it, and those who have experienced it are no longer with us to speak of it. Of the disappeared person, immediately struck from lists and memories, people would say, charitably or cruelly, "He was taken by the Core, Yölah is compassionate," or "The Core struck him off the list, Yölah is just," and return to their devotions. Not knowing staves off fear and makes life easier.

However totalitarian it might be—and perhaps for that very reason—the System was perfectly accepted, because it had been inspired by Yölah, conceived by Abi, implemented by the Just Brotherhood and monitored by the infallible Apparatus, and finally embraced by the people of believers, for whom it was a light on the path to final Realization.

The Core, which consisted of two *mockbis* and one agent from the Apparatus, was presided over by a rector who answered to the Honorable of the Just Brotherhood, and who supervised the field of activity or the region in question. One of the most important committees was the one that evaluated administrative personnel. In the capital it enjoyed a particular aura, as well as a solid organization, inspiring a string of sub-committees that increased its action in the various services and neighborhoods of the city. They were known by their codes. The committee operating in Ati's neighborhood, the S21, in the south of Qodsabad, was called Committee S21. What was important was that it had a reputation for being inflexible but infallibly fair. Its president was the venerable Hua, rector emeritus; as a young man he had been a prodigious combatant for the faith.

Ati was very moved to be back in the atmosphere of the holy Examination. In many respects it was a simple formality (all he had to do was answer idle questions and confess to minor delinquencies) but there could be surprises in store, and this was why people were both serene and proud but also tense and anxious. The committee arrived with great pomp in a fine antique sedan driven by an agent from the Apparatus and accompanied on foot by a squadron of athletic militiamen. It was then met by high-ranking officials from the city hall, to the cheering of the crowd and the personnel massed on the square in front of the city hall. Ati did not know any of the Committee members. This was normal: they changed every two years to ensure the quality of the Inspection would not be tainted by prolonged contact between judges and judged, and Ati had been absent for two long years.

While the judges were officiating in the ceremonial hall that had been transformed into an interrogation center, the personnel did what they could to prepare themselves. Some would be revising chosen passages from the *Gkabul*, others were exchanging information that they had found on the *nadirs* and in the gazettes, particularly the *NeF*, about the state of the country; elsewhere they were perfecting their arguments, repeating slogans, fine-tuning their thoughts, polishing their phrases, reciting prayers, holding forth while pacing to and fro, or dozing in a corner wrapped in their *burni*. It was like the night before a battle; everyone was awaiting their turn to go to the front but was not really worried: they knew that nine bullets out of ten were blanks.

Ati wandered from group to group, trying to see over people's shoulders and to learn something from the hubbub in the corridors.

His turn came. As he was new at the city hall, he went last. He was introduced by the mayor in person, who had been demoted to the rank of a porter, but in another life he had been a *mockbi*, and he knew the importance of things. The examining judges were seated on a podium behind a table. On a silk-covered lectern a *Gkabul* was open to page 333 where one could read the chapter "The Path to Ultimate Realization" and in particular verse 12: "*I have established committees, made up of the wisest among you, to judge your acts and probe your hearts, in order to keep you on the path of the* Gkabul. *Be truthful and sincere with them, they are my envoys. He who attempts to hide or be clever will rue the day, I am Yölah: I am omniscient and omnipotent.*"

The files of the city hall employees were stacked on a table, by order of seniority.

The judges had judges' gazes, and voices that were in keeping with their position; they could be feared, but there was also a sort of human warmth emanating from their persons, an impression that stemmed no doubt from the president's advanced age and the complacent little air of the assessors. Over their fine woolen *burni* they wore the green stole striped with vermilion of a Moral Health judge. The rector Hua wore a fluffy jet black bonnet which emphasized the immaculate whiteness of the little tufts of his remaining hair. After glancing quickly through Ati's file, he said, "First of all, hear my greetings and my prayers, and witness my humility.

"Hail to you, Yölah the just, the strong, and to Abi your glorious Delegate. Be praised until the end of time, to the far corners of the universe, and may your ambassadors from the Just Brotherhood be blessed and justly rewarded for their loyalty. I pray unto you, Yölah, to give us the strength and the intelligence to accomplish the mission you have conferred upon us. So be it according to your law."

After a pause, he addressed Ati in these terms:

"Ati, may Yölah assist you in this examination of the truth. He sees you and hears you. You have two minutes to prove to him that you are the most loyal of believers, the most honest of workers, and the most brotherly of companions. We know that you were sick for a very long time, far from your home, you fell behind in your studies and your devotions. As Yölah has ordained, as Abi his delegate makes his daily practice, we will show indulgence toward you, this once. Speak and mind you do not prattle, Yölah despises speechifiers. After your plea, we will question you in greater detail and you will simply answer yes or no."

The assessors nodded.

In a flash, Ati let the mad thought cross his mind that he

had nothing to prove to anyone, but the surrounding reality was too colossal for him to ignore. And how could he go against his education as a submissive believer: not one of the faithful knew how to do that. He took a breath and said:

"To begin with: I join you in extending my humble saluta-tions to Yölah the almighty and Abi his wondrous Delegate, and to you, my good judges, I offer my respectful greetings.

"Great Rector, respected masters, Yölah is wise and just: by placing you in such high office he shows the love he has for you. By bringing me before you, he shows that I am small and ignorant. In a word, you have taught me so very much: that Yölah is a compassionate master—he has touched you with his grace, as your generosity toward me has shown; and that Abi is a living model, for that it is enough to imitate him to become a perfect believer, an honest worker, and a brother to every member of the community. If I am here, having returned alive from the sanatorium at Sîn after an arduous journey, I owe it to Yölah. I prayed to him every day, with every footstep, and he heard me, he supported me from beginning to end. In Qodsabad he did the same, I was wel-comed as a true believer, a sincere brother, and an honest worker. This is why I believe I am who you ask me to prove that I am, but I also know that I have a long path ahead of me to better myself. My judgment regarding my little person does not matter, it is up to you to judge me and make me the perfect servant of Yölah and Abi, under the enlightened orders of the Just Brotherhood."

The committee was impressed, but Ati did not actually know whether he had been convincing or merely eloquent.

Hua, the presiding judge, spoke again:

"In their reports, the *mockbis* from your neighborhood and your boss at the city hall say that you have shown yourself to be studiously committed to your tasks. Is this out of ambition, hypocrisy, or something else?"

"Out of duty, venerable masters, to bring myself up to date with my devotions, and to be in harmony with my brothers. For far too long illness kept me from my duties and my friends."

The assessor representing the Apparatus frowned suspiciously and insisted:

"Studying reinforces faith. Do you think it is also possible to study in order to find reasons to denigrate faith? A person who becomes closer to his idol: does he do it to love him better, or to caress him and treacherously strike him down?"

"Master, I cannot believe such people exist, the *Gkabul* is a light which eclipses even the brightest sun; no lie can hide from it, no artifice can extinguish it."

"Do your friends and colleagues think the same thing?"

"I am sure they do, masters; every day I see that they are true believers, happy to be living on the path to righteousness and raising their children according to the principles of the holy *Gkabul*. I am proud to be in their company."

"Answer yes or no," said the presiding judge.

"Yes."

"Would you tell us if one of them was remiss in his duties?"

"Yes."

"Could you explain . . . would you inflict the proper punishment on him if he was uncovered by a judge?"

"Do you mean . . . kill him?"

"I do mean that, punish him."

"Uh . . . yes."

"You hesitated: why?"

"I was wondering whether I would know how to do it. The punishment must be inflicted in a holy way, and I am not agile with my hands."

The rector Hua began to speak again.

"And now you have one minute to give us your self-criticism. We are listening. And remember we are also looking at you."

"I don't know what to say, venerable judges. I am an insignificant man, my faults are those of modest folk. I am fearful, not as charitable as I would like to be, and sometimes I yield to covetousness. The disease that afflicted me for so long also exacerbated my weaknesses, and hardship sharpened my appetite. The study and volunteer work to which I am devoting all my time help me to keep a grip on myself."

"Good, good, you may go. We will give you a good rating, in order to encourage you on the path of loyalty and effort. Go often to the stadium to learn to punish traitors and loose women, for there are surely adepts of Balis the Renegade among them; take pleasure in chastising them. Remember that it is not enough to believe: you must also act; only in this way is the believer a true believer, strong and courageous."

And before rising to his feet he added:

"To act is to believe twice over, but to do nothing is to be a nonbeliever ten times over: remember this, it is written in the *Gkabul.*"

"Thank you, venerable masters, I am the slave of Yölah and Abi, and your devoted servant."

Ati did not sleep a wink that night. The film of the Examination played over and over in his mind. It was the film of a consensual rape to which he would be subjected every month of every year for the rest of his life. The same questions, the same answers, the same madness at work. Was there any way out? Other than jumping off his roof, headfirst, he did not see one.

Ati could not get over it. Life went on the next day at the city hall as if the previous day had never happened. Force of habit: what else could it be? Everything that is repeated becomes part of the muddle of invisible routine and is forgotten. Who can see how they breathe, blink, think? A consensual rape, repeated day after day, month after month, one's whole life long: does it turn into a loving relation? A happy addiction? Or is it the principle of ignorance that goes on functioning, now and forever? What indeed can we complain about if we do not know, if nothing belongs to us? Ati would have liked to talk to someone about it—to his boss for example, who was one of the old guard, but the man had other things on his mind, he ordered Ati not to forget to finish copying the previous month's files and to archive them in the proper order in the proper boxes.

Ati was beginning to think that the only purpose of the Inspection was to keep people in a state of fear, but no sooner did he alight on this theory than he rejected it: nobody looked as if they were afraid, neither of rape nor of the idea that they could be whisked off by the Core; and besides, nobody was trying to frighten them, neither the committees nor the militiamen; all anyone, everyone, was concerned with was pleasing Yölah. How were you to make head or tail of it? Sheep heading for the abattoir are no more indifferent to their fate than men going to their Moral Inspection. Yölah was clearly the strongest.

For Ati it was urgent to determine the status of his reinsertion: had it been completed, only just begun, or had it been judged impossible, once and for all?

Ati had befriended a colleague from work, a man of considerable refinement, who acted as a true guide for him in the prickly undergrowth of the city hall. His name was Koa. He knew everything and then some; he had mastered the art of telling people exactly what they wanted to hear, and everyone reveled in his company. No one could ever say no to him. Given the widespread corruption at city hall—where it was another form of breathing—Koa knew exactly how to behave. He had learned to live in a kind of breathlessness, without ever seeming to lack for air and without ever being offended at the sight of people around him scratching and panting like dogs. He transmitted his art to Ati, and this immediately rid Ati of the acid in his stomach. "It's all in the breathing," said Koa, seeing him smile with relief. It is easier not to make enemies when there are several of you: together you can ensure you both have something to fall back on. He said: "With wolves, you have to howl or pretend to howl; bleating is the last thing you must do." But Koa actually did have one great shortcoming: he was kind, and his kindness was of the incurable sort, compounded by an ineradicable candor that he thought he kept hidden by disguising as cruel cynicism. People went crying to him in order to obtain then and there what other people would make them pay top price for and then oblige them to wait for ages. This destroyed the market and ruined colleagues, but since Koa told them what they specifically wanted to hear, people did not bear him a grudge; they would ask him one more time—and it was absolutely the last time—to redirect petitioners to the right door, before they'd even had a chance to shed a tear.

As the days and the discussions went by, Ati and Koa discovered they had a shared passion: the mystery of *abilang*, the sacred tongue, that was born with the Holy Book of Abi and had become the omnipotent and exclusive national language. They dreamt of penetrating the mystery, for they were convinced it was the key to a revolutionary understanding of life. Both of them, unbeknownst to the other, had come to the same conclusion, that *abilang* was not an ordinary language of communication, since the words that connected people went through the medium of religion, which emptied them of their intrinsic meaning and instilled in them an infinitely moving message, the word of Yölah; in this respect the language was a reserve of colossal energy that emitted an ionic flux of cosmic scope, acting on universes and worlds but also on an individual's cells, genes, and molecules, which it transformed and polarized according to the original plan. No one knew how—other than through incantation, repetition, and the loss of free exchange between people and institutions—this language had created a force field around the believer that isolated him from the world, and made him deaf, on principle, to any sound that was not the sidereal, bewitching chant of *abilang*. In the end, *abilang* made him into a different being, who had nothing to do with natural man, born of chance and scheming, and for whom he had nothing but contempt and would like to crush under his heel if he could not fashion him after his own image. Ati and Koa believed that by transmitting religion, sacred language changed man fundamentally, not only where ideas, tastes, and little habits were concerned, but also in his entire body, his gaze, the way he breathed, so that the human being that was inside him would disappear, and the believer that rose from the ashes would blend into the new community, body and soul. Never again would he—even dead and reduced to a pulp—have any other identity than that of a believer in Yölah and Abi his Delegate, and so too would his descendants assume this identity even from before their birth and until the end of time. The people of Yölah did not consist only of the living and the disappeared: they also included the millions and billions of believers who would arise in future centuries to form an army on a scale with the cosmos. Another question drove Ati and Koa: if other identities existed, what were they? And two more, subsidiary questions: what is a man without identity, who does not yet know that to exist he must believe in Yölah; and what, exactly, is a human being?

Ati had opened himself to these questions at the sanatorium, when doubt began to creep in and he watched his coreligionists living out the little life they had left in a state of total unconsciousness and inertia. What was it that turned a creature filled with the essence of the divine into a base, blind larva: now there was a question. Was it the power of words? The fact remained that in that medieval fortress, there at the end of the world with its unimaginable borders, the sounds of things and of life had a strange substratum, made of old, unresolved mysteries and stale violence; over time it had transformed patients into erratic phantoms who truly did levitate just above the ground as they wandered through the labyrinth, moaning and wheezing; then between two illuminations, or as a faint shadow slipped past them, they vanished as if by magic. It was during the very frequent power outages that Ati noticed that the sound system went on producing noise—except that it did not take that noise from some magnetic memory or some providential magneto, but from people's heads, where their words, laden with the magic of prayer and scansion and repeated unto infinity, had become embedded in their chromosomes and modified their code. The stockpiles of sound in people's genes went from their bodies to the ground, and from the ground to the walls, which began to vibrate and modulate the air according to the frequencies of prayers and incantations, the thickness of stone adding a lugubrious echo to the requiem. The very air was transformed into a sort of sickly sweet, pungent mist that drifted through the depths of the fortress and acted more powerfully upon the inmates and penitents than any hallucinogen. It was as if all this improbable, obscure populace lived inside a prayer to the dead. That is the force of infinitesimal movement: nothing can resist it, no one realizes a thing, and all the while, tiny wave after tiny wave, angstrom after angstrom, this movement shifts continents beneath our feet, and in the depths it traces fantastical perspectives. It was while observing these phenomena that defied comprehension that a revelation came to Ati: sacred language was of an electrochemical nature, and no doubt it also had a nuclear component. It did not speak to the mind: rather, it disintegrated it, and out of what remained (a viscous precipitate) it fashioned good passive believers or absurd homunculi. The Book of Abi said as much, in its hermetic fashion, in the first title, chapter 1, verse 7: *"When Yölah speaks, he does not say words, he creates universes, and these universes are the pearls of light radiating around his neck. To listen to his word is to see his light and become transfigured in the same instant. Skeptics will know eternal damnation: verily it has begun for them and for their descendants."*

Koa had followed another path. He had initially taken an advanced course in *abilang* at the School of the Divine Word, a prestigious institution open to the deserving, and Koa was more deserving than most because his late grandfather had been the famous *mockbi* Kho, of the Great Mockba in Qodsabad, renowned for his sermons, whose magnificent shock formulas (like this remarkable war cry: "Let us go to our deaths that we might live in happiness," since adopted by the Abistani army as a motto for their coat of arms) had raised innumerable contingents of good and heroic militiamen during the previous Great Holy War. Koa, still prey to a certain juvenile rebelliousness that was aimed at the oppressive figure of his grandfather, subsequently went to set himself up as a professor of *abilang* in a school in a devastated suburb, and there, as if a field lab had been placed at his disposal, he was able to see for himself the power that sacred language had over the minds and bodies of young pupils, although they had been born and raised speaking one of the common and clandestine languages of their neighborhood. While everything in their environment seemed to doom them to aphasia, degeneration, and a drifting life of dissension, after only one short trimester of learning *abilang* they were transformed into ardent believers, well-versed in dialectics and already unanimous judges of society. And this squawking, vindictive brood declared their readiness to take up arms and conquer the world. Indeed, even physically they were no longer the same; they already resembled what two or three terrifying Holy Wars would make of them: squat, stooped, scarred. Many thought they knew enough now and didn't need any more lessons. And yet Koa had not even breathed a word to them about religion and its planetary and celestial aims; nor had he taught a single verse of the *Gkabul*, other than the common salutation: *"Yölah is great and Abi is his Delegate,"* which was, after all, among happy people, simply a somewhat grandiloquent way of saying hello. Where did the mystery come from? Koa had another, more personal question: why had the mystery not affected him—he who had been born into *abilang* and the *Gkabul*, and knew them inside out, and whose forebear was a past master of mass mental manipulation? Of his two questions, which one was more dangerous: that was what he had to determine, for a start.

At last he understood that when you light a fuse, you must expect something to happen. Even if you cannot see it, there is a certain continuity in the progression of ideas and the organization of things: a bullet fired from a window is a dead man at the other end of the street, and time that passes is not emptiness, it is the link between cause and effect. On the last day of the school year, poor Koa handed in his notice as if he feared for his life among those pupils; then he went back to the city and started looking for a stable job with decent pay. He did not know the secret of language, and never would, but he knew how immensely powerful it was.

What had become of his pupils? Were they good, honest *mockbis*, lauded martyrs, admired militia, professional beggars, or wanderers and blasphemers who ended up at the stadium? Koa did not know; what went on in the devastated suburbs was still very uncertain, they were worlds unto themselves, surrounded by walls and precipices; their population changed several times over in a lifetime. Everyone had their share of disease, poverty, war, calamities, and misfortune, and even of success, which carried off the clever little schemers and set them up with the enemy; no one was spared, they all died in the end, but since just as many arrived from the other side—displaced, exiled, relegated; migrants, refugees, renegades, failures too— no one realized a thing, those extraterrestrials were all so alike, whether they were from here or elsewhere. Like everywhere, whether they were humans or chameleons, they took on the color of the walls, and there were leprous walls, and others that were worm-eaten—that was the whole tragedy of the thing. This was how Koa's cynical side expressed itself.

The two comrades went about their business in several ways. They attended the *mockba* assiduously, studying the *Gkabul*, listening as the *mockbi* commented on the legends of Abistan, inflated a thousand times over; they observed the flock as it went into a trance the moment the criers urged them to prayer with the salutation "Hail to Yölah and to Abi his Delegate," echoed in chorus by the response-givers and the mass of praying figures, all in an atmosphere of intense contemplation and discreet suspicion. Behind it all lay a sort of incredible magic trick: the more you watched, the less you understood. A principle of uncertainty governed the believers; often they didn't know whether they were alive or dead, or whether, at that moment, they themselves could tell the difference.

They also studied at each other's houses, when it was possible to circumvent the vigilance of the neighborhood civic committees, known as the Civics, who had the sovereign power to invite themselves in whenever they suspected any new activities might be starting. And conversation between friends after work was really too much of a new thing: only the Chitan could inspire such idleness. The Civics were visible from afar in their green *burnis* with fluorescent yellow stripes, but they were not above using tricks to catch any lookouts unaware, and this was why the inhabitants constantly felt afraid, even when they'd double-bolted their doors. "Open in the name of Yölah and Abi, this is the Civic Committee from here or from there!": that was the sort of call no one ever wanted to hear. No one knew how to stop the machine: a summons led to an interrogation, and then one day you ended up at the stadium, with your back to the truncheon or under a hail of stones.

It must be explained that the Civics were vigilante committees formed by citizens and approved by the authorities (in this case the Service of Public Morality of the Ministry of Morality and Divine Justice and the Bureau of Civil Self-Defense Associations of the Ministry of Public Force), who aimed to punish any deviant behavior in their neighborhood, to police the streets, and to ensure law and order was maintained; some of them were greatly appreciated, such as the Good Behavior Civics; others were despised, particularly the Anti-Idleness Civics. There were countless different committees, but many were ephemeral, seasonal, and had no verifiable purpose. They gathered in designated premises, the Civics barracks, where they rested, trained, and planned their raids on the neighborhood.

When all was said and done, Ati and Koa preferred wandering around the devastated suburbs, where a shred of freedom still reigned, too tiny to be of any use, and you need a lot of freedom to start attacking the secrets on which unshakeable empires are founded. And indeed, this was rebellion of the purest kind: they'd reached a point where they actually thought they might go one day to live in the ghettos of death, those faraway enclaves where ancient populations had survived and clung doggedly to old heresies that had disappeared even from the archives. *"I gave them life and they turned their backs on me to join my enemy, the Chitan, the wretched Balis. Great is my wrath. We will drive them back behind high walls and we shall do everything to make them die in the most horrible way"*: thus are they described in the Book of Abi.

It seemed impossible to find a way into these territories: soldiers patrolled relentlessly along the vertiginous walls that sealed them in hermetically, and they would shoot on sight. And you also had to make it through the minefield and the impermeable barrages of chevaux de frise that cut off the ghetto from the city; you had to dodge radar, cameras, watchtowers, dogs, and, what was absolutely inconceivable, the Vs. It was not simply a matter of rigorously sealing off a pestilential territory, like during a quarantine; it was vital to protect believers from the deadly miasmas of the Chitan. So to the heavy weapons was added the incommensurable power of prayers and maledictions.

Yet there was no lack of channels for making one's way

discreetly to the ghetto. They were the work of the Guild, the clan of merchants who supplied the ghettos illegally—at a high price, obviously, through dense networks of underground tunnels that were defended, so it was said, by Chitanous troglodytes whose ferocity knew no bounds. The two friends finally took the plunge: as matters stood, they might as well. They had used up all their savings, down to the last *didi*. After two years of forced infirmity, Ati had scant resources, so he had to sell a few good relics he'd obtained from the pilgrims he'd met in the mountains of Sîn.

At their office at city hall they fabricated a license under a false name and went before the local agency of the Guild, posing as merchants who wanted to do some good business with the ghetto. And one evening just after the watchman had passed on his round, they slipped out and soon found themselves standing by a fairly large well, cleverly camouflaged in the rear courtyard of a dilapidated house next to an ancient cemetery famous for all the bad rumors that circulated about it. A homunculus with perfect night vision was waiting for them; he immediately sat them in a gondola, pressed on a buzzer and two levers, and the vehicle began its dizzying descent into the bowels of the earth. More than ten hours later, after multiple detours through a cyclopean ant colony, which led them under the rampart and the minefield, they emerged into the ghetto known as The Renegades, the most extensive in the country; its very name could cause a sensitive believer to faint, and threw authorities into fits of hysteria. It was morning, and the sun was shining on the ghetto. The enclave sprawled over several hundred square *chabirs* to the south of Qodsabad, beyond the place known as The Seven Sisters of Desolation, a chain of seven misshapen and furrowed hills that ran along the edge of Ati's neighborhood. The Renegades, whom the people referred to as the Regs, called their world Hur, and they were Hurs. Koa thought these words must be declensions of *hu*, a word from the *habilé* dialect, an ancient idiom that a few dozen people still spoke, badly, in the hinterlands to the north of Qodsabad, and which Koa had studied briefly. *Hu* or *hi* meant something like "house," "wind," or even "movement." So Hur would be the open house, or the territory of freedom, and Hurs were the inhabitants of freedom, men who were free as the wind, or men carried by the wind. Koa remembered having learned, from an old *habilé* native, that his distant ancestors honored a god called Huros or Hurus, whom they represented as a bird, a royal falcon, which is indeed the image of a free creature flying on the wind. With time, and the erosion of things, Huros became Hurs, which led to Hur and *hu*. But the man didn't know why, in those forgotten times, words could have two syllables like *Huros*, or even three like *ha-bi-lé*, or even four or more, up to ten, whereas nowadays all the languages you could find in Abistan (all clandestine, in case one needs reminding) only contained words with one syllable, or two at the most, including *abilang*, the sacred language with which Yölah had founded Abistan on the planet. While some people might have thought that over time and with the maturing of civilizations languages would get longer, and gain in significance and syllables, quite the contrary had happened: they had gotten shorter, smaller, reduced to collections of onomatopoeias and exclamations, quite sparse on top of it, words that sounded like primitive shouts and groans and in no way allowed for the development of complex thought or the access to superior worlds that thought would provide. At the end of ends, silence will reign, and it will weigh heavily, it will carry all the burden of things that have disappeared since the world began, and the even heavier burden of the things that never came to light, for want of sensible words to name them. This was a passing reflection, inspired by the chaotic atmosphere of the ghetto.

It may not be the topic at hand, but a short aside is neces-sary for the sake of History: many things were said about the ghettos and their trafficking. If they had muddled everything up in order to prevent everything, they wouldn't have done things any differently. It was said that behind the Guild there lurked the shadows of the Honorable Hoc of the Just Brotherhood, director of the department of Protocol, Ceremonies and Commemorations, a massive personality who organized and governed the life of the country, and of his son Kil, known as the most enterprising of all the businesspeople in Abistan. In certain milieus there were even people who dared to suggest that the ghettos were an invention on the part of the Apparatus. The theory went that an absolutist regime could not exist and remain in power unless it controlled the country right down to its most secret thoughts—which was impossible to do, because in spite of everything they might invent in the way of control and repression, someday a dream would manage to take form and escape, and then opposition would be born, just where it wasn't expected, and it would be reinforced through secret struggle, and the people, who are naturally inclined to lend their sympathy to those who combat tyranny, would support that opposition, provided victory seemed a credible hypothesis. If power was to preserve its absolute nature, it must make the first move and create the opposition itself, then have true opponents embrace it, people whom it would create and train if need be and whom it would then protect from their own opponents—extremists, dissi-dents, ambitious lieutenants, presumptive heirs eager to get things over with, all of whom would crop up out of nowhere as if by some miracle. A few anonymous crimes here and there would help support the war machine. To be one's own enemy is a guarantee of victory no matter what. Of course it was dif-ficult to arrange, but once it was under way it ran itself, every-one would believe what they were made to see, and no one would be free of suspicion and terror. In fact, many people would die from blows they never even saw coming. For people to believe and cling desperately to their faith, war is necessary—real, never-ending war, with countless casualties and an enemy no one can see, or who can be seen everywhere without being seen anywhere.

The absolute Enemy, against whom Abistan had been waging one Holy War after another since the Revelation, had thus an even more important vocation, that of making it possible for the religion of Yölah to occupy the length and breadth of heaven and earth. No one had ever seen that Enemy, but he truly did exist, in fact and in principle. If he had ever had a face, a name, a country, or borders with Abistan, it had been during those dark times before the Revelation. Who knew what he was made of? Every day the *NeF* reported on the war in breathless communiqués which the people read and discussed avidly, but as Abistanis never left their neighborhoods, and the country had no maps on which to visualize the combat zones, it might have seemed to some that the only true reality of war was in the *NeF* communiqués. It was frustrating, but as every tree is known by his own fruit, they knew the reality of war through the commemorative steles that dotted the landscape to honor great battles, bearing the names of the soldiers who had fallen as martyrs. The names of the disappeared, whose bodies were sometimes found, scattered here or there in a ravine, a river, or a mass grave, were posted in city halls and *mockbas*. The losses were terrible, and were ample testimony to the people's attachment to their religion. Prisoners came to a sorry end; it was said that the army consigned them to camps where they soon died. Merchants told stories of how they had seen endless cohorts of captives along the roads being led to one or another of those destinations. Ati himself could testify to it: in Sîn he had seen soldiers thrown into ravines with their throats cut, and on the road home the terrifying spectacle of an endless column of prisoners being towed by an army motor brigade.

No one doubted that the Abistani soldiers the Enemy captured would be subjected to the same treatment. The question which haunted everyone's mind was this: where did the Enemy take them, and how did he manage to do it with such perfect discretion?

The Holy War is made of many mysteries.

As for the ghetto and its Renegades, they were concrete, and served only one purpose: to keep tight control on the believers in their everyday life. It takes a fox lurking nearby for close watch to be kept on the chicken coop. The chaos that reigned was a protection; it was so perfect that nothing was noticed. People put up easily with regular harassment on the part of the Civics; they could hang around in the street, go up to people and chat with them, remove their *burnis*, forget prayer time, go into one of those shadowy, noisy places that were unknown in Abistan and where, for a *didi* or a *ril*, you could obtain a hot drink, such as *ruf* or *lik*, or excellent cool beverages, some of which were greatly appreciated by consumers, the *zit*, for example, and which had the power to blur one's gaze and addle one's mind. In these places, in the back behind a pile of crates and sacks or a filthy curtain, there was always a corridor or a dark, narrow stairway that beckoned and left one wondering where it might lead.

One can't be sure all this freedom served much purpose, but it was devilishly exciting. The most astonishing thing was that the Regs, who enjoyed so much autonomy in the shambles they lived in, liked to go to Qodsabad, which they referred to as Ur, in order to sell their products and items from the past, (much coveted by the notables), and to bring treats back to their families. They too resorted to the Guild's tunnels, and paid for smugglers. The Apparatus hunted them down mercilessly, and it went without saying that those who were caught ended up in the stadium the following Thursday, after the Great Imploration. Their execution made for a first-rate show, and was the opening number at festivities. A special police force, known as the AntiRegs, had been created for the purpose, and they knew how to spot these ghostly individuals, to shadow them and catch them as was right and proper. Apparently these creatures, with their long experience of banditry and life in the wilderness, were far more reactive than the believers, who were constrained by too much strict routine. But no one talked about it because it would have destroyed a legend and undermined state security; it seemed, however, that the Vs, whose power knew no bounds, could not identify the Regs' mental signature; it became muddled with the signature of bats, whose ultrasonic waves were so powerful they saturated the Vs' radar, jamming it. What was worse, the Regs' mental flux, if it was trained specifically at a V, could cause inner bleeding that was painful and in any case humiliating for creatures who were otherwise so universally feared, renowned masters of invisibility, ubiquity, and telepathy. These were conjectures, however, topics of conversation, no one had ever seen any Vs, let alone Vs bleeding from their nose or their ears. The fact is that innocent bats periodically fell victim to mass slaughter, in which the population took an active part in order to free the skies from their waves—except that nature had endowed them with another remarkable talent: they could breed faster than lightning. So it was at twilight, when the little vampires were waking up and heading off hunting, that the Hurs left their ghetto and invaded Qodsabad, where accomplices and dogs were waiting for them, and it was at dawn that they swarmed back again, when the sated bats returned to their caves. It's easy to understand why the Hurs revered the animal.

The army had its role to play in the extermination of the Regs: its artillery, drones, and old helicopters regularly bombarded

the ghetto, particularly during major commemorative festivities, when the people of Qodsabad assembled in the *mockbas*
and stadiums were at fever pitch. Stories went around then,
too: the army helicopters had dropped their bombs at random,
on vacant lots rather than at the heart of the ghetto; on
dwellings or shelters, their bombs and shells would have an
insufficient charge of powder, they would make noise, wound
people, even kill a few but not that many, and so on; there was
no end to the speculation. The explanation was that the Guild
was militating for a symbolic destruction of the Regs, in keeping with the *Gkabul*'s spirit of goodness; to be sure, the Regs
were abominable creatures, unholy and dirty, but they were
also good customers, and they were already prisoners in their
horrible ghettos, it wasn't such a bad idea to spare their lives:
so went the Guild's plea on every floor where they had willing
listeners. Between commerce and religion there was always a
possibility for complicity, you couldn't have one without the
other. From there to concluding that the Guild was bribing
army captains and warning Regs of the raids being plotted
against them there was only one step. It was a complex equation: Abistan needed its Regs to live, the way it needed to kill
them to exist.

The Qodsabad ghetto had a certain charm, even though it
was in a deplorable state: not one single building could stand
on its own; there were forests of jury-rigged props and splints
keeping it all upright, but only just. Everywhere mountains of
rubble told of recent or earlier collapses, and in both cases, of
the unjust misfortune that ensued. Children in rags scampered
over the ruins, playing or searching for things to sell. Filth had
found its realm, and in many places the garbage was heaped to
the rooftops; elsewhere it carpeted the ground up to one's
knees. As landfill had reached its limits long ago, this garbage
could not be evacuated or burned (the entire ghetto would

have gone up in flames along with its inhabitants), and so it piled up in the open air, to be scuttled here and there by the wind; the ghetto rose higher on its rubbish and its embankments. Daytime was often dark as night. There was no electricity, and this added to the sinister sense of confinement, as did the narrow streets, the chaotic urbanism, the destruction, the wailing of alarms, the untimely bombing, the long dreary hours spent in shelters, and everything else that proliferates in a besieged city. It all made life darker, and acted as a powerful curb. Nevertheless, there was a sort of spirit, a culture of resistance, an economy of making do, an entire relentless little beehive of activity that found a way to survive and to hope. Life was just passing by, seeking, clinging, inventing, confronting all sorts of challenges, then starting over again as much as was humanly possible. There would be a lot to say about the ghetto, about its reality and its mystery, its assets and its vices, its tragedies and its hopes, but in fact the most extraordinary thing about it, something no one had ever seen in Qodsabad, was this: the presence of women in the streets, women who could be recognized as human and not fleeting shadows: in other words, they wore neither mask nor *burniqab*, and clearly no bandaging beneath their smocks. Better still, they were free to go where they liked; they went about their domestic chores in the street, dressed as slovenly as if they were in their bedrooms; they went shopping in public, took part in civil defense, sang as they worked, chatted together during breaks, and, what was more, sat out in the weak sun of the ghetto to brown their skin because they actually knew how to take the time to make themselves look nice. Ati and Koa were so moved when a woman came up to them hawking some item that they lowered their eyes and began trembling all over. It was as if life had been turned upside down; they didn't know how to behave. The women recognized them for what they were, awkward Abistani lumps who knew only *abilang*, so they spoke in their patois, a very hissing gibberish, and they accentuated their words with precise gestures, waving the item for sale in one hand and with the fingers of the other indicating the number of *rils* to disburse, while casting crafty sidelong glances at passersby as if expecting applause. As the conversation could go no further, and Koa had used up the supply of dialect he'd acquired during his language courses in the devastated suburbs, the two friends bought what they could, and after that they did their best to keep the women from approaching them—not to mention the children, who knew how to fleece a sucker in less time than it took their mothers to behead a chicken.

A few Regs in the ghetto understood the sacred language, having dealt with representatives of the Guild and being used to passing through Qodsabad on their little smuggling runs. But what they knew was limited to commerce, and was expressed through numbers and gestures. The vast majority understood diddly-squat, the sacred language had no effect on them, even if they had the entire *Gkabul* poured down their ear. Did that mean it only worked on believers? This was inadmissible, the *Gkabul* is universal and Yölah is master of the entire universe, just as Abi is his exclusive Delegate on earth. The deaf man is indeed he who does not hear.

We have kept it for the end, because the thing is horrifying even to liberated (shall we say doubting) believers: the walls of the ghetto were covered with graffiti that had been drawn with nails, charcoal or . . . more ghastly still, human excrement. Graffiti mocking Abistan, its beliefs and its practices, written in one of the languages that were common in the ghetto. There was no lack of obscene drawings, and they needed no explanation. Here and there on the walls there were graffiti in *kabilé* that Koa could decipher: out-and-out blasphemy which we will not report. They said: "Death to Bigaye," "Bigaye is a buffoon,"

"Bigaye, king of the blind and prince of darkness?", "Abi=Bia!" (in *habilé, bia* means something like: "pestilential rat" or "twisted man" (!), "Long live Balis," "Balis will triumph," "Balis hero, Abi zero," "Yölah is all talk." Ati and Koa were eager to leave these horrors behind; any memory of them in their minds would single them out to the Vs upon their return to Qodsabad, whose sonar wouldn't have to scan them for long before the circuit breaker went. Our friends trembled at the thought.

In Qodsabad everyone believed that Balis must have been hiding in this ghetto of death ever since Yölah had banished him from heaven. The great fear among Abistanis, particularly the inhabitants of Qodsabad, was that Balis and his army would escape from the ghetto and run rampant through the holy land of Abistan. Obviously, they would be powerless against Abi, who enjoyed the high protection of Yölah, not to mention his invincible Legion, but they would do a great deal of damage to ordinary people. In the end it seemed as if all this armada around the ghetto, all these controls and so-called lethal bombardments, not to mention the ridiculous blockade, were more to reassure the good folk of Abistan than to prevent the Regs from swarming down onto Qodsabad. The Apparatus were gifted at doing one thing in the place of another and at making people believe the very opposite had occurred.

Let us not forget that Ati and Koa's little idea was to understand these wooly things that had filled their heads: *What was the connection between religion and language? Can religion be conceived without a sacred language? Which comes first, religion or language? What makes a believer: the word of religion or the music of language? Is it religion that creates a special language out of a need for sophistication and mental manipulation, or is it language which, once it reaches a high level of perfection, invents an ideal universe, one which it is bound to make holy? Is the postulate according to which "Whoever has a weapon will end up using it" still valid? In other words, does religion intrinsically turn to tyranny and murder?* But it wasn't some general theory they wanted, the precise question was as follows: *did* abilang *create the* Gkabul *or was it the other way around?* There is no such thing as simultaneity, the egg and the chicken are not born at the same time, one must come before the other. In the case in point, this could not be mere coincidence, everything in the history of the *Gkabul* showed that there was a plan, right at the start, and the plan aimed to grow and expand. More questions: *What about common languages, what did they invent, and what created them? Science and materialism? Biology and naturalism? Magic and shamanism? Poetry and sensualism? Philosophy and atheism? What do all these things mean? And what do science, biology, magic, poetry and philosophy have to do with any of it? Were they not also banished by the* Gkabul *and ignored by* abilang?

They realized that on top of being futile and boring their pastime was dangerous. But what was there to do when there was nothing to do, other than futile, vain things? Which were bound to be dangerous.

And that they were, for sure, they thought, when once again they found themselves one hundred *siccas* beneath the earth in the cyclopean labyrinth of underground tunnels, and then a few hours later in the old crumbling house at the edge of the cemetery to the south of the "Seven Sisters of Desolation," just as the owls and bats were silently filling the sky with their furtive shadows. In situations like these, in such cold, gray twilights, it is the entire world that seems to be in danger of imminent death.

To be back in the light of Qodsabad was a relief, a worry, and a source of unspeakable pride. On the one hand, what the two friends had done was nothing special: they had gone on a jaunt to the ghetto, something the agents from the Guild did every day in order to collect their profits, take orders, and, along the way, dally with a Renegade woman, just as, going the opposite direction, little smugglers from the ghetto came every day to Qodsabad to peddle their wares and steal a few chickens. But on the other hand, it was an extraordinary event: Ati and Koa had crossed the border of time and space, the forbidden border; they had left the world of Yölah for the world of Balis—and the sky had not fallen.

The hardest thing for them, at work and in their neighborhood, would be to act naturally and mislead the Civics and the judges of Moral Inspection, when everything inside them, the way they behaved, the way they breathed, now reeked of Sin. Clinging to their *burnis* and their sandals was the unique, ineradicable smell of the ghetto.

They had brought four earth-shattering teachings back from their odyssey into the forbidden world. 1) Beneath the separation walls there are connecting tunnels. 2) Ghettos are populated by human beings, born of human parents. 3) The border is a heresy invented by the believers. 4) Man can live without religion and die without the help of a priest.

And they also brought back the answer to an ancient enigma: the word Bigaye, so shocking when it was found scribbled by an insolent hand on the ten billion posters of Abi plastered to the walls of Abistan: in the ghetto that word was in everyday use. The culprit must have been a Reg who had wanted to leave a trace of his incursion into Abistan before going back to his burrow. The man who had been arrested and executed was surely some poor fellow they'd plucked off the street at random. By comparison, Koa understood that Bigaye was a slang word that had come from *habilé* and it meant something like "Big brother," "Old rascal," "Great leader," or "Old buddy." The expression *"Big eye"* used in the Just Brotherhood's decree was wrong, therefore; in any case the word did not exist in any of the languages of Abistan or the ghetto, it probably came from some ancient language, one of those that had become extinct during the Char, the first Great Holy War, when all the inhabitants of the North had been annihilated, given their stubborn opposition to the *Gkabul*. Ati had concluded that the text etched in stone above the draw-bridge at the sanatorium must have been written in that language, because the fortress dated from that era, or even earlier, and the symbol "1984" might refer to something else besides a date. But in all honesty it was impossible to know for sure: the notion of dates, like that of age, did not apply to Abistanis; for them time is all one, indivisible, immobile, and invisible, the beginning is the end and the end is the beginning, and today is always today. With one exception, however: 2084. That number was in every mind as a sort of eternal truth, so it was an inviolable mystery, there would be a 2084 in the immense immobility of time, all alone, but how to situate in time that which is eternal? They hadn't the foggiest idea.

Ati and Koa told each other that they should go back to the ghetto one day to learn some more.

Book Three

In which new signs appear over the skies of Abistan, adding legends to the Legend, a miracle that will incite Ati to embark on a new journey, marked by mystery and misfortune. Friendship, love, and truth are powerful motives to get ahead, but what purpose might they serve in a world governed by laws that are not human?

I t was a thunderclap in the drowsy skies of Abistan. Oh, indeed, there was a commotion, and so much repetition! The information went around the country a thousand times in a short week of seven days—through the *nadirs*, the gazettes, the *NeF*, the *mockbas*—on call twenty-four hours a day—not to mention the town criers who spared neither vocal cords nor megaphones. Upon instructions from Abi, the Honorable Duc, Great Commander of the Just Brotherhood, decreed forty-one days of uninterrupted jubilation. Gigantic prayer meetings and an equal number of votive ceremonies were organized in order to render thanks to Yölah for the marvelous present he was offering his people. A public funding drive was launched in order to collect money for the manufacture of a worthy case for it, and by the end of the week the equivalent of the state budget had been raised. People would have given more had a communiqué from the government not appealed for moderation: something must be kept in reserve.

Setting aside what institutional voices had added to the pertinent information—several thousand pages of explanation in the press and hundreds of hours of learned commentary in the *nadirs*—one could reach the heart of the matter: *a new holy shrine of prime importance had been discovered!* After some minor work, to be financed by the funding drive, it would soon be open for pilgrimage, or so the publicity hype immediately claimed, creating huge enthusiasm among the people and a no less colossal flurry of business activity. The publicity projected the mind-boggling figure of twenty million penitents the first year, thirty the second, and forty each consecutive year. Reservations had been filled for the next ten years to come. Things had gotten out of hand, people were losing their tempers, prices going through the roof—*burnis*, satchels, sandals and pilgrims' staffs now cost a fortune, and there was a threat of shortages. A new era had begun.

That wasn't all: religious historians, doctors of the law, and Grand *Mockbis* would be very busy in the decades to come. Already they were sharpening their nibs and stockpiling paper; they would have to rewrite the history of Abistan and the *Gkabul*, revise the founding speeches, and what was more, touch up chapters in the Holy Book. Abi himself had admitted that his memory might have failed him; his life had been so complex and thrilling, he had an entire planet to govern, and Yölah was demanding.

This new shrine was no ordinary place; it would offer the unexpected, alter perspectives. One example among hundreds: in the common version of the *Gkabul*, Qodsabad was at the center of History; but the truth lay elsewhere, Qodsabad did not exist before the Revelation, in its place there had been a prosperous megalopolis known as Ur, the present-day ghetto of Qodsabad, and Abi lived in another region. It was only later, for business purposes, that he came to settle in Ur. The new draft of the Holy Book would have to integrate the fact that Abi had hidden for several years in this miraculous village after he had fled from Ur, threatened as he was by the lords of that corrupted city, now in the hands of Balis and the Enemy. In those days, Balis was still called the Chitan and the Enemy was simply the enemy; they did not have the mythical aura they have today, but were a conglomerate of degenerate, barbarian peoples whose lands were known as the United High Regions of the North, the Lig in *abilang*. It might have been enough simply to wait for them to die off, their end would have been a fairly sad one, but there was evil in them, and it might spread to the believers and corrupt them. It was in that village, in the simplicity of his new life, that Abi began to hear and make heard the message of a new god, Yölah, who in those days was simply referred to as God. His message was full of light, it could fit into one slogan: "God is everything and everything is in God." It was an elegant way of saying that the only God was God. Let us not forget that Abi himself went by another name, which we do not know; he changed his name to Abi, which means Father beloved by believers, when God acknowledged him as his unique and ultimate messenger.

It was only when the crop of converts attained a critical mass capable of setting off a chain reaction that would pulverize the ancient world that God would reveal his name: Yölah, by which he reigns over eternity. And it was also in that village that one night, in a flash of light, Yölah would teach Abi the sacred language he would use to gather the men scattered through the world and lead them, repentant and grateful, onto the path of the *Gkabul*. He would teach him that faith is not enough: however brightly it burns, the fire can go out, and men are difficult, they must be subjugated the way snakes must be charmed, one must be always be wary of them, and to do so takes a powerful language that is enduringly hypnotic. Abi added two or three inventions of his own and baptized the language *abilang*. He verified its power over his own companions: after a few lessons, poor devils that they were, terrified at the thought that God existed and was watching them, they turned into infernally charismatic commanders, juggling rhetoric and the cunning of warfare. Koa had carried out the same experiment on the children of a devastated suburb and obtained the same incredible result: after one month of lessons you could no longer recognize the ignorant little brats. *"With the holy language my adepts will be valiant unto death; they will need nothing more than the words of Yölah to dominate the world. These words made my companions into commanders of genius, and so now will they make them into elite soldiers; the victory will be rapid, total, and final,"* he says, as recorded in the Book of Abi, title 5, chapter 12, verses 96 and following. It was from this village, with this embryonic army, that Abi would start the Char, the first Great Holy War of the *Gkabul*. One might wonder how Abi could have forgotten this refuge that had been so crucial to his career and the future of humanity, but no one did wonder: Abi was the Delegate, Yölah inspired him in every circumstance.

Later, once Abi had established the Just Brotherhood and made it his cabinet and the supreme authority of state, higher than all the religious and governmental institutions, he would proclaim *abilang* to be the official universal language, and issue a decree that any other idiom to be found anywhere on the planet was primitive and sacrilegious. History does not tell us who created the Apparatus, nor what its purpose was, where it stood on the chessboard, nor who ran it; those who tried to find out failed, and did not pursue their attempts any further.

The Honorable Rob, at the time spokesman for the Just Brotherhood and Abi's governor of communications, explained through the press, and in a very moving speech at the Great *Mockba* in Qodsabad, that the dear Delegate was truly convinced that this village which had taken him in with such a display of fraternal love, assuming enormous risks in so doing, given the menace of Ur, had been destroyed in one of the Holy Wars and razed to the ground by the Enemy, and that was why he had not breathed a word about it until this year, when an angel sent by Yölah came to him in a dream to inform him that the good village was still there, standing on its own two feet, and that it still preserved the sweet smell of his passage.

Stunned by so much divine indulgence, Abi immediately sent out a reconnaissance mission. The village was indeed there, just as he had seen it in his dream, spruce and shining in a supernatural light. Abi wept when they showed him the film they had made on-site and he recognized the humble dwelling the inhabitants had placed at his disposal, and the no less modest *mockba*, a comical sight with its pagan aspect; the villagers, full of joy, had built it when Abi converted them to the *Gkabul*. Spurred by a wave of enthusiasm he urged the Honorable Hoc to order the Ministry of Sacrifices and Pilgrimages to do whatever it took to enable deserving believers to visit the blessed village as soon as possible, and find joy therein.

He asked the Honorable Dia, the mysterious Dia, a very influential member of the Just Brotherhood and head of the Department of Investigations into Miracles, to carry out all the appropriate investigations and to conclude that the condition in which the village had been preserved was nothing short of miraculous, and that this phenomenon must have something to do with the fact that he, Abi, had stayed there. Which Dia did, forthwith. The believers were unanimous in hailing it as a miracle and requesting its consecration. Once again the streets of Abistan showed their infallible forbearance. As a token of his recognition, Abi granted Dia the title of "Honorable among Honorables," along with a hereditary concession on the pilgrimage to this holy place. The Honorables celebrated their powerful colleague: his promotion implied a revision of the entire interplay of alliances; the world of the Just Brotherhood and the Apparatus would, henceforth, turn for or against Dia.

To close the festivities, several thousand prisoners were executed—renegades, riffraff, fornicators, generally unworthy individuals. The prisons and camps were emptied out, and endless processions through the streets were organized so that the people could do their bit for the holocaust. The Grand

Mockbi of the Great *Mockba* of Qodsabad inaugurated the holy carnage under the cameras' concupiscent gaze by taking the knife in his own hand to the throat of a ragged, shaggy, sinister bandit they'd found in some makeshift asylum. The wretch's skin was tough, and the frail old *mockbi* had to make ten attempts before he pierced the windpipe.

The moment the discovery of the village was announced, Ati understood that the affair had something to do with the archeological site where Nas had been working. He was only mildly surprised. The way the media were reporting it, the story had little in common with what Nas had told him during their long journey back to Qodsabad, basically that it was simply pilgrims who had discovered the village, that no angel had informed them: they had been forced off their designated route by the torrential rain which had flooded vast expanses of territory—cutting off roads, confusing landmarks, adding danger to desolation. As they skirted the disaster area, the pilgrims went through places so dreary it was impossible to imagine any human being might ever want to settle there. While they were looking for a place to shelter from the gusts, in order to rest and perform their devotions, they came upon the village. It seemed alive, even welcoming, without a single sign of decay; it looked as if the inhabitants had merely gone out on some errand and would be back in no time. The penitents soon realized the village was dead, as if embalmed; that the dry climate and its extreme isolation had preserved it from the ravages of time and mankind. It was obvious that the inhabitants had left the place in a great hurry. There were signs—tables set for meals, doors gaping wide, benches overturned in a place that looked like a *midra*—that it must have been morning, between the third and fourth prayer, when they left the place. But when? A very long time ago, that was all it was possible to say; something in the air suggested antiquity, the distant past, in everything that is uncertain and mystical about these time-space indicators. But perhaps the sense of oppression was merely due to the infinite solitude of the place. Nas had said that when he arrived in the village he felt as if he'd been projected into another dimension. The pilgrims had decided to stay there until the storm abated; they spent their time exploring the astonishing village and, at night around the fire, recalling old legends that had been banished from memory.

Once they reached their camp, they told of their discovery, eyes wide, and to support their testimony they produced various objects they'd taken from the site—trifles, but very unusual things at the same time. But what they were, no one would say, dammit! As this was no ordinary matter, the camp provost confiscated the objects, filed a report to his superior, and a few weeks later a mission arrived from Qodsabad, led by Nas. The Apparatus immediately launched another mission, via helicopter, in order to catch up with the pilgrims and put them through a rapid debriefing, followed by quarantine in a secret place. Not a single newspaper or *nadir* mentioned the mysterious disappearance of the village's inhabitants, or the strange objects found on the site, or the unjust confinement of the pilgrims. The commissar of faith, the guide, and the guards who had taken it upon themselves to stray from the official designated road were severely punished; every pilgrimage had a consecrated path, and its length and trials were as important as the goal, the shrine; no power on earth could change that path—Abi himself could not change it, nor would he.

And so it was that Nas was the first to examine the objects the pilgrims had collected, and the first to enter the village. What he found there plunged him into deep thought. He refused to say more, even as Ati urged him for all he was worth. Their recent friendship in no way authorized a failure to abide by the rule of secrecy to which Nas was bound by his position as sworn investigator of the Ministry of Archives, Sacred Books, and Holy Memories. It was as he gazed off into space, his lip trembling, that one night by the campfire he let slip that what he had discovered could shake the symbolic foundations of Abistan, in which case the government of the Just Brotherhood would resort to very drastic measures—stifling restrictions, mass deportation, immense destruction—so as to maintain order in its former innocence. This declaration had caused Ati to smile: a village is a village, a parenthesis in the desert, the story of a handful of families forgotten along the road to the city. It was the fate of villages to disappear into the dust of years, or for the city to close in on them and swallow them whole; no one laments their loss for very long. Nas had underestimated the government; he would never have imagined they could come up with the ideal solution so easily: raise the village to the rank of a holy shrine, and there you had it; consecrated and set in the limelight it would be safely hidden from any hypocritical gazes or sacrilegious questioning. The System is never threatened by the revelation of an embarrassing fact; rather, it will be reinforced by making this fact its own.

In all honesty, Nas was thinking of something else: the sad fate that awaited the witnesses, for they were doomed to disappear, one after the other—the guide and the guards, the camp provost and his adjutants. Left to their own resources, the pilgrims would be lost in the wilderness and before long they too would perish. The *nadirs* would report the tragedy, and nine days of national mourning would be proclaimed. They died as martyrs, that was the main thing, so people would say as the ceremonies came to an end. And Nas thought of himself, a key witness: not only had he seen with his own eyes, he had grasped the deep significance of what was before him.

There was no point asking for the name of the village. No one knew it—such a loss—it had been erased and replaced by an Abistani name. The Just Brotherhood gathered in a solemn assembly and baptized it Mab, which comes from *med Abi*, the refuge of Abi. Ever since Abistan was founded, all the names of places, people, or things that dated from an earlier era had been banished, along with the languages, traditions, and all the rest; it was the law, there was no reason to make any exception for this village, all the more so in that it had been raised to the rank of a privileged Abistani shrine.

Once the initial excitement over the discovery of the village had subsided, along with the surge of pride he felt in his friend Nas, whose name would forever remain associated with the miracle, Ati recalled several things. Nas had told him that the village was not Abistani, Abistanis had not built it, nor did they inhabit it, a thousand details attested to the fact—the architecture, the furniture, the clothing, the dishes. What seemed to be a *midra* and a *mockba* were arranged completely differently from in Abistan. Documents, books, almanacs, postcards, and other printed matter were written in a strange language. Who were these people, what was their history, their era, how had they ended up in Abistan, the world of believers? The archeologist in Nas was astounded by how well the village was preserved, and by the absence of any human bones. An array of theories were considered, none of which proved satisfactory. The first idea: the village had been attacked, and its inhabitants had been rounded up and deported God knows where. Perhaps, but there were no signs of struggle or pillage; and if villagers had been killed during the battle, where were their corpses? Another possibility: the inhabitants had left of their own accord, but why so precipitously? They seemed to lead quiet lives, and behaved accordingly.

Ati and Koa discussed it at length. The theory of a miracle did not convince them for one second; they preferred the fact of the unchanging dry climate to explain the condition of the village, as well as the improbable but romantic explanation for the absence of human bones, which was the possibility that the village was still inhabited by a few last survivors. The story went as follows: for whatever reason, the villagers had fled their homes one day; they perished along the way, or argued over the route to take: the fact remained that a few of them, exhausted and desperate, had turned back, and once they were home they led reclusive lives, running to hide in the wilderness or the mountains at the drop of a hat. When they heard the armada of pilgrims pouring toward them like a flood, the unfortunate survivors cried out that their end had come. If this was the case, where were they, now that their haven had been invaded, occupied, transformed, guarded like the grail? Did they die in the wilderness? Might they have made it to a mega-lopolis in the hopes of melting into the first crowd they chanced upon? In all likelihood; but what were their chances of fooling such forbidding and suspicious folk, how could they dodge the administration, the Civics, the Vs, the Apparatus's spies, the AntiRegs, the army patrols, the Volunteer Law-enforcing Believers, the Volunteer Militia, the judges of Moral Inspection, the *mockbis* and their response-givers, assorted informers, and those neighbors whom no wall, no door can discourage? These survivors, lost in an unknown world—did they know these things, did they know that Bigaye saw every-thing with his magical eye, and the *nadirs* not only broadcast images, they also filmed those who looked at them, and picked up their thoughts? Whatever way you looked at it, their end was ineluctable because, as you can well imagine, those vil-lagers were not adepts of the *Gkabul*, and spoke forbidden languages. The best thing for them and for the survival of their kind would be to head as fast as they could for the near-est ghetto, if there were any left in their region. Maybe that is what they did, maybe they found a place even more totally iso-lated than their village had been, and built a retreat that could withstand any trial. Ati knew how huge the country was, how incredibly void of life; nothing could be easier than to lose oneself in it forever, were it not for those swarms of pilgrims, blinded by their impetuous faith, crisscrossing the land from its farthest reaches to the outmost bounds.

It was these thoughts that compelled Ati to find a way to visit Nas in his ministry, the only address he had for him. He shared them with Koa, and they began to construct plan upon plan. As they had never left their neighborhood—something that was forbidden by a law that was all the stricter in that it was unwritten and no one knew the terms—they had no clue where they should go, nor whom to ask for directions to the ministry, and they didn't have the damnedest idea how they'd make it past the obstacles they'd encounter around every corner. They were well aware at present that they didn't know Qodsabad at all, that they didn't know what it looked like or what sort of people lived there. Up until now the world, to them, had been no more than the continuation of their neighborhood, but the existence of the impregnable ghetto and the mysterious village were proof that there were breaches in the System, and any number of hidden worlds. On the road from the sanatorium Ati had seen the emptiness that encompassed Abistan, an oppressive emptiness that seemed woven with the murmurs of a multitude of parallel worlds that had been spirited away by an all-powerful magic. The absolutist spirit of the *Gkabul*? The radiating thought of Bigaye? The purifying breath of the Great Holy Wars?

Yölah is great and his world is truly complicated.

Now they just had to find a way to get out of the neighborhood and reach the Ministry of Archives, Sacred Books, and Holy Memories.

The time had come to take stock. Ati and Koa drew up a list of all the crimes and misdemeanors they had committed recently. It was not a pretty sight: taking into account only the escapade to the ghetto, that infernal burrow of Balis and the Regs, there was enough to send them to the stadium ten times over. They might as well add the rest—the business with the license, the breaking and entering, the falsification of a public document, usurpation of function, trafficking in an organized gang, theft, and other petty related crimes—for good measure. There was no point hoping anyone would show the slightest understanding: the city hall, the Guild, the *mockba*, the Moral Inspection judges, colleagues, and neighbors would all turn up as fervent accusers; they would hurl accusations of deceit, wrongdoing, abjuration. The crowd at the stadium would go wild, would try to trample their bodies and drag them through the streets until all that remained were a few scraps of flesh on their bones for the dogs to fight over. The reputation of the Volunteer Law-enforcing Believers would be greatly enhanced by this coup, and they would spark a pogrom in the neighborhood that would go down in history.

And yet at no time did the two friends have any subversive thoughts, let alone heretical ones; they simply wanted to know what sort of world they were living in—not to fight it, no one was up to that, man or god—but to endure it in full knowledge of the facts, and to visit it, if possible. A sorrow that has a name is a bearable sorrow; death itself can be seen as a remedy, if one knows how to name things properly. Yes, it's true (and it is a bitter heresy), they had toyed with the hope of fleeing their world—a mad, unthinkable thing, their world was so vast that it was lost in infinity; how many lives would it take to leave it behind? But such is the nature of hope; it runs counter to any principles of reality, and so they told each other this truth in the form of a postulate: that there can be no world without limits, because without limits the world would dissolve into nothingness, it would not exist, and if there were a border, then it could be crossed, what's more, it must be crossed, at all costs, for it is eminently possible that the missing part of life is to be found on the other side. But, God of goodness and truth, how to convince the believers that they must stop importuning life, life that loves and embraces whomsoever it chooses?

Ati felt guilty for dragging kindhearted Koa into his illusions. Then forgave himself, reasoning that his friend was a born rebel, a first-rate adventurer, who obeyed an essential force. He carried within himself great suffering, the blood that flowed through his veins singed his heart, his grandfather was one of the most dangerous madmen in the entire country, providing millions of young martyrs for the three most recent Great Holy Wars, and whose murderous sermons were taught in the *midras* and *mockbas* as if they were poetry, still racking up their quota of volunteers for the slaughter. From earliest childhood Koa had stoked a burning hatred of all the self-satisfied people in the world. He had fled, but it is not enough to flee, sometimes you have to stop, and then they catch up with you, corner you. Ati abhorred the System, and Koa despised the men who served the System; it wasn't the same trial but, after all, as the two went together, he could conceive that they might use the same rope to hang the lot of them.

*

Now that they had come this far, the two friends needed to stop and consider the fact that they had crossed a line, and that to keep on in the same direction would lead them to their death. They must not act blindly. It was already nothing short of a miracle that they had carried their revolt this far without being caught. They were still protected by their status. Ati was a veteran; he had survived tuberculosis and come back from the terrifying sanatorium at Sîn; and Koa bore an illustrious name and was a graduate of the unparalleled SDW, the School of the Divine Word.

They talked, they debated, they waited for the right moment, improving their camouflage techniques with every passing day; they went back and forth through checkpoints without difficulty; they knew better than anyone how to surpass each other in demonstrations of piety and civic discipline; the neighborhood *mockbi* and the Moral Inspection judges held them up as examples. The rest of the time they spent looking for channels, tracking information, questioning theories. They understood so many things, they could see how easy it was to find things out, as long as you searched carefully, and how cheating and secrecy developed creativity, or at least reactivity. And they had already found out the following: the ministries and major administrations were all housed in a gigantic complex in the historical center of the city. They had already guessed as much, the way you know a theory, without necessarily believing it. This complex was the Abigov, the heart of Abi's government, and in the middle of it all the Kiïba had pride of place—a majestic, hieratic pyramid at least one hundred and twenty *siccas* high, spreading over a base of ten hectares, bedecked in sparkling green granite with red stripes, and on all four sides of its pyramidion was Abi's eye, watching over the city, continuously probing everything it saw with its telepathic rays. This was the seat of the Just Brotherhood. One hundred thousand bombs could not shake it. The logic behind this grouping was a concern for security, and efficiency too, why not, but the purpose was above all to demonstrate the strength of the System and the impenetrable mystery underpinning it; this was how an absolutist order was built, around a colossal, indecipherable totem, around a leader with supernatural powers—in other words, on the notion that the world and its dismemberments do not exist and only hold together because that world turns around a System and its leaders.

Tens of thousands of civil servants worked there seven days a week, day and night, and every day God made, tens of thousands of visitors—civil servants and merchants who had come from the sixty provinces—rushed to the entrances of the various administrations to drop off requests, put their names down on lists, obtain certificates and full discharges. The files were sent somewhere deep within the titanic machine, on a long journey that could take several months or years, and after that they were sent to the basements of the complex where they underwent a specific treatment—no one knew precisely what. Our friends had heard tell that these underground vaults opened onto another truly unfathomable world, that from there a secret tunnel went deep down into the earth, to which only the Great Commander had the key, and that the purpose of this tunnel was, in the event of a popular uprising, to exfiltrate the Honorables to . . . the ghetto! Honestly, people would say anything when they didn't really know what was going on. The truth was that no one really entertained the eventuality of a revolution, still less the hypothesis that the Honorables would stoop to the vulgar suggestion of going to hide in the ghetto among their hereditary enemies, when they were the masters of the universe, and had helicopters and airplanes to take them anywhere on the planet in no time at all, and constantly probing the skies were their flying fortresses capable of destroying every living thing on earth. Some information is worthless, and dissipates attention. In all likelihood the tunnel was used to reach an airport or Abi's palace, which, back in the days when the Enemy was all-powerful and was dropping its atomic bombs on Abistan on a daily basis, had served as a refuge for the Honorables and their noble families.

In an old issue of a magazine of theological science Ati and Koa found a photograph depicting the Honorable Duc, Great Commander of the Just Brotherhood, surrounded by a learned assembly of several Honorables, including the powerful Hoc, director of Protocol, Ceremonies, and Commemorations. All of them were clad in a thick green gold-embroidered *burni* and on their heads they wore the distinctive red bonnet of their rank; they were inaugurating a new administration, the Bureau of Lunar Ephemeris, which the article described as an inestimable asset for the proper observance of the rites of Siam, the holy week of absolute Abstinence. Then it added, as a sort of veiled threat: "The Great Commander has expressed his conviction that he will soon see an end to the never-ending conflict between the Grand *Mockbis* in the provinces regarding the hours for the beginning and end of the holy week of Siam." A threat which remained without effect, since the Book of Abi itself was very vague on the topic, and imposed the visual observation of the moon, a method which by its very nature was subject to error, a practice that moreover had fallen to venerable *mockbis* who were as shortsighted in the light of day as they were deaf to any form of proof. The article did not mean to imply that they were as stubborn as rocks, one must show respect, but simply wished to indicate that rocks could be more reasonable than the *mockbis* were. In the background the formidable government complex was visible, a hybrid conglomerate that was part ancient military fortress and part devastated modern city, with its towers reaching to the clouds and its wings and outbuildings nestled together in such a way as to suggest Machiavellian intentions. It was easy to imagine all sorts of mysteries and torments concealed in its interior, and what sort of downright immeasurable energy must be expended at the heart of this cyclopean reactor.

Further back in the picture one could just make out the historic city, with steep, winding alleyways, narrow buildings arched one over the other, dilapidated , peeling walls, and people who seemed to be fixed in the landscape since Antiquity, obvious signs of a ruined life. It was there in that endless labyrinth that the civil servants from various administrations lived. It was called Kassi, the Kasbah of Civil Servants. Like ants devoted to their queen, they belonged to the System body and soul. They went to work through a mass of dimly-lit tunnels which, at the heart of the Abigov, branched onto a network of stairways that was just as complicated, leading them to their assigned floors; thus, of their world they saw only bowels, spine, and cavities. There was something of the automated war factory in it all; it was frightening but also a guarantee of punctuality. Through a colleague from the garbage collection service whose great-uncle was a civil servant at the Ministry of Virtue and Sin (and who, following a poorly implemented reform, had been sent one day to the stadium with one hundred other colleagues, preceded by the Minister and his entire family), Ati and Koa learned that each administration had its own residential zone. The employees of the Ministry of Archives, Holy Books, and Sacred Memories occupied sector M32. So that was where Nas lived.

They also learned that the Great Mockba, where the Honorables took turns officiating during the Thursday Imploration, was just beyond the Abigov; it could hold up to ten thousand worshippers. Every week one Honorable, chosen by his peers according to a protocol that was too complicated for the common people to understand, led the prayer, and after that commented on a verse from the *Gkabul* having something to do with current affairs, in particular with the current Great Holy War, or the one that was being prepared in secret. The faithful punctuated his words with powerful, virile cheers: "Yölah is great!" "The *Gkabul* is the way!" "Abi will win!" "A curse upon Balis!" "Death to the Enemy!" "Death to Regs!" "Death to traitors!" After which, cleansed of their sins, the flock headed joyfully toward the great stadium that could hold as many people as chose to show up.

Koa knew of these places, but had no memory of them. As the grandson of a prestigious *mockbi* who was rector of the Great Mockba, and as the son of a brilliant questor of a sacerdotal loge belonging to the Honorable Hoc, he had lived in the enclave of Honorables. There one has the eyes of a master, one does not see ordinary people, or hear them, one does not know the world. At the School of the Divine Word, adjacent to the Kiïba, in such close quarters with God and the saints, Koa had come to forget that he was living on earth—and in truth he had never known, no one had ever told him that people were human beings. But one day more miraculous than all others it came to pass that he opened his eyes and saw these poor folk at his feet writhing in pain. Since that moment the fever of rebellion had not left him.

After many hours of discussion our friends concluded that there was a chance that something that had worked once might work a second time. So they manufactured a summons enabling them to go to the Abigov on a special mission. And now they were ready to run through the streets like good honest laborers, only too happy to kill themselves at the job.

It was a time for the unexpected. Just when their bundles were ready, and the road was more or less clear, Koa was summoned to the district tribunal. The messenger's eyes were shining and his nose was running because it was an important matter: Koa had been summoned by none other than His Serene Excellency the Head Bailiff. Once he got there, an imperial old fox with a white beard and a well-polished *burni* informed him that the ABBN, the Assembly of the Best Believers in the Neighborhood, had unanimously and in the name of Yölah and Abi nominated him, Koa, for the position of Destroyer in the trial of a slattern accused of third-degree blasphemy, and the nomination had already been ratified in high places. Whereupon he had Koa sign his confirmation and handed him a copy of the file. This was a significant event: the last witch trial had been long ago, it had not even occurred to anyone that they might be conducting such an investigation any time soon; but religion weakens and loses some of its virulence if nothing comes along to give it a rough time. Religion draws its vitality as much from the stadium and battlefield as from quiet study at the *mockba*. During a quarrel between two women, neighbors, the accused, a shameless young woman of fifteen, dared to say, as she slammed the door, that Yölah the just had failed miserably by giving her such nasty neighbors. It was as if there were a sudden clap of thunder in the sky. Every shrew in the neighborhood testified against her with one accord, and the Civics came running in wholehearted support.

There could be no doubt about the matter, it would take only five minutes to reach a verdict, the issue would be debated merely for the pleasure of watching the bitch pass out and piss herself. While they were at it, they'd picked up the husband and their five children; they would be heard at a later time by the Committee for Moral Health; they would also have to testify and deliver a self-criticism statement before submission of their case, if necessary, to the Council of Reformation. A doomsayer with a substantial halo was required for a trial like this, the best to be found, and Koa was a perfect fit. His name—and that of his grandfather, above all—was like a beacon, lighting him from afar. It would be a signal honor for a tribunal in a peripheral neighborhood to officiate under such an emblem. The courtroom would be full, the matter would go down in history, justice would triumph as never before, and faith would be strengthened a millionfold, visible all the way from the Kiïba. The blaspheming slut would bring fortune in her wake; there would be a flurry of promotions in the ranks of justice.

"What to do?"—that was the question. The two friends discussed it for hours. Koa refused to be associated with what amounted to a human sacrifice foretold. Ati was fully behind him. He was of the opinion that Koa should go and hide in the ghetto or in one of the devastated suburbs where he used to enjoy hanging out, long ago. Koa hesitated, however: he thought it might still be possible to get out of the summons from the tribunal, that somewhere a decree from the Just Brotherhood stipulated that the Destroyer had to be a man of a venerable age, who had served for at least five years in an accredited assembly of emeritus believers, or had taken part in a Holy War, or had a career behind him of enviable positions such as *mockbi*, response-giver, psalmodist or incantator, conditions that Koa did not meet: he was barely thirty years of age, had no glorious feats to his name, had never taught religion, been part of any corps of sectators, or borne arms against anyone, friend or enemy. The problem was that if he were to put forward this argument, it would indicate he refused to assist the law, and that he approved of sacrilege, and he would end up at the stadium with the condemned woman. "What to do?" was indeed the right question. Ati suggested they try to make the most of their upcoming appointment with Nas to ask him to intercede in Koa's favor. As the discoverer of the most famous shrine in all of Abistan, he must surely have the grateful ear of his minister, and on his order Koa could be hired at the ministry, and at such a stratospheric level one is exempt of chores, and unaware of the world far below. Koa was skeptical. Nas might have the ear of the minister, but there was nothing to prove that the minister would listen; he might even hear quite the opposite.

Koa shuddered and said, "They want me? All right, I'll show them, I'll destroy where it hurts."

Ati gave a shiver. Koa's heart was full of rage.

The Destroyer was a key participant in the witch trials. He was not in court to plead someone's cause—that of the accused, or society's, or the plaintiff's; he was there to proclaim loud and clear the wrath of Yölah and Abi. Who, if not the offspring of the late Grand Mockbi of Qodsabad and former pupil of the splendiferous School of the Divine Word, would have the eloquence and intonation to express the fury of the Most High and his Delegate?

No one knew where the expression "Destroyer" came from; the official title was "Witness of Yölah," which skeptics transformed into "Yölah's Fool." "Destroyer" certainly emerged because long ago, in those obscure times dominated by the Enemy and the hordes of Balis, the Witnesses of Yölah systematically applied torture by impalement to nonbelievers, which did indeed destroy the sufferer just as a lumberjack's wedge splits the trunk of a tree. Regular attendants at the court gave the Destroyers another, gentler name, on the basis of their imprecations: Father Woe or Brother Woe, given the fact that all their tirades began with "Woe to ye who . . . !" or "Woe to those who . . . !" In fact, quite simply, they spoke the way the *mockbis* did when they were calling for a Holy War. The great Destroyers—and some of them were so good at their calling that they moved even the accused—were declared to be "Friends of Yölah and Abi," a title which entitled them to the greatest privileges. In light of his name, knowledge, and energy, Koa was sure to make a triumphal entry into that pantheon, and earn a great deal of money and respect; but there it was, he had chosen to be poor and rebellious, and, basically, to live in uncertainty.

At the end of their meeting, the two friends decided to pursue their first idea: they would go looking for Nas and seek his help. If they failed, they would see where they stood: Koa would either vanish into the ghetto, melt into a devastated suburb or . . . confront his destiny and destroy to his heart's content.

Time was of the essence; the hearing was fixed for the eleventh day of the next moon. This was inauspicious, for it fell on a day when people went mad, to celebrate the annual DCR, Day of Celestial Reward; there would be more disappointed souls than chosen ones, the tribunal would be overrun with crowds, and the road to the stadium would be more thronged and swarming than ever. There would be nothing tidy about the shameless woman's stoning, she'd already be ground to bits by the time she was halfway there. Considering one thing and another, the judges clearly wanted to amplify the chaos and woe, with a view to reaping considerable benefit, and everyone knew what that meant: they wanted to be noticed by an

Honorable, perhaps the Great Commander himself, why not Abi while they were at it, and to be raised one day to the dignified rank of "Friend of Yölah and Abi," the first rung on the ladder to ennoblement. Yet another rung and they would receive the right to possess a stronghold, a court, and a militia, and the extraordinary privilege of speaking at the *mockba* during the Great Thursday Imploration, in order to harangue the community.

And so, two weeks before the fateful day, early in the morning, at the hour of the *mockba* crier, carrying their bundles and armed with richly stamped documents testifying to their condition as honest civil servants on a secret mission to the Ministry of Archives, Sacred Books, and Holy Memories, Ati and Koa crossed the last boundaries of their neighborhood; their hearts were pounding fit to burst, but off they headed, straight for the Abigov. They even had a map, sketched for them by old Gog, the guardian of archives, who seemed to recall that one day, not long before the third Great Holy War, or just afterwards, when he was working as personal messenger boy to the *ômdi*, his excellency the Bailiff, he had gone with him to the Abigov, and had seen such marvels there, impressive buildings like granite mountains with endless corridors and tunnels that vanished into the subterranean night; indescribable machines, some as noisy as cataclysms and others that were ever so stressful, just blinking and jangling in a sort of never-ending countdown; file sorters and networks of pneumatic tubes more complex than a human brain; industrial presses that spat out the Holy *Gkabul* and Abi's poster in millions of copies; and everywhere, on their own or in teams, there were masses of people, all highly focused and stiff in their gleaming *burnis*: visibly, they belonged to a transcendent species. They were inhabited by a cold wisdom, but perhaps it was just extinguished madness, ash after fire. They did not speak, looked neither to the right nor to the left, each one did exactly as they were told. Life in them was cold, absent, at best residual, in any case very basic; habit had settled in instead and had created a very precise system of automatic interaction. It was these robots who made Abistan work, but they were not necessarily aware of the fact; their sense of smell was not strong enough to sniff out such things, and they never saw the light of day: the religion they served and the rules of the System forbade it. Between labor and prayer they had just time enough to hurry to the tunnels that would take them back to their kasbahs. The local siren sounded only once, and the convoy wouldn't wait. Outside their routine, from which they never deviated, they were lumpish and blind. If they stumbled or strayed, they were discharged from service and discarded or scrapped. As potential misfits they would worry their colleagues, neighbors, and loved ones, who in turn would become misfits. Through this method of preventing contagion, the ranks thinned rapidly, as worry and awkwardness were epidemics in themselves. That is how things were in Abistan; the country had its destiny, it believed in Yölah and Abi in this faithful, intransigent way, which incited it to believe ever more fervently, ever more blindly.

In the space of only a day or two, the friends had acquired a solid confidence, going from one street to the next as if there were no borders, no taboos, no rules of good neighborly behavior. They were amazed to discover that the people were just like the inhabitants of their own S21 neighborhood, with the exception of their accent; here they spoke in a singsong way, there the language was guttural and jerky; in other neighborhoods it might be nasal, whistling, or breathy, and it all revealed a great secret: behind the apparent uniformity of people and things, the people were in fact very different, and when they were at home, among their family and friends, they spoke other languages besides *abilang*, just as they did in the S21.

Their accent betrayed them, as did their smell, their gaze, and the way they wore the national *burni*; but the official inspectors, Civics, Volunteer Law-enforcing Believers, Volunteer Militia, and Patrollers affiliated with the police or the free guards could not hear those false notes in their accents, as they themselves were local, and confined to the same zone. The Vs surely could, they had so many powers—but did they really exist?

Ati and Koa were protected by their official permits, covered in very official stamps, but all the same—careful, careful—they tried as best they could to adopt the accent and manners of the land, or played sick and mute, or even the dunce who was hard of hearing.

All things considered, it was the street that deserved credit: it was a living chaos, you wouldn't recognize your own brother there. The inspectors were in constant demand, wearing themselves out, running this way and that, letting go of one prey to catch another, and in the end they added nightmare to confusion.

As strangers, Ati and Koa attracted attention the way a magnet attracts a nail. There they were, surrounded once again by a group of inspectors. The crowd came running and formed a circle around them. They didn't want to miss a thing, and did not hesitate to prompt the inspectors with the right questions. But all in all the interrogation remained very conventional: Ati and Koa knew it off by heart.

"Hey! Hey, you, strangers . . . yes, you . . . come this way."

"Greetings, brothers, honorable inspectors."

"In the name of Yölah, Abi, and the Great Commander, not to forget the Honorable of our fiefdom, salvation be upon them, who are you, where have you come from, and where do you think you are going?"

"Praise be to Yölah, Abi, and our Great Commander, not to forget your Honor, we are civil servants of the State on a confidential mission, we have come from S21 and are bound straight for the Abigov."

"S21? What is that?"

"It is our neighborhood."

"Your neighborhood? And where is it?"

"That way, to the south, three days' walk from here . . . but maybe only one hour as the crow flies."

"Birds have no neighborhood that I know of. And in holy Qodsabad there is no other neighborhood than ours, the H43. So you have come from another city. What is your business at the Abigov?"

"We are taking private files to the Ministry of Archives, Sacred Books, and Holy Memories."

"And what is the Abigov?"

"It is the government, the Just Brotherhood, and everything else . . . "

The crowd was vigilant, and came in at the right moment: "Hey, inspector! Ask 'em for their papers, search 'em, there've been a lot of thefts in the neighborhood these days."

The inspectors took things in hand.

"Show us your papers, your travel permit, your Booklet of Worth, and the enrollment card for the *mockba*."

"Here you are, brave and tireless inspectors. Our cards were examined by your *mockba*, where we said our morning prayer, and where we will spend the night in meditation and fasting."

"I see you have good ratings and are in the top ranks for your prayers, that's a good sign."

The crowd renewed their attack: "Watch out, they're clever, ask them to recite the holy *Gkabul* . . . and search them, by Yölah!"

"Let's see, then: recite verse 76 of chapter 42, title 7, of the Holy *Gkabul*."

"That's easy enough, it says: *"I, Abi, the Delegate by the*

grace of Yölah, hereby order that you submit honestly, sincerely,
and totally to the inspectors, whether they are from the Just
Brotherhood, the Apparatus, the Administration, or the free ini-
tiative of my loyal believers. Great shall be my wrath against
those who act, hide, or conceal. So be it."

"Good, good. You are good, honest believers. Do you have
any money to give us, before we validate your travel permit and
let you continue on your way? We accept relics if they can be
converted to cash."

"We are poorly paid civil servants, we can only offer you
two *didis* and a talisman from Sîn, it will protect you from
tuberculosis and the cold, it will surely buy you a caramel or a
honey fritter."

A nd so it went, their journey across Qodsabad: truth be told, there were not many good things, given how vast it was, or its status as a multimillennial city, a thousand times holy: a constant exhausting press of crowds, obligatory stops at all the *mockbas* along the way, inspections at every intersection, pious ceremonies one after the other, improvised jamborees of aspiring pilgrims, from time to time spectacular brawls and arrests, of Regs, madmen, or fugitives; and also a host of depressing sights: condemned people being led to the stadium, convoys of prisoners headed for the camps and forced labor; and then there were the obligatory stops at the *nadirs* (if, exceptionally, the Great Commander was live on-screen). In front of posters of Abi, and there were thousands of them, the custom was to recite a little verse then back away; and let us not forget the beggars, it was exhausting trying to keep away from them, the place was crawling with them and the law required giving every one of them a little something— a *didi*, a crust of bread, some salt, a saleable relic, or for lack of anything better, some item they could exchange or sell.

On the whole Ati and Koa were doing well: their fake papers were better than authentic ones. The crowd may have denigrated them, but they had no trouble convincing the forces of law and order. While the Civics were more irksome than others, it was out of ignorance: those poor devils ought to be put out of their misery—they didn't know how to read, let alone understand, you had to explain, repeat, articulate, and every other sentence congratulate them on their excellent, surpassing piety. With a travel permit mandating them to go to the Abigov on State business, Ati and Koa had every right to look down on the Civics and tell them to sweep the street ahead of them, but they refrained from doing so: a sudden reversal of fortune was always possible, and their revenge would be terrible.

The main thing was to continue on their route and keep their wits about them, all the way to the Abigov, whose famous, dazzling Kïïba could be seen from all four horizons like a rising sun. It was still a three-day walk from there.

Along the way, the two friends discovered the city and did not miss a thing. In fact, it was nothing more than replicas of their own poor neighborhood, as far as the eye could see, but the various parts, brought together in this disjointed way, in an atmosphere of the beginning or end of the world, constituted a realm of absolute strangeness. Old Gog had warned them, with a shiver: "We're better off in our neighborhood, people know you here, you have things to do, and there will always be someone to bury you. Out there, who's gonna pick you up, who will keep the dogs off?"

Qodsabad was beyond imagining, a vast expanse turned upside down, where there reigned an unchanging order that left nothing to chance. The impression that emerged from this paradoxical organization was that of a final, universal disaster, transformed by the madness of things into a promise of heavenly paradise, where believers would find an exact replica of their life on earth. The Great Holy War, therefore, would be waged in every world, Here below and There above, and happiness would always be an unachievable aspiration on the part of humans, be they angels or demons. To believe in Yölah under such conditions required more than a miracle: it took the power of a fantastic publicity machine to make dream and reality one. But once you were caught in the phantasmagorical web, Qodsabad was a home like any other: one day you could feel as wretched as a rat and the next day as glad as a lark, and so life went on, not totally disappointing; everyone had a fifty percent chance of dying happy.

The two friends stood out, and so all along the way curious passersby rushed up to them and plied them with questions, always the same, perfectly banal: "Who are you, dammit, where do you come from, where are you going like this?" People did not understand how someone could leave their home, their *mockba*, and their cemetery, where their family were buried, other than to go on a pilgrimage or to fight in a Great Holy War; they'd never heard of a neighborhood called S21, or of the famous "Seven Sisters of Desolation" which formed the border and separated it from the ghetto—which many people had heard of, by reputation. They lived in M60, H42, or T16 . . . which Ati and Koa had never heard of, and they thought that their own neighborhood was all there was to Qodsabad the holy. The ghetto did not worry them much, since they did not know where it lay hidden; what was terrify-ing to them was Balis and those accursed Regs who by night kidnapped children and believers to perform witchcraft with their blood. All, however, shared that fine Abistani quality, hospitality, and it was as natural as could be that they invited the voyagers to come and pray with them at their *mockba* and to join in volunteer activities, thus adding substantially to their tally of points, with a view to the upcoming R-Day. They also offered them food and drink, and the money they asked for in exchange was simply a courtesy, tit for tat, generosity met with generosity. But in the presence of the forces of law and order, whether it was a war tactic or simple human weakness, they set aside their kindly disposition and heaped abuse on strangers.

A s Ati and Koa drew closer and closer to the Abigov, the pyramid of Kiïba began to unveil its majestic, fantastical grandeur. With every step they took in that direction the pyramid gained two *siccas* in height, and before long the tip vanished into the incandescent depths of the heavens. From this close up, you had to crane your neck horizontally to see the summit.

At last they had nearly reached their goal: only one neighborhood left to cross, A19, an unbearable shambles of the kind that used to exist around medieval domains—shabby creatures living one on top of the other in narrow, insalubrious slums fit to drive a leper away. The reason for this lies in the history of slums, if there is one. People camped out at the edge of the city to hire out their services to the rich lords, building their fine houses, putting up ramparts and dungeons to ensure their safety, and once the work was done they found themselves back outside where they started, caught in the trap. Being a slave without a master was worse than anything. Where could they go next? The family was getting bigger, they'd forged ties with their neighbors, as poor as they were, "If you leave here you die"; so between unemployment, odd jobs, and assorted trafficking they'd settled into a long-term provisional existence, piling sheet of metal upon sheet of metal, plank upon plank, using wattle to stop up the drafts, just so they'd feel cozier, as if they were at home, and they prepared their children to take over from them. A19 was only at a very primitive stage of development, as neighborhoods went; some day they'd have proper permanent houses, and streets with gutters and over-flows, and squares for markets and celebrations, and shelters for tramps, and masses of inspectors.

The two friends walked straight through, astonished they were able to do so without being stopped or pulled over every third step.

Once they'd left the last slum behind, the governmental city—the City of God—appeared before them: enormous, titanic. None of it was on a human scale; people had been working for God, here—and Yölah was the greatest—for all eternity, all infinity. It was a human endeavor, but it surpassed all human understanding. One surprise took their breath away: the City of God was enclosed by a wall as high as a mountain, of a thickness of several dozen *siccas*! How on earth would they get over it, confound it! Gog hadn't mentioned it at all. There had been gaps in the archivist's memory, and this was a major one. The other explanation was that the wall had been put up after Gog's visit. He was barely fifteen years old when he went to the Abigov, and the little messenger boy for the Bailiff, running faster than his shadow, didn't see everything; now he was a doddery old man, with little control over his memory. So much had happened since then—invasions, Holy Wars, including a nuclear one, the mother of all battles, which had unleashed upon the planet the greatest swarm of bandits and mutants in all of human history; there had been grandiose revolutions and titanic repressions that had engendered mad-men and vagrants in the millions; there had been famines and worldwide epidemics that had devastated entire regions and caused millions of wretches to flee before them. Extreme cli-mate change had taken care of the rest, radically transforming the geography of the planet—nothing was where it used to be—oceans, continents, mountains, and deserts had all been whirled out of place as never before through all the geological ages, and all in a single human lifespan. Yölah the almighty was not enough; it also took a wall of this dimension to protect the Just Brotherhood and its disciples. All that was left alive from that era when Gog visited the Abigov for his pleasure was Abi, but he was the Delegate, immortal and immovable. And there was Gog, an insignificant mortal, nearing his end.

That's how it goes, a problem remains a problem until a solution is found. Sometimes there's no need to look, the solution comes along on its own, or the problem just disappears, as if by enchantment. And that is what happened: on seeing the two friends moaning with despair at the foot of the colossal wall, a passerby laden with his burden turned to them and said: "If you are looking for the entrance, it's that way, to the south, roughly three *chabirs* from here, but it is tightly watched and the inspectors are strict and incorruptible. We have tried, often enough . . . If you're in a hurry or have things to hide, you can get in through the mousehole, it's a hundred *siccas* from here on your right, it leads to the civil servants' kasbah. We use it to go sell them vegetables and smuggled goods, and to buy documents and authorizations from them, which we sell all over Abistan. If you want to get into a ministry or the Kïïba, you need a summons or a travel permit. You can buy them from Toz, you'll find him in his workshop, just next to the *mockba*. Tell him I sent you, Hu the porter, he'll give you a good price. If you need anything else at all, you can find it at his place. Here in A19 you can move around freely, there are no inspectors, they toe the line, but there are a lot of spies, so watch out. Good luck, and may Yölah be with you."

And in no time the two friends covered the twenty *siccas* to their right. The mousehole was there. It must have been for a whopping great mouse, or else over time the hole had grown bigger to let in handcarts and trucks: a few specimens remained of those antediluvian fire-belching monsters which generations of stubborn smugglers had miraculously managed to keep alive.

The City of God was an architectural ensemble that defied the imagination, labyrinthine and chaotic to a fault, it has been said. And very impressive: all the power of Abistan was concentrated behind its walls—and Abistan was the entire planet. According to Koa, who knew a thing or two about ancient history, the Kïïba of the Just Brotherhood was a copy of the great pyramid in the twenty-second province, the land of the Great White River. The Book of Abi informed believers that its construction was a miracle Yölah had accomplished back in the long-ago era when his name was just Râ or Rab. He had come to convince the men of the River to abjure the adoration of idols and worship only him; he had to perform a few miracles to prove what he'd been saying. Which he did. The monument had been erected overnight, with neither fuss nor dust. The effect was immediate, masters and slaves threw themselves to the ground, reciting the formula he had just taught them: "There is no other god but Râ, and we are his slaves," which would make them into free believers, and before long they would smash the statues of their former gods and break the chains of the false priests. To secure their attachment to him for all time, and to reassure them about the future of their descendants, Yölah promised to send them a delegate, and quickly, who would teach their children the known and the unknown and help them to live in joy and submission.

The ministries and major administrations had grown even larger over time, somewhat randomly, spreading in height and breadth, and Abistan itself did not stop expanding in every direction, to the farthest reaches of the planet. One day, backs to the wall, it became evident that there was not one single square span of open space left in the entire city of the Abigov on which to build any access roads or housing for civil servants. That being the case, the surrounding villages were requisitioned and integrated within the walls of the City of God, and allotted to the civil servants, who had been recruited among the most loyal believers in Abistan and trained the hard way; thus the traffic routes were laid out underground. Security had been designed as if for an ant colony, and the principles of the labyrinth, obstacle, dead end, checkpoint, bottleneck, and constriction had been applied for all they were worth. No one could go in or out without a duly authorized guide, and on that basis a system for transporting personnel had been conceived that would move people freely between kasbah and office along tunnels then up elevators opening directly onto the corridors of the administration buildings. Someone—it could only have been Abi or Duc the Great Commander—deemed that the personnel no longer needed to leave the City of God, which was protected from all want, and by the same token sheltered from any outside influence. As things evolve by force of habit, necessity, or tropism, the civil servants became troglodytes and gradually turned into ants. Veiled in their luminescent black *burnis* and brought to life by the same signal emanating from a single center, they could show real ants a thing or two.

In his own hesitant, archaic words, Gog had explained that the little he had seen had left him with the impression that the Abigov was a gigantic factory of mysteries; those who served there didn't know themselves what it was for or how it worked; they had been programmed to execute, not to understand. Gog had used a word that was unknown in *abilang* and fairly difficult to pronounce: he had said that the Abigov was an "abstraction," but he had been incapable of providing even a rough definition. It is hard to forgive old people, said Koa with annoyance, age should at least serve to teach a thing or two, otherwise what's the point in getting old? But there you are, there's culture and there's culture, there's the one that adds to your knowledge and then there's the more common variety that adds to your ignorance. For a long time Gog had a recurring nightmare: he saw himself wandering through an infernal tangle of corridors, tunnels, and stairways, where there were strange noises, and he was tormented by the impression that a shadow was following him, or was just ahead of him, and sometimes it came and blew down his neck with a disgusting smell. He always woke up at the same time: he was running flat out down a narrow tunnel when suddenly with an infernal racket two heavy grilles fell like blades in front of him and behind him. He was done for. He let out a desperate cry and . . . woke with a start, streaming with sweat. Just the memory left him gasping for breath.

Mustering all their courage, Ati and Koa went through the mousehole to the other side of the wall.

There was a crowd on the other side, a friendly crowd; it was market day, the civil servants were stocking up on fresh vegetables that stank to high heaven of polluted earth and stagnant water—scrawny carrots, mushy onions, wrinkled potatoes, and some sort of mutant pumpkin covered in pustules. Lying through their teeth, the vendors touted their wares as perfect and delicious. The market was held in a narrow passage piled high with the rubble left from a construction site, between two windowless buildings. Ati and Koa were impressed by everything they saw in the crush of people. The civil servants' extreme pallor and the absence of any inspectors nearby suggested secret things: the Apparatus itself must have instigated this marginal trafficking, or encouraged it, because it allowed the civil servants to get some fresh air and improve their sustenance, and because the soulless, parsimonious fare the government provided them with consisted of nothing more

2084. THE END OF THE WORLD · 147

than a grayish flour made from who knows what, and a red-dish, oily concoction drawn from who knows where. The resulting mixture was a pinkish gruel that smelled of poison-ous mushrooms and undergrowth after rain. Ati was already well acquainted with it, as it had been the only meal served at the sanatorium morning, noon, and night, day after day. The gruel wasn't as innocent as it looked, for it contained secret ingredients: bromides, emollients, sedatives, hallucinogens, and other additives that enhanced an appetite for humility and obedience.

The pap the common people fed on five times a day, *hir*, was poor in nutrients but rich in taste and aroma; it could be obtained by sprinkling lightly roasted flour with a green liquid, water in which various herbs had macerated, along with two or three substances bordering on poison or other narcotics. That hardly mattered, people loved the stuff, that was the main thing.

From time to time a tradesman might turn up with prod-ucts that were unknown in Abistan—chocolate, coffee, pep-per. The civil servants had grown dependent on these drugs, which they paid for with important administrative documents. Some had developed addictions to pepper or coffee, which they chewed and sniffed with passion; they were sold under the table for up to twenty *didis* a gram.

It was a fine opportunity so the two friends seized on it: they could see how happy the civil servants were to be out in the fresh air, gazing at the vegetables—an intoxicating sensa-tion—so they went up to one of them, who seemed slightly more alert than his colleagues.

"We would very much like to stop in and see a friend of ours, a famous man who belongs to the Ministry of Archives, Sacred Books, and Holy Memories . . . You might know him, his name is Nas . . . "

The good civil servant was startled; he blushed, then mumbled, "I . . . uh . . . no . . . I . . . I don't know him," glancing over his shoulder. Then he rushed off without waiting for his change.

Others reacted in similar fashion, giving a start and taking to their heels. Speech does not come easy to people whose tongue has been severed or whose cerebral lobe for language and reasoning has been disconnected. The last person they approached fell over himself in contradictions: " . . . I . . . uh . . . never heard of him . . . I . . . I . . . don't know him . . . He disappeared . . . and his family . . . we don't know anything, leave us alone!" And he disappeared in turn, without even looking back.

Ati and Koa were crushed. The enormous risks they had taken and their extraordinary journey across Qodsabad had been useless. They'd become outlaws, and to no small degree; the stadium would be waiting for them upon their return, they would be the stars of the show; the judges had invested too heavily in Koa's name, and such mortal humiliation would call for swift revenge of the best kind—the reinstatement of impalement, or of cauldrons of boiling oil. Ati and Koa could not envisage going home again.

Over and over they said, in every tone imaginable: "Disappeared!" . . . "Disappeared?" They didn't understand the damned word, it was terrifying: "Disappeared," what did it mean—that Nas was dead, or that he'd been arrested, executed, kidnapped? Or had he run away? Why? What else? Did it mean that people were looking for him, was he wanted? Why? And his family, where were they, in prison, in a mass grave, hidden away somewhere? "Disappeared!" . . . "Disappeared?"

"What to do?" was once again the pressing question. Not at all sure where their steps were taking them, they ended up outside the *mockba* Hu had pointed them toward. It was tiny, cozy, rustic, the floor covered in fresh straw, and praying in that place was like feeding in a stable. They suddenly felt the fatigue they'd accumulated while crossing Qodsabad; they needed calm and fresh air to stop and think. Their situation was desperate; there was no going back, and no way to go forward.

The *mockbi* came up to them, as he could see that something was troubling these new worshipers.

"Hu came by and told me about you—I can see you're upset and don't have a place to go. You can sleep here tonight, but you'll have to leave first thing in the morning. I don't want any trouble, there are spies everywhere. The best thing would be to go and see Toz, he'll know how to help you. Tell him Rog the *mockbi* sent you, he'll give you a good price."

But who was this Toz everyone was recommending? They would go to see him the next day, and find out if he existed and really had a solution for everything.

They spent the night thinking. The *mockba* was full of snoring souls, sound asleep; in every corner there was a shadow wrapped in a *burni*—penniless travelers, people who were down on their luck, the homeless, perhaps even fugitives. An unpleasant impression came over Ati and Koa: that of a sticky, painful fear, for the future was dark, headed toward tragedy, and they could feel the crushing weight of the mystery in all its power, there at the foot of the monumental Kiïba of the Just Brotherhood. They had never tried to find out what that thing was, whether it was a truly useful institution or rather just an immense mystery between four walls, and to tell the truth, no one really cared, beyond the strict submission it implied, for people had their own everyday woes to deal with. Habit erases anything that initially seems out of place. The two friends were beginning to realize that the Just Brotherhood reigned over Abistan in a strange manner: it was total yet cowardly, omnipresent and distant, and in addition to the absolute power it had over people, it seemed to possess other unknown, enigmatic powers that were turned toward who knew what parallel, higher world. The Honorables were men, but they were like Abi—to a lesser degree, obviously, but they were also immortal, omnipotent, and omniscient. Demigods, basically. How else could anyone explain the extent of their power on earth? There was nevertheless an underlying paradox: if they were gods, or demigods, what were they doing among men, who were such insignificant creatures, full of lice and problems? Do men mingle with bedbugs, worms, and other weak creatures that live for only a day? No, they crush them underfoot and continue on their way. Such comparisons are not always relevant, I'll grant you that; life is a question, never an answer.

Just before they finally nodded off, they agreed they would go to see the renowned Toz as soon as possible. If he knew everything and could do everything, and if he was as available as was said, then he would help them find out what had happened to Nas—to get to him if he was alive, or to his family, if he was dead or in prison. They would also ask Toz to find them a refuge, which must not be difficult in A19, where order did not seem to have ever been established. Koa had one item that was worth its weight in gold, and a believer could hardly refrain from sacrificing everything to have it: a letter from Abi himself to his grandfather, congratulating him on his commitment to the Holy War.

T oz was a chameleon, you could tell right away; he had the gift of wearing the appropriate face for the circumstance. So he welcomed Ati and Koa as a concerned friend. "Brother Hu and Rog the *mockbi* have told me about your troubles, come in, come in, make yourselves at home, you're safe here," he said, waving his arms. They were overwhelmed with trust.

Another astonishing thing was that Toz did not wear the national *burni,* and there was nothing indecent about it: he was the first person they had ever seen like this. The *burni* was not just a piece of clothing in Abistan; it was the uniform of a believer, to be worn the way he wore his faith: he never took the one off, nor did he abandon the other. It's worth taking a few words to describe it. It was Abi himself who invented and perfected the *burni* at the beginning of his career as Delegate. It was his duty to set himself apart from the mass of ignorant, flea-ridden people, and to preach with presence and confidence. Legend has it that in order to confront the ungrateful crowd who were demanding an explanation regarding this new god he was trying to sell them, he tossed the first thing that came to hand over his shoulders, which happened to be a green sheet, then he strode out to confront the unruly ruffians of little faith. When he appeared, majestic with his cape flapping in the wind and his long, fiery beard, the crowd were gripped, transfigured, and without further ado they acclaimed him as their prophet. When he came the next morning to the people to edify them, they cried out, "Oh, Abi, where is your cowl? Put in on, so that we might listen to you telling us the truth." That is how it all started: the people learned that just as the cowl makes the monk, so does faith make the believer. Abi's improvised cape, tied around his neck with a little string, flared out as it draped toward his calves; it soon became the uniform of the Honorables, then the *mockbis*, then all agents with authority, and eventually it was de rigueur for everyone—men, women, and children of the people. To signify who was who, the hem of the cape was adorned with three parallel stripes of different colors: the first one indicated gender, white for men, black for women; the second was profession, pink for civil servants, yellow for tradespeople, gray for inspectors, red for clerics; and the third one indicated social class—lower, middle, upper. Over time the code evolved to take into account the diversity of situations; stars were added to the stripes, then crescents. Then there was the headgear—scarves, caps, fezes, skullcaps, or bonnets, and the sandals, and the beard and the way it was trimmed. One day, in the wake of a fever that had decimated several regions, the women's *burni* was lengthened right down to their feet and reinforced by a system of binding straps that compressed the fleshly, protu-berant parts of the body, then finished off with a hood that incorporated blinkers and wrapped the head firmly; it was called a *burni qab,* the woman's *burni*, which made *burniqab*; it was black with a green stripe for married women, white for vir-gins, and gray for widows. *Burni* and *burniqab* were made from an off-white woolen cloth. Honor to whom honor is due: the Honorables' *burni*, known as the *burni chik*, was made of vel-vet, caparisoned, gilded, and shiny, with a silk lining and trim-mings of gold thread, worn with an ermine cap and sandals of day-old kid leather stitched with silver thread. This vestment was complemented by a royal staff in rosewood, whose crozier was encrusted with precious gems. The Honorables' scribes

and guards were also heavily bedecked. So one single look sufficed for all to know whom they were dealing with. Underlying
the principle of submission was the principle of uniformity and
branding. But reality was somewhat different; people were not
that disciplined, and the poor did not particularly favor colors,
still less anything bright and shiny; their *burnis* were uniformly
gray, dirty, and heavily patched, but they were content with
them. Abistan was an authoritarian world, but there were few
laws that were rigorously enforced.

Toz seemed perfectly at ease in his strange clothes. As these
things did not exist in Abistan, he referred to them using
words he'd made up or found who knows where: the lower
part for the body from the waist down was clothed in *trousers*
and his torso up to his neck in a *shirt* and a *jacket*; his feet were
clad in waterproof *shoes*, and everything was buttoned, over-
lapping, knotted, or belted. It was a getup fit for a clown. To
go out into the street, he reverted to the norm; he took off his
shoes, rolled up the legs of his *trousers* as far as midcalf,
slipped on some good all-terrain sandals, then tossed the *burni*
befitting a prosperous merchant over his shoulders—and there
he was, invisible in the anonymous crowd.

He hastily pushed the two friends into the back of his
shop; it was full of curiosities that seemed to have come from
another planet. He had done his homework, had found a
name for every item, and knew what it was for. In the course
of their conversation—and Toz was talkative—he pointed
things out to his visitors, informing them that they were sitting
on *chairs*, around a *table*, and that the pieces of wood hanging
on the wall were *paintings*, and over there, on the *sideboards*
and *pedestals*, those little things that cheered the gaze were
called *knick-knacks*. And on he went, without ever hesitating
or making a mistake, calling each thing by its name. How
could he remember so many names, of so many unfamiliar

items, and in a language that no one knew? It was a mystery, one the two friends simply did not try to comprehend.

Encouraged by their friendly astonishment, Toz relaxed, and became good-natured and expansive.

"These things surprise you, I can see that, but if you knew, you would see that there is nothing here that is not perfectly ordinary, for this is how people lived in that vanished era you have never heard about. With patience and considerable difficulty I have managed to reconstruct in my shop and my house a little of that world that fills me with nostalgia, even though I never knew it, other than . . . but perhaps you don't know what these are, they are *books* . . . I will show you some, my room up there is full of them. I've also got *catalogues*, and *leaflets*, they are so lovely to look at, you'll know instantly what they're about. I only show them to friends . . . and to be honest, I don't have any in these parts . . . True pleasure is selfish . . . When I sell them, I transmit my pleasure to the customer and then I look for other pleasures."

Ati and Koa were fascinated. Toz really was remarkable; they were ready to listen to him the whole blessed day. They had never imagined such people might exist on earth. They were happy, and flattered; Toz trusted them as much as they trusted him, he told them everything . . . like an open *book*.

Then he got down to the purpose of their visit. In few words, he showed them that he knew everything and had guessed the rest; they didn't need to waste time on explanations.

"I know you're looking for a friend of yours, Nas by name, an archeologist with the Ministry of Archives, Sacred Books, and Holy Memories. A brilliant young man who was in charge of the investigation into Mab, the village where our marvelous Delegate, may salvation be upon him, received the revelation of the holy *Gkabul*. At the black market by the mousehole you alarmed a few honest civil servants with your questions, and naturally they informed their bosses and the Moral Health judges of what you were up to. It's unfortunate, they were punished severely for being there and listening to your questions . . . And from that point on the information traveled by word of mouth and in the end reached me. That's the way things are, everything eventually ends up with me, I'm friends with everyone. Well, tell me now how you met Nas and tell me about yourselves. If you want me to help you, you have to tell me everything."

Ati and Koa did not hesitate for a moment. Ati told of how he had met Nas somewhere on the way back to Qodsabad from the sanatorium at Sîn, how they'd had long conversations about the mysterious village the pilgrims had discovered. Nas had been uneasy, he said strange things that Ati didn't fully understand—that his discovery was the very negation of Abistan and its beliefs. Koa took over and told his own story, how he'd rebelled against his genocidal family; how he withdrew—and this became a rite of passage for him, in the devastated suburbs or lost villages; he talked about their escapade into the ghetto of Balis and their journey across Qodsabad that had left them with the firm conviction that Abistan did not exist, that Qodsabad was merely an artifact, a stage setting that hid a cemetery, or worse, that filled their minds with the terrible sensation that life had died long ago, and that people were so damaged by their uselessness that they failed to see they were just vague traces of life, painful memories wandering in a lost time.

They concluded with the terrible business that had compelled them to leave their neighborhood and come to ask for Nas's help: Koa's appointment as Destroyer in the trial of a young woman, the mother of five children, who was accused of blasphemy and doomed to the stadium.

For most of the day they talked about these matters, but as simple conversation is not enough to express things that are beyond our grasp, they began to philosophize about life in general, which helps pass the time and stimulates the appetite. Toz offered them an unusual sort of meal, food they had never seen, *white bread*, *pâté*, *cheese*, *chocolate*, and a bitter, burning drink he called *coffee*. At the end he took a basket of fruit from the *buffet*—bananas, oranges, figs, and dates. Ati and Koa nearly jumped out of their skin, they thought these things had disappeared off the face of the earth long before they were born, and that the few remaining crops were reserved for the Honorables. After that Toz reached into his pocket for a little pouch, and with its contents he fashioned a white stick the length of four fingers, filled with dried grass; then he placed it between his lips, lit the other end, and began to produce smoke. The horrible smell did not disgust him, but seemed on the contrary to delight him. He used the words *cigarette* and *tobacco* and said that this was his one small sin. It was hard to admit something sinful to oneself in a world where sin could be fatal.

There were no two ways about it, Toz lived in his own world, and it had nothing to do with Abistan. Was he even Abistani? Where did he come from, where had he acquired his power, what was he doing in such a mediocre neighborhood, where people only lived and survived on what the Abigov tossed over the side from the top of its ramparts? Toz himself didn't look like anything special, he was short, stocky, stooped, his neck was scrawny, his hands were ridiculously small, and he must have been in his fifties, already flabby and graying. The only things that shone about him were his gaze, his culture, his intelligence, his charisma, and that aura of mystery that surrounded him. How had these qualities come to him: was he just born like that, like a genie emerging fully armed from his magic lamp, or had he acquired them over the course of a life-time? In any case, it was these qualities that had made him who he was, the king of the neighborhood.

He remained silent for a long while, the time it took to smoke two cigarettes and sip two coffees, then he turned to Ati and Koa and said firmly, "Here's what we're going to do. I will get you settled in a safe place, a warehouse that belongs to me, right nearby, for the time it takes for me to find out about your friend. After that, we'll decide what to do next."

Then, with a little smile in his eyes: "What will you give me for my pains?"

Koa reached into a hidden pocket in his *burni* and took out a rag, unfolded it, and handed the paper that had been hidden there to Toz. Toz read it, looked at them, and burst out laughing. He slipped the paper into a drawer in the table and said, "Thank you, this is a very precious present, I will add it to my collection of fine relics. Right, I have to go out now, I have a client to meet. Follow me, I'll have you stay upstairs for now. Don't make any noise, don't go near the windows, please . . . I'll be back at the end of the day. After nightfall I'll take you to the warehouse."

Without further ado he put on his sandals and his *burni* and vanished into the dusty streets. There was a furtiveness about his gestures that seemed to suggest something, but everything about him was so elegant and tactful that it erased whatever that something was.

Left to their own devices, the two friends took the oppor-tunity to explore the dwelling of the warm and mysterious Toz. They were all at sea, everything they saw had come there from another planet. How to name these things, in what language? Like in the back room at the shop, there were *chairs*, a *table*, a *sideboard*, *paintings*, and many very amusing *knickknacks*. And other truly strange objects. If there were any similar dwellings in Qodsabad, they must belong to very rich dignitaries—who else—and these very rich dignitaries were bound to know Toz, their supplier: there could be no one else in all of Abistan, he had said as much himself. The law prescribed uniformity for all, and Toz was the miraculous exception that confirmed the rule. It was truly a mystery, to find such a unique man among the dense mass. The people had no knowledge of such unusual items, they were all in the same boat, a drab world of ruined neighborhoods, crumbling buildings, worn-out houses, wobbly hovels, one or two bare rooms, a single toilet, everything was done on the floor—cooking, eating, sleeping; the rule was one *burni* per person, to be mended over and over until the final day, when it would be turned into a shroud, and one pair of sandals that were resoled for as long as possible. A dismal process was at work: since no one knew how to repair the old with the new, they did it with the old, using the same vintage, and thus everyone merely added to the woes they had been hoping to eliminate. Indeed: but where to find new ideas in an ancient world?

Toz came back at the end of the afternoon, just as furtively. He looked depleted, pensive. He collapsed on his chair, poured two coffees, and smoked two cigarettes to raise his spirits. Then Toz caught them unawares: they had been watching spellbound as he blew smoke out of his nose after swallowing it through his mouth, when he abruptly asked them a strange question:

"Have you ever heard of a certain Democ?"

"D . . . dimoc? What's that?"

"A ghost . . . a secret organization . . . no one knows . . . Apparently people talk about it, now and again," he said with a certain weariness, on the verge of boredom and incredulity.

Ati and Koa didn't understand. They looked at each other in astonishment, almost frightened; they were becoming aware that if they were to discover the world, they must venture into its complexity and feel that the universe was a black hole welling with mystery, danger, and death; it meant discovering that in fact only complexity existed, that simplicity and the apparent world merely camouflaged it. It would, therefore, be impossible to understand; complexity would always know how to find the most attractive simplification in order to prevent all understanding.

Ati had a flash of inspiration. Memories were coming back to him . . . the sanatorium . . . cold, solitude, hunger . . . and delirium as he slept . . . Yes, he remembered . . . the caravans disappearing up there, so close to the sky, in the latticework of summits and mountain passes, beyond something you didn't actually know . . . a border . . . an imaginary line . . . soldiers tortured and killed . . . the people's silence . . . they didn't speak because they had never spoken, because they knew nothing and had no way of knowing . . . And yet, behind those disappearances and murders and that atmosphere heavy with menace there had to be something, someone, there was bound to be . . . a shadow . . . a ghost . . . a desire . . . a secret organization . . . Could it be that thing . . . that person . . . Democ . . . Dimoc? Ati was sure he had heard the word, or something like it . . . but that was a sick man's rambling . . . Someone had talked about . . . demo . . . democ . . . demon? . . . He had talked about torture, too . . . but didn't know what the word meant . . .

Once night had fallen, Toz took them to the warehouse, which was not just by the shop as he had said, but clear on the other side of the neighborhood, and they reached it via a labyrinth that obeyed absolutely no reasonable human logic. A labyrinth is an eminently intelligent thing, but not in this case; the path followed the wind and was constantly changing. In the deserted streets darkness came close on their heels as here and there furtive shadows slipped past. Toz seemed guided by instinct. Ah, they'd arrived. This lugubrious place, this huge dark mass was the warehouse, a cube, a concrete base on which a clutter of rusty sheet metal had been erected. They could only make out what a moonless sky with a sparse scattering of stars allowed them to see: ghostly storage sheds to the right and to the left, with a dusty alleyway sandwiched in between, prowling with tribes of dogs and cats exhausted by hunger, scrofula, and beatings, like all the dogs and cats in Qodsabad. In the distance—or was it right nearby—they could hear something magical in the ponderous void, a baby crying and a woman singing a lullaby. Toz opened the door. A metallic sound rang out. He struck a match; giant shadows emerged from the night and began dancing madly on the walls. They were overwhelmed by the stuffiness of the air, a complex smell: something rotting, rusty, fermented, a dead creature, mold-encrusted objects. He struck another match and lit a candle in a heavy candlestick. A scant light flickered, yellow and black, surrounded by quivering shadows. Here and there were pieces of furniture, and trunks, bags, barrels, jars, machines, statues, and crates overflowing with knickknacks. At the back was a metal stairway, and upstairs, two low-ceilinged adjoining rooms. In the second one a crate contained some dishes; against the wall were a chest and a bench, and piled on a shelf, some blankets; in one corner a bucket full of water stood next to a chamber pot. On the outside wall was a fanlight which Toz hastily concealed with an old rag. "My employee, his name is Mou, will bring you some food after dusk. No one will see him coming and going, he knows how to make himself invisible. He'll leave the basket in a corner by the entrance to the warehouse. Don't speak to him, he's deaf and a bit simpleminded. Be discreet, don't go out, don't open for anyone, the spies are all on edge, they'd love to make themselves some money off of you . . . Someone got them going, a *mouaf* from the Apparatus . . . or someone high up," he said, once they were settled.

Before leaving he added, "Be patient . . . I have to be cautious, it's a delicate matter. Very delicate."

The two friends explored the place, groping their way around; the darkness could only be penetrated with their hands.

The warehouse was a dreary place; it must have witnessed a thousand bankruptcies in its lifespan, and it wobbled and creaked everywhere. The antiques it stored only added to the desolation. Toz cherished them as if they were treasures; to his eyes only old things were of any value, and that value was proportional to their age. If Toz collected so many things, it was in order to sell them, and if he sold them then he must have buyers: that was another mystery. "Mystery" was the word that came most often to their minds.

That night they slept as they never had before. A surfeit of fatigue, tension, waiting, and so many riddles in the air.

At some point during the night, as he was recalling that time of slow death he had spent at the sanatorium, Ati again heard voices in the distance, a baby crying and a warm-voiced woman singing a lullaby. In a dream he thought, life was not altogether dead.

The waiting went on and on. Eight endless days had gone by in perfect vacuousness. The two friends were beginning to worry themselves sick, constantly wondering whether Toz was neglecting them or whether his investigation had gotten bogged down somewhere. They were reassured when, in the evening, sometime around the seventh prayer of the holy day, they heard the faithful Mou come furtively into the warehouse, put down his basket with a jerry can of water, and disappear in silence. Their host had not forgotten them, at least as far as their daily bread was concerned. Having experienced the difficult joys of Qodsabad, they had no trouble imagining what an exploit it must be merely to get into the Abigov. Questioning machines that had never known they could talk if they wanted to, going up to leaders, who were surely daunting and invisible, in order to obtain secrets from them, simply belonged to the realm of the impossible. But Toz was Toz, and impossible meant nothing to him.

Very quickly, in only a day or two, they had learned how to live the old-fashioned way: sitting with dignity at the table, and on chairs without feeling dizzy; eating food they could not identify off individual plates, unable to determine whether it was harmless or lethal, licit or illicit; drinking coffee that kept them awake all night, as if they were owls. And they were beginning to miss the *hir*, the national gruel, in the most dreadful way. Sometimes, when the wind was blowing the right direction, its aroma of burned spices would drift up from the street and come to titillate their nostrils. So they would leave the fanlight ajar to allow a bit more of the scent to reach their nostrils, and they would sneeze with pleasure. The aroma came wafting over to them from the old tumbledown house across the way, whence now and again, when the silence of the night amplified sound, they could hear the baby's crying and the very gentle singing that accompanied it so loyally.

One morning brilliant with sunshine and balmy air they caught a glimpse of the invisible woman with the melodious voice. She was in her courtyard, ten square *siccas* of concrete, with bric-a-brac in one corner, a water cistern in the other, a basin in the center and next to it a cauldron on a tripod above a wood fire; against the wall stood a dead tree where laundry was drying. The matronly woman had enough volume and curves for an entire family, with huge, blindingly white breasts that could feed an entire litter of little Gargantuas; the baby would have no cause for concern regarding his food or his comfort, and he slept soundly in a basket hanging from a low branch of the tree. The happy mother was squatting by her basin, and this emphasized the particularly well-endowed shape of her posterior as she pounded the laundry with gen- uine delight. This was how she filled her time, washing diapers and bibs, singing a romantic little tune whose refrain went, roughly, "Your life is my life and my life is your life and love will be our blood." *Abilang* is full of rich rhymes; the word for life is *vî*, for love is *vii*, and for blood *vy*. So that gave, *"Tivî is mivî i mivî is tivî, i vii sii nivy."* Let there be no mistake, this declaration of love was addressed to Abi, the wonderful verse was from the holy *Gkabul*, title 6, chapter 68, verse 412, but the deepest intention was something else altogether, as it hap- pened. The faithful mother had too much to do to lose herself in religion; her life and her happiness revolved around her child and he was a difficult crybaby, who knew how to get what he was owed. There was also a husband in the matter. The two friends had seen him once, a fleeting shadow drifting past in a tramp's *burni*. He came home late at night and the way he coughed and gasped suggested he was not long for this earth. A household that was the very image of domestic life: heartwarming and tragic.

Another day they heard gunshots. By guesswork they located their origin two *chabirs* away, in the direction of the monumental entrance to the Abigov. Then there was an explosion (rocket, bomb, grenade?) that made the whole warehouse shake. The mother, sweeping her little courtyard and humming, did not hesitate for one second: she buried her baby between her shockproof breasts and with her head lowered she rushed in to take shelter in her house that the mildest of storms could have blown away just like that. The two friends thought it might be Regs trying to invade the Abigov or, why not, an eventual return of the Enemy. Then they instantly forgot about the event; alerts were common currency in Qodsabad and never had any consequences, people knew what was going on, the purpose of these warning shots was to frighten sluggish believers and remind them of their duties. Under the reign of the *Gkabul* faith began with fear and continued with submission; the flock had to keep together and march straight toward the light, and the good sheep certainly must not pay for the bad ones.

The boredom became oppressive, and there was nothing to relieve the pain. The contents of the warehouse, for all that they were astonishing, could not distract two such minds for long, avid as they were for action and the real truth. All these months gone by, Ati and Koa had had no lack of adventure, despair, or earth-shattering questioning, and this forced repose in confinement and darkness was more draining than anything.

They were threatened with the syndrome of the hermit. They must react, of course—but how?

On the ninth day of their reclusion, as they were drearily eating their food, an idea came to them in the dark, so exalting that they acted upon it at once: to hell with risk or caution. They would go out for a walk and, better still, they would go as far as the main entrance to the City of God, simply in order to get a closer look at the impressive Abigov and the holy and most extraordinary Kiïba: so mysterious and alluring on all four sides of its pyramidion, all the way at the top and close to Yölah's sky, the magical eye of Bigaye stared relentlessly at the world and the souls who lived there. They would also see the beautiful, elegant Great Mockba, where for three whole decades the *mockbi* Kho, Koa's grandfather, had officiated. That was where his magical voice, relayed by powerful loud-speakers, had beguiled the crowds, tens of thousands of people massed all around, bewitching them and packing them off to die for Yölah. The vast majority of troops for the last three Great Holy Wars had left from there, their ears ringing with the *mockbi* Kho's heroic cries.

The two friends reckoned they could not have come so far nor confronted so many strange follies only to fail to reach their goal: it was there, close at hand, only two or three *chabirs* away. As they said this, they recalled a precept in the form of a quatrain they had learned at the *gkabulic* school, which taught that:

To pray at the foot of the Kiïba
And in faith swear loyalty to Abi
Redeems a thousand sins, great and small, when death comes.
And with your spirit light, go to the bosom of Yölah.

Koa remembered that at the same time some of his co-disciples at the School of the Divine Word, all sons of noble princes and very rich merchants, and devilish composers of pastiches, had come up with a bawdy ditty and that one day, in the end, it had earned them a thousand lashes, equitably distributed, with a silk whip:

Take it to heart to pull on your cock
And in faith play marbles in the raw
Relieve a thousand sins, great and small, and then some.
And with your spigot light, put it back in your drawers.

They laughed about it; what else should they do? There was neither blasphemy nor lying in their vivacious lines.

Like shadows, they slipped out into the night. Somewhere, a dog was barking furiously; they supposed he was promising death to his loyal little enemy who was without a doubt perched at a safe height, replying now and again with a short and innocent miaow.

They went over to the little house that so enchanted them with its crying and its songs of love and they stood there, as if in a dream, listening to the purr of domestic life, feeling its soothing warmth, inhaling its odors and perfumes, those of a gentle burrow.

The air was ominous with torpor. They roused themselves and went on their way.

Further along, beneath the awning of a dilapidated building that seemed to be, or had once been, a *midra*, or a *soku*, a covered market, they noticed a group of men conversing with restrained ardor, some carrying bags, others baskets, bundles, or crates, which they exchanged hastily, from hand to hand. Ten paces behind them, here and there, leaning against the walls, were shadows, their right-hand men whose job was to keep watch and ensure the safety of the bigwigs. There could be no doubt: a black market had been set up there, an encounter among hardened professionals—tradesmen, fences, and smug-glers. And there were Regs there too, they were everywhere, in on everything, they excelled at business and always closed a deal before anyone else; because it was so confined, the ghetto's only resource was trafficking, and the profession was handed down from father to son. But how had they managed to come this far without getting caught? Their smell and their gaze, like that of a nocturnal bird, would betray them to the first comer.

The two friends continued on their way; they had nothing to buy or sell, and no wish for any trouble.

The surprise awaited them around the corner, one *chabir* ahead. A grandiose, heart-stopping vision: there at last was the unique, incomparable City of God, the Kïïba, the Great Mockba, and the Abigov, the all-powerful government of believers on earth. What a thrill! Here was the center of the earth, and of the universe, the point of all departures and all arrivals, the heart of holiness and power, the magnetic pole toward which all races and individuals turned to praise their Creator and implore his representatives.

The atmosphere in this place was so intensely mystical that a fervent atheist would have lost his mind right then and there; faith would have seized him and rid him of all vain pretention, throwing him to his knees, brow to the ground; with tears and quivering he would have heard himself utter the profession of faith that would have made him into the most fervent of believ-ers: *"There is no god but Yölah, and Abi is his Delegate."* In this formula there was no mention of the man himself, happy believer or unfortunate zombie; he had nothing to do with the transaction between Yölah and Abi, that was a private matter. Yölah had created Abi and Abi had adopted Yölah, or vice versa, and that was all there was to it.

Ati and Koa felt crushed by the majesty of it all, so colossal, excessive, beyond human dimensions. At the foot of the fortress a square covered a boundless expanse, richly lit and so vast that no gaze could encompass it all at once; paved with translucent tiles of every shade of green, it measured over a thousand square *hectosiccas* and bore the sublime name of the Square of Supreme Faith. The entrance to the City was marked by a cyclopean arch known as the Great Arch of the First Day, its summit lost in the clouds. Its pillars were in keeping with the rest of the construction, sixty *siccas* wide and a range of three hundred *siccas* underneath the arch, and they fit into the enormous rampart that encircled not only the City of God— the fabulous showcase for the Kiïba, the Abigov, and the Great Mockba—but also the barracks for the prestigious Abigovian Guard and, further along, hidden in their own shambles and connected to the city by invisible tunnels, the civil servants' kasbahs. All the substance of the world was there, concentrated behind those immovable ramparts: eternity, power, majesty, and mystery. The world of men was elsewhere; one day it might exist.

Another surprise: the square was teeming with people. The two friends had never seen so many before, even in dreams. The square was always like this, day and night, all year round, and always had been. People came from the sixty provinces of Abistan in entire flocks—on foot, by train, by truck, and at the entrance they were duly checked, counted, assigned their place. The swarm was divided into three blocs, separated into pens by corridors of metal barriers in which, like so many petty kings in their fiefdoms, guards were armed with whips and *kovs*, machine guns that dated from before the Revelation: first there was the bloc of pilgrims (a few tens of thousands), who came to worship at the foot of the Kiïba before setting off on their long pilgrimages; then there were the supplicants, civil servants,

tradesmen, and simple citizens (several tens of thousands) burdened with files, who were waiting their turn to go into the
Abigov to this or that ministry or administration; and finally the
third bloc, admired by the crowd of onlookers and children
who were held back at the edge of the square, the bloc of volunteers (several thousand), some of whom were applying for an
immediate departure to the front, and others who had come to
enlist for the next Holy War, which they preferred to experience right from the start to know all the joy it could offer. And
everywhere, all around, eager and buzzing, and ever so
resourceful at deceiving the guards, were snack vendors, water
sellers, blanket renters, washermen, healers, kids touting places
in the lines or renting their services to keep a place, as the waiting could go on for weeks or months. Here there was neither
night nor day, there was a constant rush year-round. Legends
spread throughout the ranks, it was a way of passing the time,
there was often talk of one old man who had spent a little over
a year in the line of supplicants who on finally reaching the
entrance window could no longer remember why on earth he
was there. And without a motive, there could be no entrance
ticket. The man was forgetful, but not stupid; he put his place
in line up for auction. It went to a very rich tradesman; he
couldn't be away from his business for more than a day, having
left things unattended. Now that he had made his fortune, the
old amnesiac bought himself a roof, and got married for the
seventh time, to a sweet nine-year-old kid who had just begun
to bleed, and he gave her seven or eleven jolly babies and lived
happily to his dying day. On his deathbed, although no one had
said a thing, he recalled in a flash what it was that had driven
him one day to stand in the line of supplicants: he had come to
inquire about the status of his request concerning accommoda-
tion . . . or was it employment . . . or emergency assistance . . .
over a year old . . . or had it been ten years, or thirty.

The two friends found out that there was a fourth bloc, located one *chabir* further to the east, a dark, silent place, the bloc of prisoners, several thousand of them chained together by the hundreds, waiting to be blessed and sent to the front. Some were prisoners of war taken from the Enemy, who had refused the death camps and chosen to convert to the *Gkabul* and go back to the front, but on the right side this time; the others were Abistanis condemned to death—riffraff, rebels, highway robbers who did not want to die in the stadium or the camps and had decided to become suicide bombers; they would be sent to war, to the front lines, to blow themselves up among the Enemy. A place in this bloc was a favor that was not granted to all the death row prisoners (and never to Regs) but only to those who had demonstrated a true desire to serve Abistan in the name of Yölah and Abi, may salvation be upon them. An old passerby had explained all this to Ati and Koa; he said that he himself had a son who'd managed to avoid the stadium by volunteering to go and greet the Enemy. "He died a martyr, which means I have a good pension and priority access to the State stores," he said proudly, with a burst of laughter.

Ati was moved as he thought of Nas, his friend and travel companion. He lived here in grandeur and mystery, in dark madness and absolute servitude. What had become of him, where was he? Ati was counting on Toz to find out and come to his aid.

A man came up to them, a professional: he truly looked the honest, efficient trafficker he strove to appear, his own mother would have been none the wiser. He'd been observing the two friends for a while already, and they'd noticed him. He said, "If you want a good place in line, I have some excellent ones to offer you . . . I'll give you a good price."

"That's fine, brother, we're just passing through . . . "

"I can also get you papers, appointments, hard-to-find items, and all sorts of information . . . "

"Well then, let's see. What can you tell us about a certain Nas? He works for the Abigov, in the archeology service."

The merchant of goods and services smiled as if he were preparing to reveal a great secret.

"What do you want to know, exactly?"

"Whatever you can tell us about him."

"And then what?"

"Where does he live, for example? We'd like to go and see him."

"Give me an advance and come back tomorrow, you'll get your information. And for a small supplement I'll lead you to his door, or even bring him here to you."

The two friends quickly wearied of playing "may the more clever one win." It was time to go back to the warehouse if they were to be there before daybreak; the spies would soon be on the warpath.

They hadn't gone ten paces when their sixth sense, sharpened in the course of their absurd, perilous voyage through Qodsabad, tipped them off: they turned around and saw the merchant of services pointing them out to the patrol. The merchant was also a spy and a Judas.

They did not hesitate for one second and took to their heels. Nor did the guards hesitate; they began shouting and pointing their guns in every direction. Ati yelled to Koa, "Let's split up! You go to the left, run, run! I'll see you at the warehouse, run! Hurry!"

They had their experience of the dark, narrow labyrinth in A19 in their favor, but their pursuers had strength in numbers, and they were already joined by reinforcements springing forward from the crowd of onlookers.

Night swallowed them up around the first corner.

From time to time they could hear shots, then . . . then nothing more.

Ati ran as fast as he could, for an hour, two hours. His feet ached terribly and as a former consumptive his lungs were on fire. He went down a narrow dead end and collapsed behind a pile of garbage guarded jealously by a dozen particularly sinister-looking tomcats. They hissed at him, fangs bared and claws drawn, then when they saw how pitiful he was they returned to their sprawling lookout at the top of their pantry.

An hour later, Ati set off again; hobbling along, going out of his way, getting lost, he eventually reached the warehouse just as the *mockbas* were sounding the call to the faithful for the first prayer of the holy day. It was four in the morning. At the other end of the city, night was letting in the first rays of dawn. Ati found his bed, rolled up in his blanket, and fell asleep. He just had time to think that Koa would not be long now, and he'd be glad to see his friend safe and sound, snoozing away as if nothing had happened.

The sun had not completely emerged from the night when Toz burst into the warehouse and unceremoniously pulled Ati from the nightmare in which he was struggling. Ati leapt up from his bed as if ten guards had pounced on him to strangle him. He scarcely had time to recover before he relapsed into despair: he saw that Koa had not returned; his bed was empty.

"Wake up, dammit, wake up!" shouted Toz.

Toz was not the type to waste time arguing; he kept a cool head. He grabbed Ati by the collar and shook him hard. There was enough authority in his voice to make an entire unit of rebels stand to attention.

"Sit down and tell me what happened!"

"I . . . uh . . . we went out for some fresh air . . . and we went as far as the Abigov . . . "

"And now you see what has happened, the entire neighborhood is in a state of siege, the guards are searching everywhere and people are bending over backwards to denounce each other . . . This was the last thing we needed."

"I'm sorry . . . And Koa? Do you have any news?"

"None for the time being. I'm going to move you somewhere else, this warehouse isn't safe anymore. It's impossible to go out now, you'll have to hide in a storage room downstairs that I arranged behind a fake wall for hiding rare items. And tonight or tomorrow someone will come and get you to take you to another hiding place. His name is Der, follow him and don't ask any questions. Right, I have to run, I have to make arrangements."

"And Koa?"

"I'll find out. If he's been arrested or killed by the guards, I'll find out soon enough, otherwise we'll just have to wait. Either he's hiding somewhere and he'll eventually get in touch . . . or he's dead in a ditch and his body will be found before long."

Ati took his head in his hands and burst into tears. He was angry with himself, it was all his fault, he realized he had had a bad influence on Koa and yet had never even tried to curb his natural enthusiasm. Worse still, he had taken advantage of Koa's naïveté, he'd encouraged him with all his speeches about good and evil, like some recruiting sergeant, like some dispenser of justice on a quest for truth. How could Koa have resisted? He was a born rebel, all he had needed was to find a cause.

Ati paced feverishly in the warehouse. He had located all the holes and interstices in the building's sidings and at the slightest sound he would run from one to the other to try to see what was going on outside, ready to go to his hiding place if need be. On peering through the fanlight he saw a shadow behind the window of the little house across the way, the silhouette of a rather large woman. He got a shock because she was looking at him and pointing him out to someone standing behind her. He leapt back. He did what he could to put his mind at rest: it was just an impression, an optical illusion, he thought, the good mother was innocence made woman, she was going about her household chores, a reflection on the window of the fanlight had attracted her attention, or she was showing something to her baby to distract him, a funny cloud, a lizard running along the wall, a pigeon gently preening in a gutter on the warehouse.

Ati went back downstairs and locked himself in the storage room, trying to breathe deeply in order to still the pounding of his heart and overcome his fear. His spirits were aching and his body was a raw wound. Before long his breathing slowed, and he foundered in a deep lethargy.

And so he spent the day between nervous sleep, deep oblivion, and semi consciousness.

He woke as the day was ending, taking on the sad colors of twilight, and as the cracking sounds in the warehouse were turning sinister and getting louder. He tried to get up but his limbs would not obey him; he felt pins and needles all over, and his mind was blank, anesthetized by pain.

The moments ticked slowly by while in his head a faraway voice said over and over, tirelessly, *Get up . . . get up . . . get up . . . get . . .* Eventually it managed to touch a sensitive nerve and make contact, he opened his eyes slightly, and a bit of light entered his brain. A sharp, shooting pain radiated through his body, while the voice spoke ever more urgently: *Get up . . . You're alive, dammit . . . get ready.*

With a jolt of determination he got up and began limping from one end of the warehouse to the other to rid his legs of the pins and needles and clear his head.

He filled his mind with nervous excitement by swallowing the entire jug of coffee left over from the night before all in one go. He needed to think; there was something fishy going on. Even several things.

He went back over the film of events. And for a start he saw how careless he and Koa had been. Of course it was obvious, after the fact—the Square of Supreme Faith was under high surveillance, with cameras everywhere and legions of guards and hyperattentive spies, what else did they expect, the site was hypersensitive. When, in addition, you got into the habit of living outside religion and the law, in a world that was steeped in tyranny and the most archaic forms of piety, you were bound to appear a little abnormal in the way you walked or spoke, it would be plain to see, plain to hear, it would disturb people, and from that point of view the two friends were as heretical as they came, and not at all law-abiding. And if on top of it you showed an interest in someone like Nas, whom special laws had placed among Abistan's prime enemies, you were bound to appear suspect, and to find yourself branded as a great enemy of Abistan. That was the whole problem: was it because they looked exotic that the vendor of goods had noticed them and pointed them out to the patrol, to be on the safe side, so to speak, or had he denounced them because they were interested in Nas? In that case, there was a very significant question: how could a poor devil who lived off petty trafficking at the expense of the stupefying, sheeplike crowds who haunted the periphery of the City of God know about Nas? There weren't many archeologists, and Nas was one civil servant among a hundred and fifty thousand agents in the Abigov. And what was even stranger: how could the vendor know that Nas was mixed up in a top-secret matter of State that might have had him arrested, killed, deported? Was the petty trafficker actually a top-ranking policeman or the head of something—a specialized cell of the Apparatus, an agency connected to some clan or other of the Just Brotherhood? Did he give an order to the patrol when he pointed out Ati and Koa, or did the guy act the flunkey to get some sort of favor from them? Or maybe he'd even been trailing them for a long time. Yes, he probably had . . . from the moment they left the warehouse . . . or even before, when they arrived at Toz's place. Or when they were asking about Nas at the market by the mousehole . . . or before that, maybe others had spotted them, as they crossed Qodsabad, shadows had been relaying each other from neighborhood to neighborhood, all the way to the trafficker . . . Or even before then . . . for a very long time . . . since the time they went to the ghetto, they'd have been denounced by some auxiliary from the Guild or a Reg who occasionally worked for the AntiRegs . . . Or before that: where Ati was concerned, ever since he left the sanatorium and arrived back in Qodsabad . . . which might explain why he'd been given a position as a subsidiary civil servant and a lodging in a solid building . . . He remembered perfectly, the doctor had written, "Keep under close scrutiny," and underlined it twice, at the bottom of his discharge papers. But the real question would not go away: who was Ati, in their opinion, to deserve so much surveillance, and why?

As for Koa, he must have been under surveillance from the day he left the family fold; his name made him an icon, a collector's piece. He was a child of the System, and the System looks after its own. The guardian angels were all the more careful to cocoon him in that they knew he was turbulent, and full of fury against his family, while they all prospered from the reputation of the famous *mockbi* Kho.

It was all so patently clear, if only you opened your eyes; everything fit together perfectly.

Then suddenly an even more troubling question sprang to mind: how did Toz find out so quickly what had happened up by the City of God, since at the time only the protagonists were present, in other words Ati and Koa, the petty trafficker who had denounced them, and the patrol who had gone after them? Who had informed Toz, then? The denouncer or the patrol? How, and why? And if the point was to catch them or to kill them, why had they waited so long? And why now?

In fact, it could all be summed up in one question: *Who was Toz, really?*

Once it's been turned on, there's no stopping the doubt machine. In no time at all Ati found himself overwhelmed with a thousand unexpected questions. And suddenly he felt a chill down his spine because he was beginning to realize what all these questions implied: he would have to take important decisions and did not know which ones, nor whether he would have the strength and the courage to go through with them. Without Koa he was lost; for months now they'd shared everything, their lives and their information; they had reflected and acted together like indestructible twins. On his own he was severely disabled, incapable of understanding or of making a move.

And suddenly his doubts took another leap forward, completely unexpectedly, showing him that nothing was sacred, there were no exemptions, no exceptions, but this was simply inconceivable, it wasn't allowed, Ati felt like throwing up, screaming, smashing his head against the wall . . . The nasty, insidious little voice was talking about Koa, his brother, his friend, his companion, his accomplice! He could hear the voice murmuring: "Who's to say that the brilliant young man was not commissioned to win your friendship, which he managed to do, and brilliantly . . . " But what would be the point, dammit? I'm nothing, I'm Ati, a poor devil who has one hell of a time just trying to live in this too perfect world . . . Why should I be worthy of the State or whoever it is devoting so much time and effort into watching me? So, nothing to say? "Ah, dear Ati, you've become so forgetful . . . Yet you know why, you thought about it a lot when you were at the sanatorium, up there on the roof of the world . . . Time immemorial has gone by since the spirit of judgment and revolt disappeared from the earth, it was eradicated, and all that remains, floating above the swamps, is the rotten soul of submission and intrigue . . . Men are sleeping sheep, and they must stay that way, you mustn't disturb them. Yet there in that scorched desert they call Abistan a little sprout of freedom has been growing in the feverish mind of an exhausted consumptive, and it can withstand cold and solitude and the unfathomable

fear of heights, and in very little time it comes up with a thousand impious questions. Mind you, that's what's important, the
exuberant nature of doubt and its counterparts, curiosity and
challenge, all those questions you went around asking, that was
just it, in a manner that was elusive or unspeaking but perfectly
audible to people who had never asked questions, so their vir-
gin ears were hypersensitive, and you went asking questions
left and right, interrogative words and gazes, which those
patients and nurses and pilgrims and caravan drivers and all
the eavesdroppers standing by overheard and reported, while
the bureau of surveillance scrupulously took note . . . not to
forget the Vs, who day and night were raking through your
brain. And they don't go tearing it out right away, that mad
weed—on the contrary, they are fascinated, they want to know
what it is, where it came from, how far it can spread . . . Those
who killed freedom don't know what freedom is; in actual fact
they are not as free as the people they gag and disappear . . .
but at least they understood that they would never gain any
understanding of freedom unless they left you free to move
around, that they would learn while watching you learn . . . Do
you realize, my friend, you have been the guinea pig for an
extraordinary laboratory experiment: great tyranny is learning
from you—a little nonentity of a man—learning what freedom
is! It's crazy! They'll kill you in the end, of course; in their
world freedom is a path to death, it goes against the grain, it's
disturbing, a sacrilege. Even for those who have absolute
power, it is impossible to go back, they are prisoners of the
System and of the myths they invented to dominate the world,
they made them the jealous guardians of dogma, eager servants
of the totalitarian machine.

"The most extraordinary thing in all this is that someday,
somewhere at the heart of the Apparatus, someone—high up,
obviously—while reading a report taken at random from the
multitude of insignificant reports the machine receives non-stop

and archives by the ton, just in case, that someone might have said, 'Well what do you know! This is new for a change!' By studying the commentary written by some scribbler living in dust and boredom, and by launching a quick little investigation of his own, he reached a conclusion that absolutely bowled him over. He discovered a free electron, an unthinkable thing in the cosmos of Abistan: 'This man is a new sort of madman, or a mutant, he is the carrier of an argumentative spirit that disappeared long ago, I'll have to take a closer look.' As it is not against the law to wish oneself well and guard one's own discoveries jealously, he might have gotten it into his head to baptize a new ailment of the soul with his own name, and fill a few lines in the History books about Abistan. He might have come up with something like 'the heresy of Ati,' or 'the Sîn deviancy,' since those are the two things the Apparatus fears above all, heresy and deviancy.

"This rebellious mutant, dogged by madness, the possible carrier of a new plague: that's you, dear Ati, and I'm willing to bet that your file has traveled way up the ladder in the hierarchy of the Apparatus, even as far as the Just Brotherhood, why not. At those levels they are not unintelligent, they're even too intelligent, it's just that they're a bit sleepy, they've never done anything but rehash what is old, rancid, and dusty, and now here's something new that's going to wake them up, excite them, the discovery of a revolutionary village, capable of abolishing the founding truths of Abistan—and it has taken on a very special significance in no time. Your meeting with Nas was in itself so unlikely . . . What were the chances that an insignificant man like you would meet an eminent archeologist like him, and inspire him to share such dangerous secrets? It is all the stranger for having been merely fortuitous; that would mean that it was written in the deeper process of life, which commands that like attract like and opposite attract opposite; sooner or later the little drop of water reaches the sea and the mote of dust lands in the dust—in other words, it was the explosive encounter between Liberty and Truth. Nothing like this had ever happened since Abi perfected the world through the principle of submission and worship. What the Just Brotherhood had always feared, without being able to name it, was there before them, at an embryonic stage, carried by a reclusive patient in the most isolated place in Abistan and a civil servant who was too wise for what he was supposed to be doing there."

But thinking something doesn't mean you believe it. Ati didn't care about any of that, they were the thoughts of a sick mind—gratuitous theories, wild, far-fetched imaginings, too improbable to even be true. Dictatorship has no need of learning, by its very nature it knows everything it has to know and has virtually no need of a motive to hold sway; it strikes at random, that is where its strength lies, for it makes the most of the terror it inspires and the respect it garners. It is always after the fact that dictatorships conduct their trials, when the condemned confesses to his crime in advance and shows gratitude toward his judges. In this case, no need to look any further: Ati and Koa would be convicted as *makoufs*, nonbelievers affiliated with the contemptuous sect of Balis. Those who end up at the stadium are guilty, because the people know that God has never punished an innocent; Yölah is strong and just.

It was late. Der, Toz's agent, had not come. Ati ate what was left from yesterday's meal and slipped under his blanket. He did not have the faith of a believer but he prayed with all his strength to the God of victims, if he existed, to save his dear brother Koa.

The day went by in boredom and sadness. Yet another day. Ati could not stop playing and replaying the film of events from two days earlier in his mind, and every time he found more food for thought. It served no purpose but what else could he do, he had to occupy his mind; he missed Koa terribly and a bad sense of foreboding was making him queasy.

Der arrived just before the seventh prayer. The neighborhood *mockbas* were sounding the horn and the call to gather the faithful. There could be no dawdling about, there was a meaning to this prayer, it marked the end of the day and the beginning of the night; an entire symbol.

Der was not the talkative kind. Mou before him had not been, either. No sooner had he come in than he set about picking up everything that might indicate someone had been staying in the warehouse. He wiped away every trace, as if covering someone's tracks. He filled a bag with potential clues, tied it firmly, tossed it over his shoulder, and then, after one last inspection, told Ati to follow him, as if it were nothing special, and to stay a distance of fifteen to twenty *siccas* behind him.

They set out, walking briskly for a long time, avoiding the vicinity of any *mockbas*, which were constantly crowded with idle people only too eager to call out to passersby and ask them to join in their fine conversations. Along the way, Der tossed the bag onto one of those piles of garbage that adorned the city in the less salubrious neighborhoods. Once they reached a paved road, Der and Ati took shelter in a doorway and waited in silence. To their left cats were meowing, dogs barking to their right. Above them the moon shone without much conviction; they could see, but indistinctly. Odors of *bir* and hot pancakes wafted from the houses, perfuming the streets. What lucky people.

One hour later, two headlights on the horizon penetrated the night. As it drew nearer, the vehicle flashed its lights, and Der replied, waving his arms and standing in the middle of the road. The vehicle stopped short right in front of him. Silent, spacious, majestic, it was an official car, green with pennant bearers on the front fenders, displaying an Honorable's coat of arms. Imperious, too: who would have dared stand in its way? The driver opened the door and told Ati to get in. What an honor, what an incomprehensible honor! Der's mission was complete, he turned on his heels and went off into the night without saying a word. The car took off in a squeal of tires and quickly gained speed. It was the first time in his life that Ati had been in a car, and this was one of the best there was. He smiled to himself with pride; in his unfathomable misery he had suddenly attained that more than perfect happiness reserved for the very privileged, the high life, but very quickly he ordered himself to remain calm and humble. Only top-ranking officials in the hierarchy owned such marvelous vehicles, or fabulously wealthy tradesmen whose acquaintances with the synarchy were unquestionable. No one ever knew where these dream machines came from, who manufactured them, who sold them: the secret was inviolate. For lack of information, people said they came from another world, that there must be a channel; they still spoke of invisible borders. The purr of the engine was so gentle, the seats so comfortable, the whole car smelled so good, and the bumps in the road were so sweetly cadenced that before long Ati felt quite drowsy. He resisted as best he could but not for long; he slipped into a blissful sleep despite the anxiety gnawing at him. Where were they taking him, what was awaiting him there? Toz was as secretive as he was strange.

When Ati awoke, somewhat surprised to find himself flying in a state of weightlessness, the car was still moving, like an arrow of love piercing the air with grace and luxurious pleasure. Ati reckoned they must have gone about a hundred *chabirs*.

In the distance he saw lights, a geyser that reached as high as the clouds, setting them ablaze, a veritable riot of light, something that was rare in Qodsabad. Electricity was rationed and so expensive that only top leaders and rich merchants could afford it; the former did not pay for it and the latter made their clients pay. The air was moist, and there was a cloying odor, a mixture of salt and something else that was cool and fresh. From the depths of the night came the sound of a mass of water breaking against rocks or a wall. Was this the sea—did it really exist, did it come this far, was it true you could approach it without being carried away or engulfed? The road went no further. The car went through a gigantic gate, guarded by an entire army, and into a vast park with majestic trees, romantic copses, charming flower beds, dreamy arbors, lawns, and ponds as far as the eye could see. Along the way magnificent lampposts, regularly spaced, cast a gentle light onto the shadows. The car tires crunched on the gravel (in daylight, he would discover it was pink). The house, lit by huge spotlights cleverly arranged, was enormous, filling the horizon from one end to the other. It actually consisted of one main building, a royal palace of symmetry and harmony, and on either side, at a certain distance however, numerous outbuildings, both large and small, tall and low, round and square. Among them was a magnificent *mockba*, embellished with green marble and finely worked stucco. Everywhere in the park, on terraces and roofs, or perched on watchtowers, were heavily armed guards, soldiers in armor, and civilians wearing the clerk's *burni* covered with a coat of mail. Dog handlers patrolled with terrifying mastiffs of an unknown race, half bulldog, half lion. In the distance, on a mound enclosed by barbed wire, stood a pylon thirty *siccas* high or more, supporting impressive hardware consisting of some sort of drum, satellite dishes facing all four directions, and an enormous rotating metallic structure.

Further away there was something which Ati, like ten Abistanis out of ten, had always dreamt of seeing close up: flying machines. Outside a huge hangar a row of airplanes was neatly parked (one big one, some medium-sized and small ones) and an equal number of helicopters of varying shapes and sizes. He had only ever seen any of these aircraft far away in the sky, dots passing with a quiet roar, and like many people he had eventually no longer known what to think. Were they machines, birds, magic, holograms? Friends, enemies? Is what you see always real, and how were you to interpret those unknown sounds? There was another, smaller hangar, and an impressive parking lot full of cars, carefully arranged—little cars, sedans, trucks, special vehicles. Where did all this materiel come from, from what world, through which channel?

No matter how hard he stared, Ati could not take it all in. The domain was huge and the car was speeding along; clearly it knew where to go. They stopped a long way from the center, in a residential zone that consisted of several dozen houses, each one more beautiful than the next, surrounded by artistically pruned trees. The driver asked him to get out and follow him into an immaculate white bungalow, number 15. A vestibule gave onto a large central room, with a kitchen, bathroom, and three bedrooms on either side of a discreet corridor; all of it was luxuriously appointed and filled with furniture and

186 · BOUALEM SANSAL

paintings and knickknacks of the sort Toz collected with such loving nostalgia. Ati had never dreamt such dwellings could exist, nor that anyone could live there and feel at home. There was nothing of the sort in Qodsabad, people would have been uncomfortable, even unhappy, they liked to feel the earth beneath their feet and have an open view; above all they liked to be in the same room to share bread and *hir*, to save on heat, to pray and prattle with one voice.

The driver informed Ati that he would be staying in this bungalow until further notice. In the kitchen two men stood to attention, dressed in neatly tailored white *burnis*. They were easy to tell apart: one was black, sturdy, with a wide nose, and his name was Ank; the other was short and pale, with slanting eyes, and he was called Cro. The driver, who was white, elegant, intelligent, and went by the name Hek, introduced them in an offhand way as servants. There were two or three of them in every bungalow, he said, they were at the disposition of the guests of His Lordship. Ank and Cro acquiesced and nodded to Ati. "Who is His Lordship?" asked Ati, timidly. The driver answered, full of self-importance, "His Lordship is HIS Serene Lordship . . . the Honorable Bri!"

After a quick nibble, Ati went to bed and spent most of the night struggling with his thoughts and fears. He felt trapped, and dreaded the worst. Fatigue finally overcame him just as the sun was beginning to rise above the horizon. And almost immediately he was woken by the horn from the *mockba*, the call to the first prayer. Ati was still trying to recover his wits when Ank came to tell him that a young clerk was waiting at the entrance to drive him to the *mockba*. Which he did. The *mockba* was full of people. Everyone had their assigned place: dignitaries in the front rows, followed by high-ranking administrative officials, and so on down to the last secretary; servants and workhands performed their prayers at their workplace, and guards in their barracks. They were very keen not to miss it; surveillance never stopped, and the punishment was the same for everyone, one hundred lashes to the lower back with a stick, and more for repeat offenders. Ati was seated in the wing for guests. The dawn prayer was important, everyone hurried to attend, it marked the end of night and the beginning of day; an entire symbol.

Later he would find out that His Most Serene Lordship had his own *mockba*, in the palace, adjacent to the throne room. The *mockbi* was chamberlain to His Lordship's *mockba*, and it was his adjutants who took on the roles of beadle, crier, response-giver, incantator, cantor, and psalmodist. On Holy Thursday, when he was not tired, His Lordship went to the *mockba* in the camp and led the prayers himself. This was a signal honor for the population of the fiefdom. No one missed roll call. When it came his turn to lead the Great Thursday Imploration at the Great Mockba in Qodsabad, commonly known as the Kho Mockba, he went there in full procession, with an impressive security detail, leaving his territory in a state of extreme desperation. But his return the same afternoon was cause for an even more incredible celebration. When His Lordship was absent for several days, in particular when he went to the Kiïba, where his official cabinet, court, and multiple services occupied several stories, the camp went into hibernation and wept day and night over the master's absence.

Once the prayer was over, the clerk drove Ati to a huge building that was near the royal house. "This is the seat of the government of the fiefdom, run by Viz, His Excellency the Great Chamberlain to His Lordship. Ram, his cabinet director and highly valued councilor, is expecting you." On "highly valued" the young clerk, whose name was Bio, placed a grave stress, which was not the right tone, but perhaps he meant to imply that Ram was more than just valued by his chief, that all

188 · BOUALEM SANSAL

he had to do was open his mouth for him to listen. They went in through a service entrance, down a long underground corridor, and came out in a labyrinth of stairways, corridors, and offices where clerks who all looked strangely alike were religiously bustling about; this labyrinth opened onto a vast, luxurious, and very silent corridor that led to the Chamberlain's office. Ati, whose observational skills had become keener through his experience of danger, noticed that the signage here was in an unknown language, that it was finely wrought, full of delicate flourishes and embellishments, very different from *abilang*, which at the time of its artificial birth proclaimed itself a military language, conceived to inculcate rigidity, concision, obedience, and a love of death. Truly, how many strange things there were here in the heights of Abistan. What must it be like at His Serene Lordship's, and all the way up there at the Great Commander's? Let alone at Abi the Delegate's place: where he reigned, everything was mystery and incomparable marvels.

Ati was ushered into a room which was sparsely furnished with a chair, an armchair, and a coffee table. His mission accomplished, Bio withdrew, smiling faintly.

Might as well relax; Ati sat down in the armchair and stretched his legs. He waited a long time. He had gotten used to this form of torture, which had been abundantly inflicted upon him lately. At the sanatorium, he'd scaled the Himalayas of patience. He had learned to wait; he went into his thoughts and spent the time unraveling them, and this brought on aches in his head and fear in his gut.

The torture came to an end: a man entered the room— short, delicate, with a friendly air, of indeterminate age, probably in his early thirties. He was wearing a black *burni*, which was unusual. Ati jumped to his feet. The man planted himself before him, hands on hips, as if trying to seem teasing, and stared at him for a long time, right in his eyes, until suddenly he said with a smile, "So you're Ati!" and added, slapping his chest, "I'm Ram!" There was something else, deeper, in his gaze, hidden by his fine manners: a coldness, cruelty perhaps, or simply the vacancy which confers such a disquieting gleam upon a gaze.

"Right, have a seat and listen to me without interrupting!" he ordered, pushing the chair next to the armchair; he sat down, spread his legs, and with his elbows on his knees he leaned toward Ati as if about to share some grave secret.

"For a start, and I will tell you this without pulling any punches: your friends Nas and Koa are dead—it's sad, but that's the way it is. It is so that they will not have died in vain that I have come to ask you to join us in what we're doing . . . I'll explain later, but first I have to tell you a few things and let you think about them. Nas committed suicide, that's the official verdict; the discovery of Mab seems to have upset him profoundly. We hid his death in order not to upset his colleagues at work; the Abigov needs serenity to carry out its difficult mission. It was a mistake, because people imagined the worst scenarios. Why he committed suicide, we don't exactly know. He left a letter for his wife but it was not explicit, it just says that he'd been beset by doubts regarding his faith and could not live in uncertainty and pretense. He was a man of great integrity, and reacted like one. One day he disappeared, leaving his family, neighbors, and colleagues in distress. They searched for him in vain. His wife Sri and his sister Eto were very brave, they struggled to learn the truth, but the tragedy quickly became an affair of State at the highest level, involving the Just Brotherhood—a state secret, in other words. What had been going through his mind—we'll never know, one day, suddenly, he went back to 'his' village, we don't know why— to think, to check something, to finish some research, hide some evidence—in any case it was there, in one of the houses, that his body was found by workers who had come to prepare

190 · BOUALEM SANSAL

the site for the first pilgrims. He'd hanged himself. On his body they found the letter addressed to his wife.

"In the very detailed report he had filed to his minister upon his return from the initial investigation of the site, Nas had put forward the theory that Mab was not an Abistani village, but that it belonged to an earlier civilization that was far superior to our own, governed by principles that were totally the opposite of those that are the foundation of the *Gkabul*, the Holy Submission. Worse than that, he is thought to have found clues which led him to believe that the *Gkabul*, our *Gkabul*, already existed at that time, in other words before the birth of Abi, our Abi, the Delegate, which is impossible, and that everyone had already denounced it as the gravely degenerate form of a brilliant religion of that epoch, one that History and vicissitudes had placed on a downward path revealing and amplifying everything about this religion that was potentially dangerous. It would seem that this civilization was so damaged by the *Gkabul* that it died as a result. The planet was nothing more than chaos and violence, and the *Gkabul*, despite its triumph, did not bring peace on earth. If a single word of this report is true, then it would mean the death of Abistan, the end of the world, it would mean that we are the heirs and perpetuators of that world of madness and ignorance. The report showed how gravely confused Nas's mind had become; he had reversed the order of things, it is not the revelation of Abi that is dubious but the past beliefs which Abi's teachings came to refute . . . As the matter was of capital importance, the Great Commander naturally transmitted copies of the report to all the Honorables in order to gather their opinions . . . It stirred up a terrible storm in the Kiïba. They wanted to raze that cursed village to the ground, close the Ministry of Archives, Sacred Books, and Holy Memories, scatter their personnel, arrest all those who might have gotten wind of the story . . . and you were at the top of the list, as you were the one who had spent the most time with Nas when he was on his way home from his investigation, with his head full of strange ideas and, no doubt, a desire to confide in someone. Only the personal intervention of Abi himself extinguished the fire; he remembered having lived in that village, and that it was there that he'd received the revelation of the *Gkabul* and of *abilang*. The controversy was suppressed, but not the conflict of interest.

"In accordance with the rules of our holy religion, Nas's remains were incinerated and his ashes were scattered in the sea. As he doubted our faith and committed suicide, he could not be buried in the earth of Abistan, sanctified by the *Gkabul* and the blood of millions of martyrs. After we made sure that they had not been contaminated by the doubts of their husband and brother, we arranged marriages for his wife Sri and his sister Eto to good, honest believers, one a civil servant at the Abigov, the other a tradesman. I say 'we' because the decision was made by the Great Commander in the name of the Just Brotherhood. Now that their sorrow is behind them, they lead healthy, happy lives. We will see what we can do, you can meet them if you so wish, if they and their husbands agree to it; they most certainly will, since you were Nas's friend . . . Eto lives in the Kasbah in the City of God, and Sri is in H46, a quiet neighborhood just next to A19."

To give Ati the time to recover, he paused for a moment before delivering the next blow.

"Are you all right?" he asked, patting him on the shoulder.

"Mmm . . . "

"So I'll go on, then. As for Koa, most regrettably, he died in the most horrible way. During his flight he fell in a ditch and impaled himself on a stake which tore his side open . . . He bled to death in a sort of burrow where he had gone to hide . . . Some children found his body two days later. The dogs, those scourges of Qodsabad, had begun to devour him. In recognition of the merits of the Grand *Mockbi* Kho, a beloved friend of

His Lordship's, we have buried him here in the fiefdom. You will be able to go and pray at his grave.

"Toz informed us of your presence in A19 the moment you got in touch with him. He is a distinguished member of our clan. He's something of an original—he prefers living in the filth of A19 rather than here among his friends and his own kind. The investigation is ongoing, but it would seem we are not the only ones to show an interest in the fate of Nas, and in yours and Koa's. Several Honorables feared for their position, or wanted to take advantage of the situation. The Honorable Dia, who was granted a hereditary concession on the pilgrimage to Mab, could not tolerate the slightest doubt about the holiness of any of the pilgrimage sites, let alone that of the very place where the Revelation was born. It is a source of colossal revenue for him, so enormous that it threatens the equilibrium at the heart of the Just Brotherhood; his arrogance knows no bounds. He managed to get Commander Duc and Abi himself to agree to withdraw all the copies of the Nas report and have them burned. At his request a closed-session, white-gowned Abi Jirga was organized. You won't know what that is: it's a solemn reunion of all the Honorables, including the Great Commander, at the home of Abi himself, during which everyone pledges to Abi and on the holy *Gkabul* their absolute submission, which in this case meant a full, total, and loyal execution of the order to destroy the report and erase every trace of it—which, as you can imagine, had regrettable consequences for anyone who might have been in contact with it. I think that that was a mistake and a loss: to silence and hide and suppress is never a solution. I suppose that Nas had realized something was going on at the highest level and that he risked much, so fear compounded his helplessness. Perhaps Dia put pressure both on his minister, who also died in circumstances that were strange to say the least, and on Nas, to refute his findings.

"So much for Dia, but he is not the only one who's been

plotting. Some of our great Honorables—in particular the terrible and very ambitious Hoc, director of Protocol,
Ceremonies, and Commemorations—are not sorry to see His
Lordship Bri, the Honorable in charge of Favors and
Canonization—and I might mention in passing, leading con-
tender in the order of succession to the Great Commander,
whose fragile health is declining by the day—being given a
rough time over this business that occurred in his fiefdom—all
the more so in that it was in A19, where the City of God is to
be found, of which His Lordship is the governor and police
chief. Our investigation, led by our best spies and sleuths, has
shown that there was a conspiracy: the man who denounced
you to the so-called guards works for an organization with
ties to that dog Dia, but also to Hoc and his son Kil. We had
him kidnapped by one of our most secret organizations so
that, should the need arise, we could prevent His Lordship
from being implicated. Some skillful questioning got him to
confess everything. We worked our way back through the
network and stepped up our alarm system to keep us
apprised of anything that might be brewing against our clan.
We've got him close at hand in a secret place and are endeav-
oring to turn him, and slowly and patiently we're preparing a
response of the sort that the Honorable Dia and his friends
will remember for a long time.

"But anyway, these are internal issues relating to the Just
Brotherhood, and they're none of your business.

"You are the last survivor, your friends are dead, I understand your sorrow and the terrible solitude in which you find
yourself. You have to help us destroy our enemies the way we
helped you escape from them, and help us prepare the radiant
future that Abistan will know—the sooner the better—when
His Lordship becomes Great Commander of the Just
Brotherhood, with the help of Yölah and Abi, may salvation be
upon them. Under His Lordship, the holy *Gkabul* will truly be

the only real light in the world, we won't allow anyone to undermine it with nonsense and daydreaming. Amen."

"And how can I help you? I'm nothing, just a poor fugitive at the mercy of the first assassin to come along . . . If you put me out, I wouldn't know where to go. I don't even have a home anymore."

Ram's expression turned mysterious, superior, and friendly, all at once.

"We'll tell you at the right time and place. Go and pray on the grave of your friend Koa, go and see Sri and Eto to offer them your condolences—we'll arrange it for you—take a walk in the park and go and see the sea, it is five *chabirs* from here, only two if you go through the park. Get some rest and put your mind at ease, you are safe here, you are in our fiefdom for a radius of three hundred *chabirs*, not even a bird can get in here without my permission. Bio, the young clerk who brought you here, will accompany you everywhere it is allowed, just tell him what you'd like, he'll know how to arrange it. See you soon!"

At the door, he turned back:

"What was said in this room was never said. You and I will not survive a single day if so much as one word of our conversation gets out, even into the corridor. Don't forget that. May Yölah preserve you!"

Book Four

In which Ati discovers one conspiracy can hide another, and that truth, like falsehood, only exists insofar as we believe in it. He also discovers that the knowledge of some does not make up for the ignorance of others, and that humanity models itself upon the most ignorant of all its members. Under the reign of the Gkabul, *the Great Work has been achieved: ignorance dominates the world, and has reached a stage where it knows everything, can do everything, and wants everything.*

On the corner of the kitchen table, beneath Ank and Cro's watchful gaze, Ati devised a program. It included no less than six points: 1) go pray on Koa's tomb; 2) take a trip in an airplane and a helicopter; 3) visit His Lordship's palace; 4) see the sea and dip at least one finger into it; 5) meet Sri and Eto and tell them how much he had loved and admired Nas; 6) have a serious meeting with Toz, and ask him, in passing, why he burst out laughing when Koa, to thank him for his services and hospitality, gave him the letter of congratulations Abi had sent to his grandfather Kho, the *mockbi* of the Great Mockba in Qodsabad.

Bio came back the next day with a program Ram had revised downward. He explained that the airport and the palace were extremely sensitive places: no one could get near, no point even thinking about it, it was a zone where you'd be shot on sight if you so much as put your finger through the surrounding fence. No problem for the rest. The organization of the meeting with Sri and Eto would, however, require some time, the problem was complicated, because if they asked the husbands for permission to visit with their wives, they would balk and turn against the women, and to ask the wives directly—women who never left the home of their lord and master—would put them in danger, they would have to tell their husbands and explain why a stranger who claimed to be the friend of their late husband and brother wanted to see them to present his condolences when their mourning had ended long ago and both widow and sister had been wed. But not to worry, Ram had come up with a very innocent plan. Not to worry about that secretive fellow Toz, either, he came to the camp every Thursday to have lunch with his family, his older brother was none other than Bri himself, His Serene Lordship, and his twin brother was none other than Viz, the Great Chamberlain, and his nephew was none other than Ram, the son of Dro, a brother who died under mysterious circumstances a long time ago in one of the worst episodes of the clan wars. The deaths had numbered in the millions all over Abistan, but no one remembered those wars and History had kept no records. Peace was restored one day and what is inevitable about peace is that it erases memories and wipes the slate clean.

So they headed for the cemetery, which was itself a sensitive zone, because that was where the plots of martyrs, top leaders, and the reigning family were located, carefully closed off and guarded; the reigning family's plot was on a mound covered in flowers, and that was where His Lordship went to pray once a month. The graves of the common people were open to everyone. The cemetery was perfectly maintained, which was a good sign regarding the values in force in the fiefdom; but in truth everything in the camp was perfect, it really was how Ati imagined paradise. Only two or three things were missing, in the realm of leisure, frivolousness, and other indulgences; the holy *Gkabul* forbade them in this life, but duly and explicitly promised them in the next.

Koa's tomb was in a plot a little ways off to one side, where the dead who did not belong to the clan were buried. It was a very simple grave, in keeping with the funerary traditions in that region of Abistan: a burial mound where a flat stone stood, with the dead man's name, in this case, "KOA."

Ati was moved . . . and full of doubt: he wondered who really lay in this grave. A name is not an identity and a grave is not proof. Ram's story had so much that was truthful and simple about it that one was left hungering for more. Where was the reality in it all? For the report to have caused turmoil within the Just Brotherhood, that was obvious; the theory of a brilliant civilization surpassing the eternal perfection of Abistan was not an easy pill to swallow; believers are only too eager to think they are the best. And then, besides, there were interests, animosities, ambitions, vices—in short, everything that made man base and unworthy, but still, the brilliant Ram was far too knowledgeable and powerful to be the guardian angel he wished to appear. In fact, everything about him suggested the perfect conspirator who knew how to link one intrigue to the next, how to cunningly weave them together to kill two birds with one stone without ever leaving his office. His purpose this time, if Ati had understood it correctly, was monumental: he hoped, all at the same time, to bring down Dia, humiliate Hoc, ruin his son Kil, overwhelm Duc the old patriarch with such poisonous worries they'd finish him off, and hasten the succession in favor of his uncle Bri—and his own succession—in a near future, and then, without even pausing to catch his breath, to eradicate everything that posed even a distant or marginal threat to the perfect order of the *Gkabul*. If there were any exceptional men of ambition who held four aces—knowledge, power, intelligence, and madness—in this never-ending game of intrigue and death, Ram was one of them, and no doubt the best.

Ati roused himself to banish these circumstantial thoughts from his mind, then went down on his knees, rubbed his hands on the ground to cover them with dust, and crossed them over his humbly lowered head, as was done during the Great Holy Thursday Imploration, then began to murmur:

"Whoever you might be in this grave, oh dead one, I greet you and wish you the best the Hereafter can offer to a man of good will. If, as I believe, you are not Koa, forgive me for troubling you with my words . . . but I must confess and alleviate my sorrow, so allow this unfortunate wretch to address you as if you were him . . . If, as we believe, the deceased are united in the Hereafter, please convey my message to him.

"Dear Koa, I miss you, and I am suffering terribly. I have so many questions about you, I find it hard to believe you died falling into a ditch, the way that smooth talker Ram would have it, that's not like you, you were both nimble of body and of spirit . . . and you never lacked for courage, even gravely injured you would have found the strength to make it back to the warehouse, and then I would have done everything possible to save you . . . Or you could, more easily, have knocked at the door at the first house you came to and asked for help . . . People would not have refused to help you, not everything inside them has died under the skies of Abistan . . . As long as people go on having children, finding a roof for shelter, and lighting fires to keep warm, it means they have life inside them and therefore an instinct for self-preservation. I am so angry with myself, dear Koa, it was my idea to split up when we had to flee, I thought that way we'd increase our chance of making it, but in fact I divided it in two and left you with the bad half, I should have gone to the left and let you go to the right . . . On this side there were no obstacles, other than a few dogs sniffing at my ankles . . . When I got to the warehouse and didn't see you, I should have gone straight back out to look for you. And what did I do, wretch that I am? I wrapped myself up in my blanket and slept. I'm ashamed, Koa, I'm ashamed, I'm a coward. I abandoned you, my brother, and because of that you died in some dog's burrow, or murdered by professional killers. I'm not trying to lessen my guilt but I don't know why I go on hoping, deep down, that you are alive somewhere, maybe held prisoner; it's a hope without any illusions, now that I know a little about who the Honorables governing this poor world are. I learned that Nas—I wanted so much for you to meet him—is dead too, supposedly. They say he committed suicide in that mysterious village that had no business being in our sacred land of Abistan. I don't believe that for one second, Nas was a scholar, a coolheaded man who wanted to know and to learn, and he didn't indulge in dreams and illusions. He was assassinated by the people who were upset by his discovery . . . and he knew that this would happen, he told me so, one night around the campfire. As for me, I'm numb and wandering, full of troubles. But every cloud has a silver lining: from where I stand, at the mercy of the Honorable Bri's clan, I have a slight chance of learning something about your death, and Nas's. They want to use me in some plan of theirs, so at some point they'll have to light my lantern. They won't show much restraint, either, because they know the end they have in store for me. But I don't care about my fate, I despair of this world, I have nothing to keep me here, nor do I want anything, not at any price. I'll soon be with you, dear Koa, and in the Hereafter—with complete impunity, I hope—we'll continue our adventures and our impossible quest for the truth. I embrace you and will see you soon."

Ati bowed down four times, as was the custom, dusted himself off, symbolically to return dust to dust, and went to join Bio, who was off to one side waiting for him, lying under a tree, blissfully chewing on the stem of a daisy.

"Thank you, dear Bio, for waiting so patiently. Let's go now, back to the world of the living—those who we are sure are alive; I told my friend Koa what I had to say to him, he'll think everything over. Since our leader Ram has agreed, you can drive me to the sea. I've always thought the sea must exist but I could never picture it for myself. It is hard, believe me, when all you've ever seen around you is sand, dust, and struggling fountains. I wonder how you manage in your vast fiefdom, with fresh water running day and night, you waste it as if it fell from the heavens and cost nothing."

"It's easy," replied Bio with a broad, knowing smile, "we rerouted the river so the flow is just for us, and we have giant cisterns where we stock water, gasoline, and all sorts of other things. Life can never stop here, it has everything it needs."

"That's reassuring, my dear Bio! Let's go at once to the sea, and let's hurry, you never know, it might not wait for us!"

They took the road through the camp, as it was shorter. About their short walk of two *chabirs* over a flowering lawn, in the shade of the woods, there was absolutely nothing terrifying.

The sea appeared on the horizon; it was as if it took its source in the sky and came down on earth from there. That was Ati's first observation, and as he drew closer, the ethereal line of horizon, indistinct and trembling, became sharper, spreading, until it was a colossal, vibrant mass of water filling all the space, overflowing and rising toward him like a tide to stop short at his feet; he felt surrounded. Impossible to escape from the fascination and terror: the sea was the sum of all the opposites, it took only a few seconds to convince yourself of the fact, and then you knew that it could, in a flash, cause everything to shift dramatically, from best to worst, most beautiful to most sinister, life to death.

That day, for Ati's first visit, the sea was in a friendly mood, like the sky that covered it, and the wind playing with its little waves. A good sign.

Ati went courageously to the water's edge, where it disappeared into the sand. One more step and the miraculous contact was made. Beneath the pressure of his weight, water and sand oozed through his toes, massaging them in a way that was more than merely sensual.

But what was happening? Everything was moving, reeling, he felt the ground slipping under his feet and his head began to spin, while a faint nausea turned his stomach, but at the same time a wonderful sensation of plenitude spread through him. He was in harmony with the sea, the sky, and the earth; what more could he ask for?

He lay down on the warm sand, closed his eyes, offered his face up to the rays of the sun and his body to the sea spray, and let himself lapse into a dream.

He recalled the extraordinary mountains of the Ouâ—the summits, the vertiginous chasms, and the nightmares they had brought on, pure terror but also a feeling of exaltation inspired by the incredible majesty of those hardest of places, emerging from the farthest recesses of time. It was then that an over-whelming feeling of freedom and strength such as he had never known was born in him, and gradually, even as illness tormented him and decimated those around him, that feeling brought him to open rebellion against the oppressive, cowardly world of Abistan.

The sea, no doubt, would have produced other awakenings, other revolts. Who knows what they might have been.

"My dear Bio, let's go back, I've enjoyed enough seaweed- and salt-perfumed air for a year, if life wants to grant me that much time. I feel swollen all over and nicely roasted. I have known the immense terror of the mountains, and now I know the enchantment of the sea and the ardor of the sun on salty skin—I'm a satisfied man. It has all made me hungry and sleepy. I'm eager to move on to the next step of my program and meet the two women I do not know but whom I have loved ever since the day the husband of one of them, who was the other's brother, told me about them. I would have liked to take them with me, to cherish and protect them always, but the Just Brotherhood, in its infinite respect for life, gave them to

204 · BOUALEM SANSAL

two strangers, one of whom is an honest civil servant and prisoner of the kasbah, and the other a no less scrupulous tradesman, prisoner of his shop, since they were chosen by those who know all there is to know about integrity and love.

"So, let's set off, dear Bio, and tell me a little about yourself, you have a life, I suppose—a family, friends, maybe enemies too, and surely you have dreams, those that are allowed. I would like to know what a subject of His Lordship thinks as he goes about his everyday life."

"Thinks about what?"

"Anything, this and that . . . your . . . your work, for example. What does it consist of, are you happy, what are you going to tell Ram about our fine day out today, and so on?"

They spent the afternoon telling each other their life stories. Compared to Ati, who did nothing but encounter problems from one end of vast, mysterious Abistan to the other, dragging his friends to their death, Bio led a hazy life, which had neither breadth nor length nor density, nothing to grasp hold of; it was as if he were born for no purpose, and his life was utterly guileless. He burst out laughing when he recited the slogan of the fiefdom: "Worship Yölah. Respect the *Gkabul*. Honor Abi. Serve Your Lordship. Help your brother. Thus will your life be beautiful."

Ram had decided that the meeting between Ati, Sri, and Eto would be as secret as possible; no one must ever suspect that the clan of the Honorable Bri had anything to do with organizing it. The plan he had hatched would become worthless—worse than that, it would turn against the clan. The second reason was that Ati was currently being hunted by all the public and private police in Abistan; he could not take two steps out in the open without being arrested by the one or killed by the other. The fact that he had knocked about the entire country from the faraway mountains of Ouâ, that he had been trafficking in the ghetto, had illegally crossed thirty neighborhoods in Qodsabad to try to get into the City of God, and his ability to disappear from one place then reappear in another had added considerably to his image as a perverse monster. He was Public Enemy Number One, and all the police wanted him as their trophy, without really knowing why, at best they just knew a vague fragment of the story, but that hardly mattered, they'd received their orders.

The common people, like prisoners in a camp, are extremely sensitive, the slightest little rumor upsets them. Just let them hear that there will be a shortage of *hir*, or that it will cost one *didi* more, and the country will go up in flames, there'll be talk of the end of the world, and no one will hesitate to reproach Yölah for abandoning his children.

In A19 and inside the City of God, the climate was already worse than unhealthy; rumors and counter-rumors ran riot.

Spies, propagandists and others who fished in troubled waters were putting on the pressure, the people could do nothing about it, but they wondered what was going on. The Venerable Duc, the Great Commander, said nothing, there was no sign of him in the *nadirs*. Was he alive, was he dead? What was the Just Brotherhood doing? And where was the government? In an enclosed society the air is unclean, people are poisoned by their own miasmas. The Enemy and Balis were evoked in every conversation, in the end you could not tell one from the other. Anger was unleashed—violent, overwhelming, insatiable; Ram's agents were painstaking and organized and they did marvelous work, injecting poison at just the right moment, in just the right place, in just the right dose; it was impressive, the beast was reacting exactly the way it would in a lab test. There was talk of other wicked individuals, Honorables and ministers, who figured in every insinuation, no one ever forgot Dia or Hoc, their reputation went before them, nor did they forget the wretched Nam, Zuk, or Gu, who plundered the people and cheated shamefully with the weight and ingredients of the daily *hir*, let alone the vain Toc, or those madmen in H3, the Hu Hux Hank, or the Honorable Partisans of Total War who spoke of nothing but battles, battalions, and bombardments, Zir and Mos in particular, who were endlessly beefing up their militia and multiplying the training camps, and they never let an opportunity for provocation slip, for they were convinced that wars were won by those who started them. Zir had written a psychedelic memoir about lightning wars, and he dreamt of waging one on a grand scale; his pet peeve was the Qodsabad ghetto, just the thought that the Regs existed poisoned his every waking moment, he had a plan to annihilate the entire place in three days: one day to fill the population with fear, another to smash everything, a third to finish off the wounded and pack up; whereas Mos, in another brilliant dissertation, defended the notion that only permanent, total war, without truce, without interruption, without restraint, was in keeping with the spirit of the *Gkabul*; a state of peace was not worthy of a nation professing such a mighty faith. It would no longer be necessary to have a motive in order to strike. Did Yölah need any justification to create and destroy? When he kills, he kills, and he has a heavy hand, it is definitive and particularly cruel, and in the end he spares no one. Abi said as much in his Book (title 8, chapter 42, verses 210 and 211): *"Beware of closing your eyes and drifting off, that is what the Enemy is waiting for. Wage total war upon him, spare neither your strength nor that of your children, that he might never rest or know joy, or the hope of returning home alive."* He also said, bolstering Mos in his thirst for war: *"If you think that you have no enemy, it means the enemy has crushed you and reduced you to the state of a slave happy with his yoke. You would do better to seek out enemies than to let yourself think that you are at peace with your neighbors"* (title 8, chapter 42, verses 223 and 224).

It was all irksome yet perfectly usual; however, for those with sharp hearing and an eagle eye, there was something new in this chorus of droning refrain and counter-refrain. And if it was new you wanted, well then, this was really new. Completely off the beaten path, on to something enormous, unimaginable, impossible. Well done, Ram, the bigger it is the better it strikes. For the first time, there was talk of a mythical creature who'd appeared out of who knows what world, who was neither a god like Yölah nor a counter-god like Balis, but a disturbing, solar being, made all of light and reason, intelligence and wisdom, who could teach something totally unknown in the land of Holy Submission: revolution, in harmony and freedom. This teaching refuted Yölah's hegemonizing brutality, and Balis's deleterious guile, opposing them with the strength of kindness and friendship. What did it all mean, and who was saying this? A name went around, from crowd to crowd, but no one had caught it properly: Democ . . . Dimuc . . . Dmoc.

There was also talk of a man, a very humble Abistani who walked among the most humble, and who was a sort of herald for the solar being; he announced the Return. "The return, what return?" asked people in the street. The return of a bygone era, when other gods reigned on earth, and other men populated the land. Life was difficult, to be sure, gods and men are hard to get along with and don't rub along well together either, but nothing, not a thing, during all those millennia of suffering and boredom, had ever managed to destroy hope, and hope was what enabled gods and men to resist their own negation and, sometimes, to accomplish beautiful things—a miracle here, a revolution there, elsewhere an exploit, which at the end of the day meant that life was still worth living. In those days, people used to say, "hope keeps you going" even when times were desperate. Did the Return mean a return of hope? Or rather, the return of the idea that hope existed, and that it might, perhaps, help us to live, we're just humans, after all, simple mortals, we can't ask too much of life. It was said that the messenger's name was Ita the Abistani, and that he already had a first apostle, whose name was Oka the Rebel. In a world born of religion, every messenger is a prophet, everyone who accompanies a prophet is a long-suffering apostle; anyone who quibbles and wonders is a heretic.

The tireless Ram was in his element amid this wonderful commotion. This was his world, and his dream, his plan, was to control it from start to finish. The pieces of the puzzle had long been in place for the final onslaught, but what was missing was the little escape device that would enable him to launch the operation and secure his victory. Ati's meeting with Sri and Eto would provide it. If a grain of sand can jam the most sophisticated machinery, removing it can relaunch it more smoothly than ever. This was the principle behind Ram's method: insert a hindrance, remove it, and then the plan will move ahead.

His office had been working on it, diligently and precisely, ever since the day Ati and Koa arrived in A19. What Ram knew about those two itinerant phenomena was strictly nothing: a few hazy remarks dropped by the so-called almighty Ministry of Moral Health and its half-baked subcommittees; a few alerts issued by one of the thousands of supposedly infallible civic observation cells run by the Apparatus—a bunch of obscure bureaucrats who, with their obsessive filing, produced an untranslatable racket—a few insinuations drawn from the vast amounts of piously redacted notes which that unbelievable General Inspection of the *mockbas*, the rite police, had recorded on the state of the believers' piety, to which were added two or three clues unearthed in the flood of notes emanating from who knew which sub-bureaus, specialized in nothing, etc. But each clan had its own instruments, firmly concentrated on the subject—and these were the only useful ones. Bri's clan was well-equipped in that regard, and Ram oversaw personally the perfect functioning of the machinery. Without chance, there could be no grain of sand. Unlike the other clans who invested their colossal fortunes in pomp and brute force, the Bri clan invested in analysis and forecasts, in organization and efficiency, in lab work then tests in the field. Very early on, therefore, Ram had grasped the necessity of following those two spirited eccentrics and nudging them in the right direction. They would prove useful for something. That was how they came upon Toz, directed by a passerby, who was not all that anonymous after all, since he said his name was Hu, and by the *mockbi* Rog, who by the looks of it was more of a middleman for trafficking clandestine migrants than a saint practicing an honest vocation. They were expected, and their subsequent itinerary had already been set down as their destiny, as willed by God.

End of the first stage. Good old Toz, he had wound them up to perfection, imprisoning them in his warehouse by pretending to be helping them to get away, and they'd fallen for it, and cheered him on. Nice work.

What was interesting was that the two eccentrics did not belong to any clan—they professed anything but Unique Thought, and what was more, they were determined and audacious, as naïve as two big babies. In addition, they each held one important trump card: one of them had known Nas and heard him speak of the existence of the mysterious village, the other was the grandson of a major figure who had marked the history and imagination of Abistan, the *mockbi* Kho. They would bring to the plan a background of mystico-religious terror that would impress the people and the judges. With players like these, the cabinet could manufacture a clock capable of giving everyone the exact hour of their death.

The micro-plan for organizing a meeting between Ati and Sri before chosen witnesses, without having any collateral effect on the Bri clan, required the intervention of a third person, a particular individual who could satisfy a host of delicate conditions: he must be known to be secretly linked to the Dia and Hoc clans; he must not have ever had anything at all to do with the Bri clan; he had to know Nas, Ati, and Koa, or at least have been in contact with them and know enough about them; and finally he had to be a talented actor. Ram had just such a rare bird at hand: the vendor of services from the Square of Supreme Faith, the spy who had denounced Ati and Koa to Dia's guards, their shared employer. Ram's specialists of mental manipulation had finished turning him and were actively prepping him for his first mission, the mother of all missions if ever there was one, in the service of the Bri clan. For the needs of the script, his name would be Tar, a name so

common as to sound like a cover, and he would play a prosperous, ambitious tradesman with offices and warehouses in
H46. He would have a wife, they'd call her Nef, Ore, Cha . . .
or better still, Mia—that suggested a strong-minded woman,
cruel and manipulative.

The plan, committed to paper right down to the last
comma, consisted of setting up a business relation between the
tradesman Tar and the tradesman Buk. The latter, who specialized in the manufacture of basins and commercial dinner-
ware made of tin, was Sri's husband. On D-day, Tar would
introduce himself and make an offer to buy his production for
the next ten years, if Buk would give him a reduced price, as
Tar himself had a ten-year contract with a firm belonging in
partnership to Dia and Kil, where they rented and sold can-
teens and portable kitchen equipment to the organizers of pilgrimages and jamborees (they all sailed under Dia's flag, or
that of an allied clan in charge of the media hype, whose
famous business slogan was, in case one needs reminding,
"Neither too little nor not enough"), as well as to army battalions, clan militias, and local warlords. Buk would be blown
away by the offer that had fallen in his lap, and would surely
be eager to invite Tar to celebrate their alliance, and before
long they were bound to become inseparable friends, in that
way businessmen know how to do when there's a certain
urgency. Tar would force the issue if need be, increasing their
opportunities to meet. They would visit each other at home,
among friends, and give each other presents. Eto and her husband would be invited and they would come if they managed
to obtain the authorization to leave the City of God. Mia
would be as sweet and thoughtful as could be toward Sri and
Eto. When their business and family relations were at their
peak, Tar would introduce his cousin Nor (this will be Ati's
role), who had come to visit, both out of affection and also on
business; he would explain that his relative was a prosperous

tradesman connected to the Kil group and occasionally the Dia group. In an aside that Mia would arrange, Nor would inform Sri that he had been a friend of Nas's, that he had met him when Nas was working on the site of the mysterious village the pilgrims discovered, and that Nas had come to him one day to entrust him with a report, asking him to keep it until further notice—and then never came back. Since learning of Nas's strange disappearance, Nor had constantly been puzzling over what to do with the document, and now just by chance, through Tar, he had found out that the wife of his friend and dinner companion Buk was none other than Nas's widow. What a strange and wonderful coincidence! And then the very event for which the entire plan had been so carefully made would take place: Nor would give the report to Sri, enjoining her not to tell anyone about it, in keeping with Nas's wishes, except perhaps her sister-in-law Eto. He would not forget the promise he'd made himself: to tell her how much he had admired Nas, an upstanding individual from whom he had learned that to tell the truth, whatever the cost, is an excellent disposition of the spirit, for otherwise truth would be taken for falsehood; and to denounce falsehood whatever the risk, for otherwise it would be taken for truth. But he would not tell her that he had found her beautiful and charming; that was not done, in the husband's house.

This would be the end of the performance and the end of the mission for Ati; it would last two hours, the time of a dinner at Buk's house, including two minutes aside with Sri to give her the aforementioned report, hidden in a rare gift, a *sila*, a piece of silk from Upper Abistan.

Ati would not know that this film would be followed by the darkest of sequels, and that it would end in a world war. Once the dinner was over, and the report had been transferred, and goodbyes had been said, he would be exfiltrated from H46 and taken back to the camp of His Lordship.

*

The second episode would unfold in an atmosphere of impenetrable mystery: from deep in a throat trembling with righteous anger, a voice would be heard revealing to the world the unimaginable infamy committed by two great lords of Abistan who were cherished by Abi and the Great Commander. It would bring proof that Dia and Hoc, those snakes, were the leaders of an incredible plot against the Just Brotherhood and, what was an immense, terrible blasphemy, against Abi and Yölah themselves. Those scoundrels had betrayed the Abi Jirga and kept a copy of Nas's report in their possession and then, driven by their dark designs, they'd had the poor archeologist abducted, whereupon they proceeded to falsify his report by inserting their own conclusions; finally they killed him in that same village where Abi had received his holy Revelation. They then went on to assassinate Koa, the worthy descendant of the *mockbi* Kho. The Voice would not stop with the facts alone, it would also reveal the ins and outs of the matter: Dia and Hoc were working to achieve nothing less than the destruction of Abistan in the most terrifying way, by calling the truth of the *Gkabul* into question. This was absolute proof that they were in the service of the Enemy and of Balis.

Nothing could save Dia and Hoc and none of their family would be spared. They would be led by the hundreds to the stadiums and by the thousands to the most sinister camps, extermination camps run by the Regs, who would be relieved to discover that they were not the most vilified in the world, and they might even be glad to have them as companions in their tumbril for the final journey. The Great Commander Duc would be compelled to commit dignified *akiri* on the Square of Supreme Faith, or to retreat as a hermit to the most inhospitable of wildernesses to expiate his sin, that of having so poorly defended the Just Brotherhood and allowed two snakes to sully the Kiïba and soil the *Gkabul*.

With a sigh, the Voice would add that His Lordship Bri would never have allowed such a thing; he knows that the truth is the truth and the order underpinning it must never be allowed to weaken, not even for the blink of an eye, otherwise it is no longer order and never will be so again; it is disorder, and the essence of mendacity.

In reality, give or take a few details, everything happened just as the scenario had predicted. No sooner did Ati return to the camp than a letter sent from an anonymous post office was expedited to inform the authorities, some of whom had already been made aware by eminent, discreet individuals whom Ram had put into action, that the Nas report was going around the country like a poison treacherously injected into the people's blood, and that the Honorable Dia and Hoc were behind the crime, along with others acting as accomplices. A second letter sent from another impossible-to-locate post office provided the investigators with the elements—although they were perfectly obvious—that they had been incapable of seeing with their own eyes, namely that Nor, an accomplice of Tar's, had given Sri the report, and that Tar had gotten it from one of Dia's men, who said he'd been commissioned by Nas not long before Nas's disappearance. The letter explained that Dia and Hoc's plan was to seize power and proclaim themselves Commander and Vice-Commander. A touch scornfully it added that those useful idiots were in fact none other than pawns in an apocalyptic plan conceived and implemented by the Enemy and Balis, whose ultimate plan was to replace Abi by Democ, and the Just Brotherhood by an assembly of representatives, and in time to make the Abistanis, the sincere worshippers of Yölah, into vulgar Balisians—heretics and free men.

Ram's cabinet had rehearsed the scenario a thousand times, and proceeded to make all the necessary arrangements in the field. Tar was already in residence and at that very moment was negotiating with Buk to buy several thousand braziers, cooking pots, basins, and other large utensils. The list of those who were doomed to disappear had already been drawn up and the executants were stationed, ready to go into action; one of them (Mia?) had been assigned to help Tar commit suicide point-blank, the very day the report was to be handed over to Sri; the first link in the chain had to disappear before all others so that the last link would be preserved. It was the beginning of the end; the clans would soon embark on a long and merciless war.

Sri, in the matter, would inevitably be in danger. Ati blamed himself for letting his brother Koa die, but he could never accuse himself of having wronged him. When he had put Ati in charge of giving Sri Nas's report, Ram promised him that she would be delighted to receive this testament from her late husband. Ati must also act in a discreet yet casual manner in order not to antagonize the husband, that was logical. Ati would no longer be there when they came to interrogate the couple, triggering a vast operation of arrests all over Abistan, at every level, from the most humble servant to the greatest lord.

Never in the course of human history, except perhaps in some ancient life, had there been such a grandiose roundup in such a short time. Once it got up to full speed, the machine would quickly reach an industrial phase: arresting and exterminating such quantities of people would no longer be a simple police matter, the question of the logistics would in itself become vital and determine everything.

Ati would never know that the film in which he'd made a brief appearance would go on to have such a colossal end. Naïveté, like stupidity, is a permanent state. Ati had never asked himself these questions—obvious even to a child—and

he believed that Ram's strategy had only one purpose: to
enable him to meet Sri without shocking her husband, and to
present her with his condolences, and while he was at it, hand
her Nas's report, per Ram's request. How had the report ended
up in Ram's possession? Had the worthy and Honorable Bri
lied to the Abi Jirga and kept a copy to himself? Why, then,
would he suddenly release a document he'd kept hidden for so
long, and which Ram had said could revolutionize the world?
Was the document given to Sri the genuine report? What conclusions did it offer the reader? Why had they chosen Ati to
give it to her? Who, really, was this Tar who had driven him to
Buk's house and who behaved at table as if he were his cousin?
There was something about him, a sense of déjà vu, that made
Ati feel his question was perfectly legitimate. It would seem
that beneath his fine prosperous tradesman's *burni* there
lurked a worthless good-for-nothing.

One explanation might be that the deaths of Nas and Koa
had destroyed Ati's defenses, and announced his own; and Sri
and Eto's marriages had stifled any secret hope he might still
have had of devoting his life and strength to Nas's widow and
bereaved sister.

A nk and Cro were very proud to be serving a celebrity. When he got back from H46, Ati had a long audience with Ram, who conveyed congratulations from the Great Chamberlain and encouraging words from His Lordship. By agreeing to give Nas's report to his widow, without the clan being directly involved, Ati deserved such praise. "The whole matter was a real nuisance," confessed Ram, "it was putting us in an awkward position vis-à-vis the Abi Jirga and the Just Brotherhood. His Lordship didn't know anything about it, nor did the Great Chamberlain, they don't deal with trivial matters, so it fell to me, but we did indeed receive two reports, the official one, which we restored to the Great Commander at his bidding, and another, sent by we don't know who, some distracted civil servant or a discreet friend with our interests at heart, and we didn't know what to do with it . . . How could we explain its presence here? What would our friends in the Just Brotherhood think, who had always trusted us? We could destroy it, but was that appropriate, it was a rare document, the report of an archeological investigation at a unique site, an element of our heritage that was all the more precious in that this was the last and only copy, as the others had been burned in the presence of Abi, the Great Commander, and all the Honorables. That was when we came up with the perfectly natural idea of giving it to his widow, it will be a testament, a keepsake for her and her descendants. Anyway, all's well that ends well, our minds are at rest."

Ram had a talent for making everything seem clear and simple, and this matter of the second report appearing out of nowhere and leaving again by the back door did indeed require some enlightenment.

Etiquette being what it was, Ati, as a stranger to the clan and a man of modest origins who had neither fiefdom nor fortune, nor high position, could not obtain an audience with such high dignitaries. His Lordship and the Great Chamberlain deeply regretted it. There was no disdain implied, propriety simply had its rules, and besides, Ati was not there to seek honors; but he would have liked to meet these larger-than-life characters, to observe them as they dominated the world, to admire their fine palaces, which he pictured laden with heavy, luxurious embellishments; perhaps, on the contrary, they were overflowing with magnificent, exuberant simplicity.

They philosophized for a long while; times were hard and there were so many rumors weighing upon people's lives, nothing good could come of it. That they agreed on. Indeed, there was something in the air, more rancid and acrid than ever, an atmosphere of the end of the world which had clung to Abistan from the day of its birth. They both agreed that this dissoluteness was not superficial but belonged to the deeper nature of things—but were they speaking of the same things? Deploying a tone filled with real energy for the future, Ram implied that the country would soon be transformed from top to bottom, rid of its old woes; the new Abistan would need new men, and in that context Ati, if he so desired, could carve out an enviable spot within the clan, for he had that deep sense of freedom and dignity that makes for an outstanding servant of the State. Ati remained silent. He nodded his head and bit his lip; it helped him think. What did he really want, what did he hope for? He questioned his heart and mind . . . but nothing came, a few echoes from childhood, obviously unfeasible. He raised his arms to the sky: he couldn't think of anything, didn't want anything. To be honest, he would have preferred to give back anything Abistan might have given him—but what? He had no work, no home, no identity, no past, no future, no religion, no customs . . . absolutely nothing . . . except problems with the administration and death threats from the clans . . . Perhaps he'd be content with some spare time to devote to breathing in the fresh air from the heavens and the aphrodisiacal scents of the sea. He thought he could love the sea, with a true passion, in spite of its capricious, treacherous behavior. Ram was rather optimistic to think that Abistan would change. Hens would have front teeth before then and would be singing in *abilang*. In truth, nothing and no one could change it, Abistan was in the hands of Yölah, and Yölah was immutability itself. *"What is written is written,"* or so it said in the Book of Abi, his Delegate.

Ram begged Ati to think about it. "I'll see you later, I have a lot to do, the change will soon begin to take effect," he said, getting up, then he added, giving Ati a pat on the back: "Better not to venture outside the camp. You're at home here." He was joking but his eyes were shining with a hard, intense gleam, and in his voice there was something of a war chant.

That morning, Ank and Cro had both come into Ati's bedroom to tell him that Bio was at the door, bearing extraordinary news: "His Excellency Toz has the honor of inviting you to visit his museum," they said, in unison.

"Museum? What's that?"

Those poor devils did not know. Like Ati, they were hearing the word for the first time. It was not *abilang*, because according to a recent decree from the High Commissariat for *Abilang* and *Abilanguization*, presided over by the Honorable Ara, an eminent linguist and fierce adversary of multilingualism, which he saw as a source of relativism and impiety, common names deriving from an ancient language that were still in use would have to adopt either a prefix or a suffix, as appropriate, from among *abi* or *ab*, *yol* or *yo*, *Gka* or *gk*. Everything belonged to religion—beings, things, and names, too; it was therefore appropriate to mark them. "Museum" was either an exception, which the edict allowed for or would tolerate for some time yet, or it came from one of the ancient languages, prohibited but still in use in enclaves here and there, and these ancient languages had neither breviaries nor dictionaries. There was also the fact that people still spoke however they liked in private, despite the danger of denunciation by children, servants, or neighbors, and the fiefdom was as private as could be, it was even sovereign.

"Why is this extraordinary? I know Toz, I had coffee at his house in A19, and I lived in his dark warehouse; you won't know about it because you never leave the fiefdom," said Ati, pulling on his *burni*.

"But . . . but . . . he's never invited anyone to his museum. Just once, at the beginning, for the inauguration, his brothers—His Lordship and the Great Chamberlain—and his nephew, master Ram who runs everything, no one else since then, not a soul . . . "

Yes, now it was becoming fascinating.

Bio was even more excited; the poor messenger boy thought he might be able to dissolve into Ati's shadow and go with him into the museum, and see at last what had been going on there for so many years. In the camp they'd always seen the trucks coming and going to the museum, delivering crates, removing shipping material, and shuttling workers hired from faraway cities who, for the time of their employment, bustled about inside the building without ever showing their faces outside.

There really was envy in the air. As he crossed the domain, Ati could see that everyone was full of kindhearted curiosity; their gazes said, "How lucky you are, oh stranger, you are going to see something we shall never see . . . Why you and not us, when we belong to the clan?"

Bio and Ati walked at a good pace for a full hour, which made their legs somewhat heavy, crossing a vast housing estate where, Bio informed him proudly, the technicians for the electric power plant and the waterworks lived, then an industrial zone where there was no lack of noisy, juddering workshops; then they went past wasteland that was solidly fenced off, where His Lordship's army trained and held maneuvers, in which according to Bio's mathematical calculations there was enough space to contain at least three villages. Finally they ended up in a huge green expanse, in the middle of which stood a magnificent white building surrounded by an impeccable lawn. Ati would learn later from Toz himself that the building was the fifth copy of an ancient, prestigious, gigantic museum called the Louvre, or the Loufre, that had been ransacked and razed to the ground during the first Great Holy War and the annexation of Abistan by the Lig, the United High Regions of the North. He would find out that the only country that had resisted the forces of Abistan, because they were governed by a mad dictator called Big Brother, who had thrown his entire nuclear arsenal into the battle, was Angsoc, or Angsok, but in the end it too had fallen and they had drowned in their own blood.

Toz was there, half sitting, half lying on a strange seat, a piece of canvas stretched between four bits of wood. Ati heard him refer to it quite simply as a "chaise longue." Was it a pleasant way to sit? He would have to try it. Toz was smiling, there was something mischievous in his gaze, as if to say, "I got you there, you and Koa, and I apologize, but as you can see, my

222 · BOUALEM SANSAL

intentions were good." His gaze clouded over and a sort of bitter grimace distorted his face. Ati understood that he was thinking about poor Koa, and that in a way he blamed himself for what had happened.

He patted Ati on the shoulder and nudged him toward the entrance to the building. "Welcome to the Museum of Nostalgia!" And with a wave of his hand he drove away the shadow of poor Bio, who was contorting himself in an attempt to peer in through the slightly open door. What had he managed to see? Nothing: a vast white vestibule, completely empty. The heavy door slammed in his face.

"Come in, dear Ati, come in. Welcome. I have invited you into my secret garden to seek forgiveness for having misled you . . . and also, I confess, because I need your help. The journey through time and the paradox I invite you to visit will help me in my own research, because I'm at a point where I doubt everything, myself included. Let's sit down for a moment . . . yes, there, on the floor . . . I would like to prepare you for what you are about to see. You don't know what a museum is, since there aren't any in Abistan. That's the way our country is, it was born with the absurd idea that everything that existed before the advent of the *Gkabul* was false and pernicious and had to be destroyed, erased, forgotten, just like the Other, if he did not submit to the *Gkabul*. The museum, in a way, is the rejection of this madness, my revolt against it. The world exists, with or without the *Gkabul*; to deny it or destroy it does not eliminate it—on the contrary, its absence makes its memory even stronger, more present, and in the long run pernicious, as it happens, because it can lead to idealizing that past, making it sacred . . . But at the same time, and you may become aware of this, a museum is a paradox, trickery, an illusion that is every bit as pernicious.

"Reconstituting a vanished world is always both a way of idealizing it and a way of destroying it for a second time, because we remove it from its context to set it down into another, and thus we freeze it in immobility and silence, or we make it say and do something it may not have said or done. To visit that world under these conditions is a bit like looking at a dead man's body. Look at it all you like, you might even resort to photographs of the man when he was alive, read everything that might have been written about him, but you'll never feel the life he had inside him or around him. In my museum there are a lot of objects from a certain era—the twentieth century, as its contemporaries called it, and those items have been arranged according to function or the use that was made of them; you'll also see amazingly lifelike wax reproductions of men and women in their everyday life, reconstituted down to the minutest details, but there will always be something miss-ing—movement, breath, warmth—and so the tableau is and will remain a still life. No matter how great, imagination can-not give life. That chaise longue, for example, that I was sitting or lying on just now, and which surprised you. It belongs to its era, it was made in keeping with a certain concept of life. If I spoke to you of vacations, of leisure, of dilettantism and supe-riority over nature, which was there to serve mankind, if you knew what that was and could feel all these things in the depth they had at the time, you would see the chaise longue for what it really was, not just a piece of canvas stretched between four bits of wood like you must have thought when you first saw it.

"Once you've visited the museum I would like for you to tell me, if you will, what you felt, what sort of thoughts the scenes inspired. I've been looking at them for so long that a certain distance has come between us—if there ever was a time when that distance did not exist . . . Sometimes I get the impression I'm visiting a cemetery I came across along the way, I see graves, I read names, but I know nothing about these dead people, who they were when they were alive, and nothing about the place and time in which they lived.

"You have to remember that all this is strictly forbidden by our religion and our government, which is why I built the museum here, in our fiefdom, and not in A19 where I live among the people. And that is also why I deal in the second-hand trade, and more discreetly in antiques, to the great displeasure of my brothers Bri and Viz for a start, who think I'm not maintaining my rank, and also of my young, intelligent, and very ambitious nephew Ram, who has to work extra on my account to ensure my security and facilitate my economic activities, something I pretend not to notice so that he won't exaggerate . . . Already I'm seen as the godfather of A19 when in fact it's Ram's henchmen who control everything around me. I've found contentment in secondhand things, in antiques, they've enabled me to get away from Abistan and work discreetly on my plan to put the twentieth century into a museum. Well then, on with your visit into the past, into impiety and illusion! I'll wait for you at the other end; I don't want to influence you."

The museum consisted of a series of rooms, more or less vast, each one devoted to one episode of human life that, perhaps for all time, people had identified as a world unto itself, hermetically sealed off and independent from the next one, and therefore Toz had separated the rooms by locked doors; each key was hidden somewhere in the jumble of the room. To get into the next room, the next episode in life, the key had to be found, and there wasn't all the time in the world, life is movement, it doesn't wait. By creating this difficulty Toz sought to place the visitor (but who could that be, other than he alone?) into man's natural state of not knowing his future and always seeking it, in urgency and difficulty.

The first room told the story of birth, from delivery to early childhood. It was like being there, the delivery room was strikingly real, you could almost hear the cries of the mother and the baby's first wailing. On display cases, tables, or the floor were the banal items belonging to this phase of life: cradle, potty, stroller, baby bouncer, rattles and toys. On the walls were paintings and photographs featuring everyday life: children playing, eating, sleeping, swimming, drawing, while their parents watched over them.

The following rooms were devoted to adolescence and adulthood, divided according to various milieus, eras, professions, and circumstances. One of them made a particularly strong impression on Ati: the vividly realistic model of a heaving battlefield, with muddy trenches, incredible tangles of barbed wire, chevaux de frise, exhausted soldiers mounting an attack. The paintings and photographs revealed other aspects of war—devastated cities, steaming carcasses, emaciated prisoners in death camps, gaunt crowds on the roads fleeing the enemy.

In another room items of leisure and sports equipment were displayed, while the pictures on the wall showed a cinema, a skating rink, hot air balloons, a shooting range, a circus, paragliders in flight, and so on. Play and performance, along with extreme excitement, were the honey of that era. All these things had vanished from Abistan after the Victory and the Great Cleanup, so Ati wondered how and where Toz had managed to find these photographs. And what he must have paid for them.

One dark room was devoted to instruments of torture and death, and another to activities related to the economy, commerce, industry, and transport. Then came a pleasing installation of the kind Ati and Koa had seen in the ghetto of the Regs: a bar counter, an acrobatic waiter running between tables, people drinking heavily, crackpots calling out to very attractive women as they flaunted their tattoos and mustaches and thick builders' biceps, and at the back of the room that ever-present narrow stairway vanishing into gloom and mystery. On the wall was an etching which had clearly served as a model for the installation: a visiting card glued to the wall said, the text in French: "French bistro: old-fashioned delinquents teasing loose women."

The etching was signed: "Léo le Fol (1924)." An antique from the belle époque.

The last room but one was reserved for old age and death. Death means only one thing, but there were numerous and varied funerary rites. Ati did not linger: he did not feel inspired by the sight of coffins, hearses, crematoriums, funeral parlors, and an anatomical skeleton, who seemed to find his situation rather amusing.

Ati did not see the time go by; he had never been on such a journey, an entire century of discovery and questioning. On his way he remembered how he had felt during his interminable voyage across Abistan, from Sîn to Qodsabad. A living museum over several thousand *chabirs*, an endless succession of regions, hamlets, deserts, forests, ruins, and lost camps, separated by borders that were invisible but symbolically as hermetic as a padlocked door (particularly if you forgot to validate your circulation visa). That great variety of races, customs, dwellings, utensils, work tools had gradually changed his way of looking at Abistan and at his own life; by the time he reached Qodsabad Ati was another man, he did not recognize anyone and people only recognized him through hearsay—he was the man who'd had consumption, the miraculous survivor from Sîn, Yölah's protégé. Was that what you were supposed to expect a museum to do? To describe life like a book, to imitate it for pleasure, to transform people? Objects, paintings, photographs, a staged scene—did they really have the power to change people's vision of life and of themselves?

At the end of the journey Ati found Toz in a vast empty room. Toz explained the symbolism behind it: Ati had entered the museum through an empty room, now he would leave through an empty room: the image of life caught between two voids, before creation and after death. Life is constrained by limits, it disposes only of its time, which is short, and is divided into segments that have no relation to each other apart from those which man drags around inside him from one end of his tenure to the other—uncertain memories of what was, and vague expectations of what shall be. The passage from one to another is not made explicit, it's a mystery, one day the lovely baby, that inveterate sleeper, disappears, and no one is alarmed, and a turbulent, curious little child, a sprite, appears in its place, which hardly surprises the mother even when she finds herself left with two heavy, useless breasts. Later on other substitutions will occur, just as stealthily: a heavy, worried man will take the place of the slim, smiling young man who had been standing there, and in turn, through who knows what magical trick, the oppressed fellow will yield his seat to a stooped, silent man. It is at the end that the surprise comes, when a dead man, still warm, suddenly replaces the mute, cold old man who was sitting glued to his chair by the window. That is one transformation too many, yet sometimes it is welcome.

"Life goes by so fast that you don't notice a thing," you'll say to yourself on the way to the cemetery.

Toz and Ati spent the afternoon philosophizing, their sadness heartfelt. Toz lived in nostalgia for a world he had not known, but which he thought he had managed to reconstitute faithfully as a still life, and into which he would like to breathe life. What would be the point? They agreed that the question was meaningless; the void was the essence of the world but did not, however, stop the world from existing and filling itself up with nothingness. That is the mystery of the zero: it exists to say that it does not exist. In this respect the *Gkabul* was the perfect response; to the absolute uselessness of the world the only response could be a human being's absolute, comforting submission to nothingness. Nothing is what one is, nothing is what one shall remain, from dust to dust shalt thou return. As for Ati, he had examined the question in another way, and come up with the notion that the end of the world began at birth, the first cry of life was also the first death rattle. As time went by, with its lot of suffering, he had become convinced that the longer an affliction lasted, the sooner its end would come and life would begin a new cycle. The point was not to wait with one's head full of questions but to accelerate the process, for to die in the hopes of a new life was more dignified, after all, than living in despair of one's impending death.

They admitted honestly that Abistan's great misfortune was the *Gkabul*: in response to the intrinsic violence of the void, it offered humanity submission to sanctified ignorance, and by pushing servitude to self-negation, to pure and simple self-destruction, it denied the possibility of rebellion as a means of inventing a world on a human scale—which, at the very least, might preserve humanity from the ambient madness. Religion truly is the remedy that kills.

For a time Toz had been interested in the history of the *Gkabul*. He was born in it, he did not see it, the *Gkabul* was the air he breathed, the water he drank, and he wore it in his mind the way people wore their *burni* over their shoulders. But before long he began to feel ill at ease; already at school he realized that public education was a calamity, the source of all calamities, such an insidious thing, as unstoppable and implacable as death. With true enthusiasm on his part, education turned him into a compulsive, vicious little confessor, prepared to swallow dark fairy tales and schoolgirl legends whole, and recite fantastical stanzas, obtuse slogans and offensive curses; and where physical exercise was concerned, he became the perfect perpetrator of all manner of pogroms and lynching. There was no time or attention left for anything else, optional branches such as poetry, music, pottery, or gymnastics. As the son of an Honorable, who would perhaps become an Honorable himself one day, he was, moreover, held to the blindness of the head conductor who is sure of his machine and what he is doing. As he dabbled in the *Gkabul*, to keep in step and reeducate himself, he lost both hope and hopefulness; the *Gkabul* was not meant to enlighten the unfortunate, it was ballast to take him to the bottom, and it wasn't the school's fault, the poor woman was teaching what she had been given to teach, and she even managed rather well, survivors were rare. It was too late, the *Gkabul* had spread its hypnosis into the body and the deep soul of the people, into their bodies, and it reigned supreme. How many centuries would it take to undo the spell—that was the only question that was truly worthwhile.

Casual as could be, Toz cleared a forbidden path and boldly set off down it. There was really only one path, the one that went back in time. Since the *Gkabul* had colonized the present for all centuries to come, it was in the past, before its advent, that one could escape from it. Before our time, humans were not all like this, wild, stubborn beasts filled with bad faith. From time to time Toz got lost along the way, History itself had gotten lost in the maquis, there weren't any decent trails, they had all been blocked off and covered over. The most hardened historians knew how to work their way back as far as 2084, no further, no more than that. How else, without holy ignorance and the total apathy-inducing possession of people's minds, could those poor folk have been persuaded that before the birth of Abistan there was only the uncreated, unknowable universe of Yölah? It couldn't be simpler: just choose a date and stop time at that moment; people are already dead and foundering in the void, they'll believe anything you tell them, they will applaud their rebirth in 2084. That will be their only choice: either to live according to the calendar of the *Gkabul* or return to their original void.

The discovery of the past very nearly killed Toz. As cultivated as he was, he did not know that 2083 existed, or that you could go even further back. A round earth is a dizzying tragedy for anyone who ever thought it was flat, with edges. The question "Who are we?" had suddenly become "Who were we?" and as a result one's self-image changed drastically, was covered in darkness and ugliness; something had broken inside, the cornerstone that held up the universe, so there was poor Toz, as if tossed up in the air, living like a ghost among ancient ghosts. No one knows how to make time linear and coherent again once these qualities have been destroyed in such a way. Toz still didn't know; he was somewhere between yesterday and today.

After a great deal of effort and research, he managed one day to break the time barrier and go back through the entire twentieth century. It was a miracle; believers, in their lifetime, cannot escape from the phenomenal pull of the *Gkabul*. Toz was gripped with wonder. He had discovered what every man who opened his eyes would hear as a first truth: before the world there is the world, and after the world there is still the world. He discovered a very rich century which was lacking for nothing—there were hundreds of languages, dozens of religions, an abundance of countries, cultures, contradictions; there was madness, unrestrained freedom, insurmountable danger, already, but there were also innumerable, serious sources of hope, well-oiled machinery, benevolent observers on the lookout for slippages, hardened refuseniks, men of goodwill who were not discouraged by effort but stimulated by it. Life is exuberant and voracious, both in good ways and bad, and it had proved as much during that century. There was only one thing missing, the simply mechanical means to rush to occupy the stars.

Toz also discovered something that all the others had perceived very early on, but which had been minimized, relativized through heaviness, fear, calculation, the porousness of the air, or simply because the doomsayers were not sharp enough or loud enough: the warning signs of what the world would soon become if nothing were done to put things right. Toz watched as 2084 arrived and was followed by the Holy Wars and the nuclear holocausts; more importantly, he witnessed the birth of the absolute weapon which one does not need to buy or build, the conflagration of entire populations as they are filled with the violence of terror. It was all so obvious, so predictable, but those who said, "Not in our lifetime," who echoed, "Never again," were not heard. As in 1914, as in 1939 or 2014, 2022 or 2050, off they went again. But in 2084, it finally worked. The old world ceased to exist, and the new world, Abistan, began its eternal reign upon the planet.

What are you supposed to do when you examine the past and see the danger bearing down on those who came before you in History? How can you warn them? How can you tell your own contemporaries, now, that if they carry on the way they've begun yesterday's tragedies will soon be upon them? How can you persuade them, when their religion forbids them from believing in their own death, when they are convinced that their place in paradise has been booked and is waiting for them like a suite in a luxury hotel?

Toz was astonished to discover the origin of the *Gkabul*. It was not spontaneous generation. It was simple, nothing miraculous about it—the *Gkabul* was not a creation of Abi's, in keeping with Yölah's instructions, as had been taught with the utmost seriousness and gravity since 2084; it came from far away, from an inner malfunction in an ancient religion which had once brought honor and happiness to many great tribes of the deserts and plains; but its inner workings had been broken by the violent, discordant use that had been made of it over the centuries, and this had been aggravated by the absence of competent repairmen or attentive guides. The *Gkabul* came into existence because of a lack of care that should have been given a religion which, as the aggregate and quintessence of the religions that had preceded it, sought to be the future of the world.

Those who are sick, are weak, and at the mercy of scoundrels. United in a clique known as "The Messenger Brothers," a group of adventurers who sensed all around them that the end was near decided to found a new religion on the ruins of the old one. A good idea: they took what was still strong from the old one to add it to the new one. The new religion drew crowds with the novelty of its discourse, its tactical game, its commercial marketing and militarist aggressiveness. Their successors did even better: they revised the major symbols, invented Abi and Yölah, wrote the *Gkabul*, built the Kiïba and the City of God, founded the Just Brotherhood, and gave themselves the title of *chik,* which means Honorable (to distance themselves from the vulgar Messenger Brothers). Once they were equipped with potent symbols and a good army, they broke with the old religion, which no longer served any purpose; it was dying off among the elderly and a few benighted scholars who believed in the miracle of Resurrection and the possibility of a Fountain of Youth. Now the idea was to put all that behind them and track down any nostalgic stragglers: they were dangerous, they might want to try to bring back the dead.

"This is all still a working hypothesis; there's always a lot that is secretive and intoxicating about religion and military strategy—to be honest they're two sides of the same coin. This requires further thought," added Toz.

Ati became aware of a strange sensation inside: he felt no interest in a question that had hitherto preoccupied him quite a bit, after all. What Toz had told him about his research into History and his thoughts about life formed an answer in themselves. If he decided to ask the question it was because this was a good opportunity, and he might not get it again.

"Tell me, Toz, I'm sure you've read the Nas report . . . Can you tell me about it?"

"Uh . . . I don't know what to tell you. Those are State secrets, I'm not supposed to know them, I have no official position, other than being His Lordship's brother, and to be honest it's very complicated, but in fact, well, here it is: the report doesn't exist. There's never been a Nas report, it's the fictitious element in a fictitious plan . . . which came about gradually. When Nas, who was aware of the danger the discovery of the village represented, got back from his mission, he made an oral report to his minister, just the two of them, in private, and I imagine his boss ordered him not to breathe a word of it to anyone. He'd let him know, he'd see, he'd think about it, was what he would have said. Then Nas disappeared and only then did people start to talk about a report . . . then about *the* report, and, as is often the case, by virtue of talking about something, you make it reality. The Nas report appeared; people called it THE *Nas report*. It evoked a whole atmosphere, a legend. At that point, something had to be done, so copies were made of the report that didn't exist, and they were distributed among the Honorables, with a view to having the Just Brotherhood deliberate what to do. This report, written by someone, who knows, from the Just Brotherhood or the Apparatus, was full of nonsense. The village was said to be an advanced outpost of the Enemy; the famous Democ was hiding there; heretics had founded a community that had pledged allegiance to Balis, and so on. To elucidate the matter I went to the village with a group of experts mandated by the Great

Commander; Bri appointed me to be part of the commission, because each clan insisted on having their own representative. With Tat, cabinet head for the Great Commander, presiding, we wrote a technical report that was instantly placed under absolute secrecy, and which in turn became THE *Nas report*. I won't be giving anything away if I tell you that we did indeed find troubling things in that village; it looked as if it had been hosting a community that was experimenting with a lifestyle and an administration founded on the free will of the individual. To many of us this was incomprehensible, a good number of us couldn't see how you could organize your life without first uniting around a leader, a religion, and an army. This story illustrates all that is wrong with Abistan: we've invented a world that is so absurd that we ourselves have to be more and more absurd with every passing day just to find the place where we left off the day before; in short, in the end we devised a report that conveyed what frightened us and we didn't want to hear about. History is dragging us into its madness. The other dramatic consequence is that the affair has divided the Just Brotherhood and altered the balance of power within it, and here in Abistan that automatically means war."

After so much philosophizing and discussion of current affairs, the two explorers of the Abistani soul have reached the point where they are bound to ask themselves, "And now, what is to be done?"

Toz has a plan he drew up long ago: he will go on doing his research, convinced as he is that it will be useful someday; when men of good will know how to recognize each other and mobilize, they will find the materials he has so painstakingly stockpiled. The rest of the time he will help his nephew Ram; beneath his air of an impenitent plotter who wants to be top dog, he is a reformer, in other words a true revolutionary who pushes through his reforms instead of just singing their praises.

In this they have very similar aims: eliminate the Just Brotherhood, dismantle the Apparatus, open the City of God, turn the Kiïba into a multimillennial museum, destroy the absurd myth about this Abi who is supposed to be alive and immortal, raise people's consciousness, set up an assembly of representatives and a government that will answer to them— now there you have an exalting future to build. The people might die as a result, they hold fast to their gods and their woes, but there will still be children, and they have their inno- cence, they will quickly learn another way to dream and to make war, we will call on them to save the planet and wage a fierce battle against the smoke traders. There is always the dan- ger that Ram might turn into a horrible top dog, and Toz knows that, so he wants to bring about a transition that will ensure the emergence of tenacious, competent competitors . . . His idea is that if they all want to be top dog, they will cancel each other out, they will be forced to get along to go on doing their very lucrative business, they will eventually understand that losing doesn't necessarily mean dying assassinated, and winning doesn't necessarily imply killing the other guy. You mustn't stop them from dreaming, on the contrary. The most dangerous ones are the ones who don't dream; they have souls of ice.

. . .

Toz goes on expounding his ideas. They are good, and real- istic, but impossible to implement and he knows it. He is try- ing to convince himself of the fact. The revolution that Ram wants will end in a bloodbath and nothing will change, Abistan is Abistan and will remain Abistan. The Honorables and their sons, who already see themselves as Honorables in the place of their Honorable fathers—they too dream and plot to become top dog. Who would willingly give up his place to the best one? They are all better than the best among them; every one of them is the genius the people have been waiting for.

Suddenly Toz pauses; he realizes he has been talking so much simply because deep down he has nothing to say; in fact he doesn't believe a single word. He asks, "And you, Ati, what do you want to do?"

Ati didn't have to think, he realized he'd known what he wanted for a long time, for several months now . . . Ever since his stay at the sanatorium in Sîn, he had not stopped thinking about it. He knew it was a bad choice, irremediable, unachievable, it would lead him to terrible disillusionment, inhuman suffering, certain death . . . but what did that matter, it was his choice, and he chose freedom.

Toz was waiting for his reply: "Yes, tell me, what do you want to do, where do you want to go?"

"Do you think, dear Toz, that Ram would allow me to leave the fiefdom . . . before his revolution?"

"Yes, surely. I'll vouch for it."

"Do you think if I asked him to leave me somewhere in Abistan he would do that?"

"Why not, as long as it doesn't endanger his own plans . . . And there, too, I'll do everything I can to get him to agree."

Ati was silent for a moment then said, "Tell me something else, Toz. Not long ago, you asked Koa and me if we knew Democ . . . who was supposed to exist without existing, or vice versa . . . I'd like in turn to ask you a question like that."

"I remember . . . I'm listening."

"Have you ever heard of—of the Border? Do you know about it?"

"The border? Which—ah, that Border. Yes, I know about it. People talk about it the way they talk to silly children about the big bad wolf, it's a ruse to discourage smugglers and clandestine migrants or vagabonds without permits. They are told the Enemy will come from there one day and slit their throats."

"Is there a chance in a million that the Border exists?"

"Not one in a billion. On earth there is only Abistan; you know that."

"Really?"

"Well . . . there might be an island, here or there, for example, that still falls outside the jurisdiction of Abistan."

"And there are ghettos. I saw the great ghetto of the Seven Sisters of Desolation. They call it a ghetto but it's a country. A small one but a country all the same, and the people who live there are men and women who are perfectly alive and not mutant bats. And there's a Border there, very well guarded . . . and I'm not talking about the Border of Borders that hermetically seals off the City of God, or of the ones that serve as a pointless separation between the sixty neighborhoods in Qodsabad or the sixty provinces in Abistan . . . "

"That's all nothing, dear Ati, a drop in the ocean, anachronisms, nonsense, demonstrations of incompetence on the part of the Apparatus, who by virtue of playing with fire became intoxicated and laid a grid over everything, with checkpoints. As for the Regs, they are, uh . . . they belong to Abistan. The people and the System need them, they need phantasmagoria like them to channel hatred and anger, and to reinforce the notion of one superior, pure, united race that is threatened by parasites. It's as old as the planet. So what is your idea, in fact? But I'm afraid I'm beginning to get it . . . it's sheer madness!"

"Yes, that's what it is, dear Toz . . . I would like Ram to leave me off somewhere in the Sîn mountains, in the Ouâ range . . . in a place where that Border has one chance in a million of existing. And if, by miracle, it does exist, I'll find it and cross it, and I'll see with my own eyes that twentieth century you so faithfully reconstructed . . . "

"It's madness. How can you believe such a thing?"

"I have hundreds of reasons to believe it, I believe it

because Abistan is based on lies, nothing has escaped its falsifications, and since it has altered History there's no reason why it might not also have invented a new geography. You can make people who never leave their neighborhood believe whatever you like . . . Since I met you, Toz, I've become more and more convinced of this. You believed in your twentieth century and you brought it back to life—there it is, shiny and beautiful in your miraculous museum . . . You know that century, you have seen how the inhabitants had science and technology and certain virtues which, in spite of all the limitations, enabled them to maintain a diversity of views, and to experience it, even when it was painful to them. As for technology, there's no lack of it in Abistan: where did it come from, since we don't manufacture it? Isn't there a border somewhere that means it's coming to us from the other side? And you also believed, Toz, that men of good will existed in Abistan and that one day they would know how to find each other and mobilize in order to save their country and their souls. You are one of them, and a lot of people think like you in wretched A19, so near yet so far from the City of God. Why wouldn't I also have my beliefs—that those men from the twentieth century didn't all disappear in the Holy Wars and holocausts and mass exterminations and forced conversions? Why wouldn't I see myself as a man of goodwill who has acknowledged the fact and is mobilizing to establish or reestablish a connection between our world and the other one? Yes, why not, dear Toz, why not? I know for a fact, because I was there, at the sanatorium in Sîn, that entire caravans disappeared behind that . . . Border . . . If they'd just gotten lost, they would eventually have found their way and come back, don't you think? And if someone made up the story about the Border to scare children and smugglers, wasn't it because they knew the thing had actually existed? And maybe there is a little bit of it left somewhere in the remote icy fringes of the Ouâ. I want to try: I've come this far, it's the only choice left to me . . . Life for me in this world is all over, all I hope and desire is to make a new life on the other side."

Toz remained silent. His lip was trembling when he finally replied:

"I'll ask Ram. Yes, I'll ask him and I'll do everything I can to persuade him. When you're on the other side, you'll let me know, somehow or other, and you'll help me finish my museum . . . and maybe one day I'll breathe life into it."

A very long silence settled over them, until Ati suddenly broke it.

"My dear Toz, just so I don't go to my grave without knowing, tell me three things, quickly—first of all, why did you burst out laughing when Koa gave you the letter Abi wrote to the *mockbi* Kho to thank him for having sent so many young people to their deaths?"

"The *mockbi* Kho was a family friend, and we all knew of his immoderate love of glory. He flooded the country with that letter: he had written it himself and given it to the Great Commander to have Abi sign it. On the basis of his work and in the light of this recognition, Bri, as the Honorable in charge of Graces and Canonizations, nominated Kho for sainthood and no doubt will obtain it one of these days; but that sort of thing moves rather slowly. What else?"

"How did you find out so quickly that we had been attacked by the guards on the Square of Supreme Faith? The question has been bugging me."

"As I told you, Ram set up a whole security network around me, and everyone who comes near me is scanned, and is driven away if there's any doubt. You were my protégés, so to speak, so you were under surveillance . . . who by, I don't know—your neighbor, her husband, my factotum Mou, who else? It was my agent Der who came to wake me up and inform me that you'd gone and thrown yourselves so rashly into a catastrophe."

"And what is that very polished language that is used in the signage in the offices of the Great Chamberlain?"

"You noticed? Well done . . . It's the language in which the holy book that came before the *Gkabul* was written . . . A very beautiful, rich, evocative language. As it had a tendency toward poetry and rhetoric, it was eradicated from Abistan, *abilang* was a better choice, since it demands duty and strict obedience. Its conception was inspired by Newspeak, from Angsoc. When we occupied that country, our then leaders discovered that its extraordinary political system was founded not only on weapons but also on the phenomenal power of its language, Newspeak, a language that was invented in a laboratory and which had the power to crush all will and curiosity in the speaker. So as the basis of their philosophy our leaders adopted the three principles that presided over the creation of Angsoc's political system: 'War is peace,' 'Freedom is slavery,' 'Ignorance is strength,' and added three principles of their own: 'Death is life,' 'Lying is truth,' 'Logic is absurdity.' That's Abistan for you, sheer madness.

"Bri and Viz criticize my nostalgia for the twentieth century but they are nostalgic for that language and its charms . . . They sometimes write poems and recite them in family circles. But careful, that's a State secret, it mustn't leave the fiefdom . . . Have I answered your questions?"

"Not completely, but there have to be a few secrets for the next life, if it exists and we're allowed to express ourselves there."

Epilogue

In which we will hear the latest news from Abistan, sourced from various media: The Voice of the Kïïba, Nadir 1-*Qodsabad Station*, the *NeF*, *the bulletin of the VLBs entitled* The Hero, The Voice of the Mockbas, The Civic Brotherhood, *the* Army Journal, *etc. These should be read with the utmost circumspection, as the Abistani media are above all instruments of mental manipulation in the service of the clans.*

The news came first of all through *The Voice of the Kiïba*. In fact, it did no more than echo the communiqué from the Ras, the bureau of the presidium of the Just Brotherhood:

> The Cabinet of the Holy Kiïba has informed us this morning that His Most Serene Excellency the Honorable Duc, Great Commander of the believers, president of the Just Brotherhood, exclusive Master of the Lordships scattered throughout the sixty provinces of Abistan, has suffered a slight malaise that will necessitate his absence for a certain period.
>
> During his absence, the interim Command of the Just Brotherhood will be ensured by His Lordship the Honorable Bri. By formal order of Abi the Delegate, may salvation be upon him, and the entire Just Brotherhood, all individuals and institutions are called upon to obey him faithfully and do everything within their power to facilitate his task.
>
> Signed: For the Just Brotherhood assembled in an extraordinary session, and on the authority of the acting Commander of Believers, the Honorable Bri, the principal private secretary, Sub-Honorable Tat.

One week later, *Nadir 1*-Qodsabad Station broadcast a still image illustrating the following information, a mass execution being held in a stadium:

We have just heard, and are waiting for confirmation from the Ministry of Morality and Divine Justice, that two hundred and fifty criminals are said to have been sentenced to death by a religious decree issued by the Grand Jury of the Just Brotherhood. We already congratulate our brilliant agents from the Apparatus for unmasking them and confounding them so quickly. If the appeal for clemency they have submitted to the acting Great Commander, His Lordship the Honorable Bri, is rejected, they will be beheaded after the Great Thursday Imploration in various stadiums around the capital. According to sources close to the Kiïba, these criminals are said to have invented the most incomprehensible, despicable, and ridiculous rumor ever heard on the sacred soil of Abistan, namely, that because of a sudden decline in his health the Great Commander Duc was evacuated during the night by presidential airplane to an unknown location designated by one insignificant word, "Abroad," where he will receive specialized treatment which Abistan could not provide even if it knew how. For shame! What is Abroad, where is it, who is it? No Abistani would hesitate for one second to carry out, himself, the just sentence the Grand Jury passed on those dangerous *makoufs*. The people unanimously call on the Great Commander to scornfully reject the appeal for clemency. Decapitation is already a great indulgence; scum like this ought really to be impaled, quartered, boiled alive. May Yölah restore the health of our Great Commander Duc and watch over our acting Great Commander Bri.

In a recent issue, the *NeF* reported the following:

According to sources close to the ministry of War and Peace, intense fighting is currently underway in the desert regions of southwest Abistan. Our sources allege that the combat involves free militia controlled by certain milieus with varying degrees of government connections. Is this fighting the confirmation of a rumor which has been circulating for some time, namely that the Just Brotherhood is meeting in conclave to elect the new Commander? According to another source the situation is even more complicated: the Just Brotherhood is said to have split in two and to be holding two conclaves in two secret locations. It is understandable that under these conditions the army, whom many have accused as the cause of all woe, are staying in their camps and barracks. Who are they supposed to obey, if they are receiving contradictory orders? In our next issue we will relay the decisive information that our investigators are obtaining at this very moment from a major government figure. It will no doubt confirm, in greater detail, what a worker at the Just Brotherhood's airport revealed to us last night, a few minutes before the newspaper went to press, namely that a medical team appointed by the cabinet of the Just Brotherhood had just boarded a jet to fly to this place called Abroad that is the topic of much discussion these days, for the purpose of verifying the demise of our Great Commander and repatriating his august remains. May Yölah greet him in his paradise.

The *Army Journal* has posted the following (unsigned) communiqué from General Staff Headquarters:

In light of the insane flood of rumors endangering Abistan's stability, the general Command of the army would like to insist upon the fact that the army is at the service of the government and the Just Brotherhood, as they are the supreme institutions of the country, united under the authority of the acting Great Commander, the Honorable Bri. The army forcefully denies the suggestion that intense fighting is under way in any region of the planet; the army's information services have observed nothing other than the usual, occasionally excessive confrontations between local leaders, or fighting between smugglers and our armed forces, skirmishes between rioters and the forces of law and order, or the settling of scores between rival gangs of delinquents. General Staff Headquarters call on everyone to remain calm and serve only the Just Brotherhood, under the enlightened leadership of the Honorable Bri, acting Commander of believers.

In the *Civic Brotherhood*, the despicable paper published by the FAC (Free Association of Civics), a strange long story was dug up. Given the level of crass ignorance displayed by the rag's piss-artist copywriters, it is clear as day that the text was written by the resident in-house phantom.

A certain Afr, a bum by trade, who has been repeatedly subjected to beatings by the Civics without ever mending his ways, showed up at the Civics' barracks in the eighth district of H46 to reveal that two days earlier he had spotted a renegade who has been on the run from his neighborhood, S21, for several weeks, a certain Ati. Intrigued at seeing him so far from his own neighborhood, which he himself came from originally, Afr followed Ati. He was in the company of a stranger, an imposing man. Afr saw them enter the house of an honest tradesman, Buk the hardware dealer. Driven by his light-fingered, impulsive nature, Afr crept into the garden of the house, and through the window he witnessed a strange scene: Ati the renegade was deep in conversation with the hardware dealer's worthy wife, to whom he was giving a present wrapped in a fine piece of silk. The husband was not in the room, so Afr suspected this must be a crime of adultery. He pictured a double reward for himself at the next R-Day, first for having located and reported a wanted renegade, and second for interrupting a crime of adultery. His day would have been well worth it. The Civics, who know everything because they live among the population and enjoy their complete trust, wanted to get to the bottom of this story, but Ati the renegade and his accomplice had disappeared. Summoned and called upon to explain himself, the worthy Buk protested that he had been framed, and said that Tar had introduced himself as a rich tradesman, there to make an offer for his production of cooking pots and basins over the next ten years, so as to honor his contract with a company belonging to the Honorable Dia, and that when Buk hosted a splendid dinner to celebrate his success, Tar showed up with a cousin of his who was passing through H46, whose name was not Ati but Nor.

The Civics filed a report to whom it might concern but, as usual, they received neither thanks nor information regarding the further developments of the matter. Later, upon learning that two suspect individuals had entered the City of God and that one of them had been killed in A19 by free guards, they made the connection with the renegade and his accomplice and, in an additional report to the authorities, put forward the hypothesis that the swindlers in H46 and the bandits in A19 were one and the same; consequently, it seemed expedient to them to transfer the file to the Civics in A19. Which is what they did, but the Civics did not get very far with their investigation, as the body of the man who'd been killed by the guards had disappeared. No body, no crime, no case; as for the other individual, he had simply vanished into thin air. Also worthy of mention, because it is regrettable, is the fact that in A19 the prerogatives of the Civics have been limited drastically by an edict from the Honorable Bri, governor and police chief of the neighborhood.

248 · BOUALEM SANSAL

This is where security in our country stands: a dangerous renegade moves freely from one neighborhood to the next, an honest hardware dealer gets ripped off by fake tradesmen; an individual is killed by unknown guards and his body disappears just when it could have proven useful (it was most certainly seen by children playing in a vacant lot), and his accomplice vanishes without a trace . . . The highest authorities are not doing a thing, they have not declared a state of emergency, nor have they sent out a search party, nor arranged to have the neighborhoods searched, nor had anybody arrested. A fine thing, Abistani justice. It makes you wonder what the point of being a Civic is in this country!

As for *The Voice of the Mockbas*, it has published a call to vigilance that is rather alarming, which reads as follows:

We have been witnessing a new phenomenon of late that cannot help but be a cause for concern: individuals who arrived from who knows where are spreading throughout the country with a call for greater orthodoxy in the practice of our holy religion. For the time being they are seeking out the small *mockbas*, because they have little or no surveillance, but these men can only grow bolder and slip through every breach, and God knows there are enough of them in Abistan. It is obvious that these cunning monkeys have a master who has trained them well: they all deliver the same speech, almost down to the very word. Our young believers, alas, seem to appreciate these diatribes, which call on them to take up arms and kill honest folk. With horror we have discovered that these demons wear bombs on their persons which are ready to explode, and the moment they are found out and cornered they set them off. This diabolical defense makes it impossible to conduct any investigation into who they are, where they have come from, or who they are working for. The Association of *mockbis* calls on its members, particularly those who officiate in small *mockbas*, to reinforce their vigilance and report to the police any individuals they suspect of belonging to this infernal horde as discreetly as possible. Finally, the Association calls on the VLBs, the Volunteer Law-enforcing Believers, to increase their influence over youths in the streets, for otherwise the Association will be obliged to withdraw permission to deploy their religious police in public places from the VLBs. It would be already more than enough if they practiced at home, on their children. It isn't enough to have a cat wandering around licking its chops in the house, it has to catch a few mice as well.

The Hero, the VLBs' newsletter, refers to the article in *The Voice of the Mockbas* to turn the argument back against them.

The Voice of the Mockbas has called on us to be vigilant. Granted, we see their point. Things are indeed happening without our knowing, we are aware of that. But they don't only say that we are not paying attention: they accuse us of having allowed evil to proliferate, and therefore of being complicit in some plot against our holy religion, and they criticize us—simple believers that we are, who offer up our own time to help our fellow citizens, our religious police, and the Inspection of Morality—of not fighting the terrorism this savage horde is seeking to impose upon the country. Are we also supposed to be militia and policemen? We know how much we owe our honorable *mockbis*, but now we must say no to their newsletter—which is their mouthpiece, since it is called *The Voice of the Mockbas*, or the voice of the *mockbis*, which amounts to the same thing, and we accuse them in turn of having failed to show vigilance and serious intent, for who teaches our holy religion to the population? The *mockba*—they themselves, in other words! Who evaluates the level of the believers' morality in the neighborhoods and districts? Once again, the *mockba*—they themselves! Finally, who is authorized to declare *rihad* and launch a vast operation to purify people's morals and their minds? Still the *mockba*—they themselves! Have they done this? Are they doing it? Will they do it? In reply to all three questions, no. So, for pity's sake, may they spare us their gratuitous accusations. We are volunteers, we sacrifice ourselves day and night for our religion, we want recognition and respect. A word to the wise is enough.

A free, mimeographed leaflet, published by a rich merchant from the Sîn region: thanks to the caravan drivers a few copies are going around the country, and it tells this little story which sounds like a fairy tale from the mountains:

Civilian guards in a Dru village have reported that a helicopter bearing the coat of arms of the Honorable Bri was seen maneuvering in the region of the Zib pass to the northwest of the famous sanatorium at Sîn. We did not know that the Honorable Bri, who is currently our acting Great Commander, may Yölah assist and protect him, had interests in the region. We would have celebrated his presence among us and facilitated his business in a brotherly and respectful manner. But no, the helicopter merely circled here and there and eventually left a man off on a plateau; he was carrying mountaineering equipment. Every day thereafter the guards saw him, spotted him, caught a glimpse; he was dressed in a very odd way, shall we say old-fashioned, and he hurried here and there and yonder, as if he were looking for something—a lost trail, a legendary ruin, a secret passage, the forbidden road, perhaps. Intrigued by his behavior, the Dru villagers put together a group of young men to go up and question him, to help him if he was in need, or chase him away if he was harboring evil intentions. They couldn't find him anywhere; he had vanished. They looked again and again and spread the word to the most remote villages. Not a thing. The Dru villagers finally concluded that the man had gone to look for the famous Border and that if he didn't perish at the bottom of a ravine or wasn't carried away by a mountain torrent or a landslide or an avalanche, maybe he had found the Border; or maybe he turned around and went home with his tail between his legs. The young people just laughed about it as they drank their tea around the fire, and it had started snowing again, harder than ever, erasing all human trace; obliged to stay in their shelter, they told stories about how they themselves and their parents before them had searched in vain for that mythical border. They are now convinced that it does not exist, or not in their parts, anyway; it must be somewhere over on the other side of the pass, to the southeast, in Bud or Raqi territory, beyond the summit of the Gur or elsewhere, because the Buds and the Raqi are practically certain that the border runs through Dru territory, or way up there among the Sher, who vie with the eagles for the sky.

This story about the Border is as strange as they come. If the Border does not exist, and that is certain, its legend does, and is still growing. The ancestors of our most distant ancestors already talked about it, but in our mountains at the top of the world the border is what separates good from evil. Nomads and smugglers know only too well that no border can separate one mountain from another, or one pass from another, one nomad or smuggler from another. The border is their connection. If sometimes caravans disappear, or are attacked and decimated, they know who is responsible, it's the caravan drivers themselves, the very same who broke with divine law to devote themselves to theft and crime.

ABOUT THE AUTHOR

Rohan Wilson's first book, *The Roving Party*, won the The Australian/Vogel's Literary Award as well as the Margaret Scott Prize and the NSW Premier's Literary Award. Wilson was chosen as one of the Sydney Morning Herald's Best Young Novelists in 2012.